80,000 WORDS

Achilles: A Love Story

A Gay Novel of the Trojan War

Byrne Fone

"The story of Troy was also a tale of love between men—of the devotion of Achilles for Patroclus…"

Dedication

For Alain: My Love Story

Book One

The Golden City

Agamemnon intoned a prayer: Mighty Zeus, grant that the sun may never set nor darkness fall until I bring down Priam's golden palace, blackened with smoke, and send up his gates in flame, and all his men are fallen in the dust and bite the earth in death.
--Iliad 2. 412 ff.

From: Dionysos of Tenedos. A History of the War at Troy

I will tell you some history—the story of the fall of Troy, the most magnificent city in the world. But I will tell you also a love story, for the tragedy of Troy's fall is also a tragedy of love. When we are young we are taught in school about the great heroes of that war, and especially about the invincible Achilles, the most ferocious of warriors, leader of the Myrmidons, he who was called Slayer of Men, the most valiant and most handsome man in the world who loved battle. As much as he loved to fight for glory, for plunder, and for blood, Achilles loved his companion Patroclus even more. Achilles and Patroclus: their names echo down history; their fame is assured; their story forever enshrined in the songs of poets; their passion an inspiration for lovers; their bravery the envy of all brave men; their tragedy unbearable even to this day. But there is another story we are never taught, and that is the one I tell here.

In a thousand ships, it is said, the Greeks came from all the corners of Hellas with the manifest intention of despoiling Troy of its uncountable treasures, razing its high walls to dust, and taking back the woman held captive there, she who was Queen of Sparta, but who all the world called Helen of Troy.

From the distant height of his Trojan walls that no army had ever breached and that not even, it is said, demi-gods could successfully scale, King Priam could see the invaders parading their arrogant power at the morning assembly, reviewed by Agamemnon, king and commander, and lord of all the Achaean peoples who had come to besiege and capture Troy.

The huge army stood at attention on the parade ground in the center of the camp, arrayed in close order, armor flashing brazenly, helmets glittering in the sun, a forest of spears rising ominously, shields like signal mirrors sending out warnings to any enemy that resistance was hopeless.

It was in the ninth year of the war that Prince Antilochus came to Troy, for he had been too young to go to war when it began. But when he came of age he went to fight at his father's side, called by duty, by desire for glory in battle, and by something stronger. He came to find the man he loved more than any other in the world. He fought not for glory or for gain, but for love. This is the story only hinted at in the ancient tales. For Antilochus loved Achilles, who, alas, loved another.

Chapter 1

Ever since I can remember I had heard of Achilles, son of Peleus, King of the Pythian Myrmidons. I suppose in the complicated web of Achaean relationship we may be cousins, for we are related to all the other royal families. Stories about him were as common as were the tales of the gods themselves, though some seemed as unbelievable. Not only is he Peleus's son, but son too of the divine Sea Goddess Thetis, at least so the priests say. Legend claimed that he was raised by Cheiron the Centaur; that he killed his first boar when he was only six summers; that he is so swift of foot that he can outrun the very stags he was hunting; that he can throw a javelin further than any man; that he is braver and more beautiful than any youth ever born; that he is invincible. Other tales even claim that he is immortal. And he is only two summers older than I. How it happened I do not quite know, but I gradually became obsessed with Achilles.

Was it because my days were spent wandering alone on the beaches of sandy Pylos that I found in a youth I had never seen an imaginary companion? I was alone for most of my hours. My father, Nestor the king, at council or with his ministers, settling quarrels with villagers who came to petition him, officiating at ceremonies, had little time for companionship, though he is a good man and loving. My mother, Anaxibia, was busy too: governing a household, keeping order among the servants. I saw no one save my tutor.

My tutor—a man in his forties-- who was tutor as well to the sons of the nobility, filled our heads with tales of love and friendship between men and youths. He told us how Zeus had taken the beautiful Ganymede to his bed, how brave Hercules loved his young companion Iolaus, how Orpheus sang of his passion for the youth Calais. He told me too that Spartan men courted handsome boys with gifts and took them into the wild where in nights of love they came erotically into manhood.

"Perhaps one day, Prince Antilochus," he would say, "You too will have such a handsome suitor."

All the other boys would laugh, and I would blush, for I hoped the same. And I have to say, as we listened to him expatiate on the wonders of love between men, there in the gymnasium where we both learned and exercised, that sometimes his teaching became quite tactile. He liked to ruffle our hair as he walked about among us, or pass a hand across our naked shoulders, letting it linger a bit, as he made a point. But we did not mind. He was not ugly and he was kind. Some of the boys, it was rumored, learned more than theory from him.

As I grew older, ten summers, then eleven, older, these stories swirled in my head. My body seemed always to be alive. Alone on the sandy beaches I would lie naked while dreams of friendship and of love overwhelmed me, the hot sun caressing me into desire. I felt ever more keenly the need for someone to... to do what? I was not quite sure. I looked at handsome men as I passed them in the streets, but they did not look at me, for all men must lower their eyes in deference in the presence of our family. Oh, how I wanted a friend and suitor too.

As the world knows, in most of the lands of Greece it is the custom for men not yet married to take younger men—youths in their late teens--as lovers until the older finally chooses a wife. And even after marriage, many men continue to have their favorites among the ranks of handsome youths and pursue and court them and of course, enjoy them. For the younger man it is flattering to be sought out by a handsome older man and it is an outlet for the burning passions that rage in the loins of the young. For the older, it allows him repeated access to the flower and vigor and glory of youth.

But it is more than that. Our world is a man's world in which women have little part. Indeed women bear our children, but they do not come into the agora and participate in the councils of men. They do not take arms and go into battle. They do not make the great

9

decisions that keep the state and our lives in motion and on an even keel. This is man's work. Women serve at home. They govern the household so that we do not need to do so. But they have little to tell us about the work of men. They are not educated as we are, and so cannot offer us the companionship of the intellect or spirit that one man offers another. It is men who train youths, and what better way to learn the arts of war and statecraft than while treading the circuitous byways of the labyrinth of love in the arms of some strong warrior.

Though men and women bear children of the flesh together, and one day some woman will bear mine no doubt, yet when two men are caught up in the nobility of love and the heat of passion, they too bring forth children, as the old philosophers say. These unions between two good men, one the older and wiser and experienced in the life of the world, the other younger and eager to learn to become a part of that world, produce true and noble offspring of the spirit and from these unions youth learns wisdom and virtue, temperance and justice, and the proper care of the the state and family. Such men are married by a far closer tie and have a stronger friendship than those who beget mortal children.

This, at least, is what I was taught in school. The theory was thrilling to hear, of course, but the reality had as yet escaped me. In fact I thought of nothing else and made lists of prospective suitors. There were several among the lesser nobles who I would have liked to teach me what I had begun to suspect could go on between two men. But that could never be. My father would forbid it, for though such dalliance was encouraged among men before they sought a wife, for a prince many things that were open to lesser men remained closed. There were no young men who I could befriend, for who could be my friend when as Prince of Pylos none were my equal?

I did not remain ignorant long. I practiced with one of the stable boys—then with two or three. Fearful of my rank, but obviously taken by what everyone said was my daily ripening beauty, first one, then another came with me to a sunny cove upon the beach or to the rich darkness of a forest grove, and soon I was reasonably sure of the possibilities and they seemed to me infinitely enticing.

But stable boys and stories of love were not enough. And thus it was that Achilles came to be central in my thoughts. Surely he was the friend and suitor worthy of my blood. I convinced myself that his destiny and mine must inevitably be intertwined. What did he look like? I had heard that he was golden-haired and incredibly handsome. I walked the sandy beaches, staring out to sea, conjuring pictures of a young man I had never seen. I tried to imagine his voice.

"Antilochus come to me," I heard him say in my imagination.

Is that how he would have said it? Someday, I was sure, he would say it. I looked forward to such a day and to an ever-golden future. For I, wise Nestor's son, had become a besotted lovesick boy gone quite mad for a man I had never met. But, I thought, I would one day be a king. Mine the crown, and in my heart I was sure that Achilles, too, would one day be mine.

But golden dreams can tarnish and reality intervenes to wake us. Rumors and reports began to come to us on Pylos. We heard stories about Menelaus of Crete and of Helen his queen, of Paris the Trojan prince, and of infidelities and abductions. But they were only stories, rumors borne on the wind or told in the market. No one knew if any of it was true. My mother sniffed that Menelaus was hardly one to complain about infidelity, and anyway, next to our family, his was but an upstart one. My father nodded sagely, but kept his counsel. It all seemed far away to me, there on the sandy beaches of Pylos, the sun hammering down day after day, the smell of olives ripe and sweet floating across the fields and mixing with the redolence of marjoram and thyme, the sound of new lambs giving way to the call of sheep at shearing, the seasons passing, and thoughts of Achilles never far away.

Then it all came home to our sunny shores. Rumors became fact. Messengers arrived from Menelaus, from Agamemnon his brother, from Peleus in Pythia, from Odysseus, lord of Ithaca. My mother grew anxious; my father grim. A war had begun and the world was turned upside down. War? Against whom? Why? Rumor told it all and rumor had been right: Helen, the world's most

11

beautiful woman, wife of Menelaus King of Sparta had indeed been abducted by Paris, a Trojan Prince, son of Priam, Troy's Great king. But what had all this to do with us? We soon learned what.

Agamemnon came to Pylos to urge my father, whose counsel he much valued, to join him in the prosecution of the battle. I had never seen such a sight. Long black ships filled the harbor, pennants flying. Soldiers lined their decks, their armor glittering in the sun. The largest of the ships rode up to the stone quay, men leaped ashore and secured it. Ram's horns blaring a salute, the king descended from the ship, wearing full battle gear and surrounded by a guard of stony-faced Achaeans.

My father received him seated on his throne under a canopy in the square in front of the king's house. He wore the diadem; his face made up, as was our custom, and he was surrounded by the priests, for my father is a Sacred King. They exchanged the usual greeting filled with titles and honorifics, and then when all was done they went together into the hall where a feast lay waiting. My father allowed me to attend him as his body servant so that I would miss nothing.

After we had made libations and dined to repletion, Agamemnon rose. I do not recall all of his long speech, but fragments come back.

"We must do battle for the honor of our people," he said.

"We must not wait to strike, for they have insulted the House of Atreus and thus every one among us in Hellas."

I can see him standing there, fists clenched, dark eyes glaring out at the assembled Lords of Pylos.

"We must crush this evil city and end the Trojan sway over the oppressed peoples of the Troad." He raised his arm in an expansive gesture and brought it down, pointing his finger at us all: "They are a threat to us all. We – all of us-- must join in a great coalition of forces against them. We must destroy them before they can take more than just a wronged king's beloved wife."

Who could resist such oratory? Most of the assembled lords broke into loud cheers, though some looked dubious. My father's face remained impassive.

"But what is this quarrel to us?" someone shouted.

Agamemnon turned and stared at the speaker.

"What is this to you?" he said, his voice suddenly soft. And then in a hoarse shout: "What is this to you? I will tell you what it is; it is the safety of your lands, of your wives and children. That is what it is."

And then, his voice sinking again to a whisper, he asked: "For if we do not strike, then how long will it be until they send out their fleets to strike at us? How long will it be before they invade us and send their vast armies into our towns and cities, into our temples, and into our homes? How long will it be before they lay waste to our homeland?"

He paused; looked around him, his eyes sweeping the hall and catching the eye of every nobleman there. Then turning to my father, he said, his voice resonating against the high pillars of the hall: "My Lord King, Noble Nestor, Keeper of the Wisdom of Hellas: Join me in a war of liberation. Let us together release the captive peoples that Troy wickedly holds in thrall. Fight with me so that our wives and our children and our homeland will forever be safe. Join me," he shouted, "to raze the walls of Troy to the ground."

The room erupted into shouts and cheers.

"War," someone shouted. "War!" someone echoed. The men stamped their feet, and the cry "war, war," resounded to the roof beams.

If any still doubted his right to command them, Agamemnon did not take long to make clear why they had no choice.

"I am Agamemnon, son of Atreus, and to my house all lords and kings of Hellas owe allegiance," he bellowed. "When I command you must obey. If you do not, by the gods I will bring the war first to the land of any who disobey!"

At this moment my father rose, full of years and dignity and, no doubt, anxious to restrain the wrath of Agamemnon whose anger everyone knew could be terrible and irrational.

"There is no need, Lord Agamemnon to bring war to any here. No need my Lord, for threats or dark words. No man doubts your right to call us when need arises. And are we not all bound, as

13

history tells us, to rise to this occasion? And for that reason we must go to war."

He meant of course what all there knew: that years ago many in the room had sought fair Helen's hand. Because they had done so they were bound in honor by the oath they all had taken then, imposed by Tyndareus, Helen's father, that obligated them to come to the aid of whomever Helen chose to wed her, should need arise.

Menelaus had wed Helen. Need had arisen. And so that was that.

Then wily Odysseus, ever at the king's right hand, made another point: "Troy is rich," he said. "It is the richest city in the world. Own it and you own all." That was all he said. But it was enough. They agreed to meet in Aulis by summer's end. War it would be; war to capture Troy, the richest prize in all the world.

Chapter 2

It was decided that my father and King Odysseus would make a recruiting tour of the islands. One stop was to be Pythia, the home of Peleus and of his son Achilles. My chance had come. I besieged my father to let me go. I would brook no argument. To my overwhelming joy, he agreed. We would go to Pythia to convince Peleus to join in the war against Troy, and I at last would see the boy—the young man-- who had been the companion of my dreams and object of my fantasies. At last I would see Achilles. My fantasy would at last become reality.

Our ship with its purple sail, its banks of oars tipped with gold, swiftly skimmed over the sea toward Pythia. Night and day Achilles was with me: in the day I imagined the moment of our meeting; at night I dreamed of him in my arms.

At last we saw the island. The boat swept into the shore. We docked. I was in a state of high excitement; I barely knew what was happening, so eager was I to catch sight of him. We were met by Peleus and the court, the soldiers at attention, banners brightly streaming, trumpets sounding a royal salute. All I remember of that moment was my heart pounding in anticipation, my head full of hope. We came down from the ship, I a few paces behind my father, the crowds cheered, the sun burned down. We walked toward the dais where King Peleus had risen from his chair to greet us. I could see a knot of men in armor standing with him. One must be Achilles. We came to the dais. My father embraced Peleus. I bowed. I looked up. Then I was presented to Achilles.

"Welcome, cousin Antilochus," he said with a negligent drawl. He looked at me with those famous eyes, a glance like a javelin hurled into your heart.

I saw. He conquered.

Achilles was splendid. He was very well built for his age—golden hair bleached by the sun, skin bronzed. His sensuous lips seemed made for the madness of kisses, yet his cool gray eyes

15

looked at me with curiously impassionate appraisal. He was at once immensely charming and yet arrogant, with even a touch of the cruel. But who could care.

Achilles smiled at me. I smiled shyly back. Our eyes met and my heart leapt. I wanted to kiss him there and then.

Then I saw, but it took awhile for me to understand what I saw. There was someone by his side, too close by his side. A gesture did it. The man next to him casually placed his hand on Achilles' shoulder. That gesture said it all. Of course it was Patroclus. I had not heard about him. How had I not heard about him?

I arrived prepared for Achilles to instantly desire and take me, though only of course after the appropriate coyness and hesitation on my part, only of course after his appropriate pursuit and offering of gifts.

But I was not prepared for Patroclus—he too was handsome in a manly, almost brusque way, taller than Achilles, with dark straight hair and piercing jet back eyes that looked through me and saw, I was sure, my secret. He had a dazzling smile and together they made a gorgeous pair. Standing there on the quayside, my father and King Peleus still engaged in interminable royal rituals, all I could do was stare at the two of them and try not to cry.

Our visit was not a long one; Peleus needed little coaxing to go to war. The days were spent in councils and feasts, games and hunting. I dutifully stayed by my father's side, went through what had to be borne and desperately wished to leave. From time to time I saw him, my Achilles as I could not help but think him to be, but they were always together. He was obviously devoted to Patroclus and he to him.

I never saw Achilles alone, and when we met he was friendly, but he treated me like a little boy even though I was only three years younger. Patroclus was older than Achilles by a year or two and treated me with even greater condescension than did Achilles, suspecting rightly that I could be a rival or at least a troublemaker. I disliked him instantly, though in fact he is much the nicer of the two. Most annoyingly, this Patroclus was highborn, but he was not royal.

But, I thought, Achilles is a prince and so am I. We were clearly meant for each other. But the fates laughed. Patroclus did not disappear as I nightly prayed that he might do during the days of our stay.

How they came to be together I learned from one of the servants assigned to attend me who was eager to gossip. Patroclus had fled to Pythia as a result of some tasteless brawl wherein he actually killed someone over a game of dice. Peleus granted him asylum and Achilles was instantly taken with him and he with the young Prince. It was clear that nothing could keep them apart, and so Peleus wisely agreed that Patroclus should be Achilles' mentor and teacher. In short, they became lovers. In matters of state and precedence, Patroclus could never be equal to Achilles. But then who could equal Achilles? They had been together for four years when I encountered them.

By the time we returned to Pylos my shock and hurt had turned to anger and determination. I could think of nothing but Achilles. I plotted how I would win him, how I would convince him of my worth. I thought of sending emissaries secretly to him, of arranging for Patroclus' sudden death. In short I was quite mad with love.

My father was busy now preparing for our force to go to Troy. He would lead it, for Agamemnon needed his counsel as well as our sizable army. I begged my father to let me go to war, since Achilles and Patroclus were also going to Troy, Achilles to command his Myrmidons, the elite fighting cohorts sent by the aged King Peleus who was too feeble to go into battle.

Fantasies besieged me: fighting side by side with him, answering his trumpet call, engaging in some act of extraordinary heroism which would far outshine the pedestrian Patroclus, even throwing myself in an ecstasy of sacrifice in front of an enemy spear meant for him. I saw Achilles pausing, wondering, being struck by my beauty and war-like manner, rejecting Patroclus, coming to my side, holding me in his arms as I died, for him.

Oh lovesick boy, for boy I was.

But my father would not let me go to war. The answer was the same: I was too young. Not yet of age, and I must stay to guard my mother. Wise Nestor forbade it and so I watched in tears as father's ship sailed into the morning, not tears for his departure, but tears for the golden lad who was the fond image of my waking hours and who I nightly embraced in my dreams.

The days and months sluggishly passed. Every day I felt myself growing stronger, more ready to fight. My mornings were spent in war-like practice with my weapons tutor; the afternoons in gymnastics. I determined to make myself a warrior. Every night Achilles rose to greet me from the cave of my desire.

News filtered in: from my father's letters, from occasional ambassadors, from rumor carried across the seas. Some we would not believe, others we could not believe. After false starts the fleet had finally gathered at Aulis. But it was becalmed. There was no wind. The ships could not sail. The priests accompanying the army claimed that the gods were angry, but priests always claimed that the gods were angry. It was said that Agamemnon had been told by the priest Calchas that the great fleet would never sail from Aulis and Troy never fall unless a suitable sacrifice was offered, and that the only sacrifice that was acceptable was Iphigenia, his daughter!

How could this be so? I could not believe it. It was barbaric. My mother held her tongue and said nothing, as a woman should. But late at night she would go to the grove of the goddess who could foretell the future and reveal the answer to any question. And one morning, having been gone all night she returned, haggard and disheveled. She said nothing. But her eyes told all. The terrible rumors were true. Iphigenia was dead, by her father's hand.

Later, after it was done, rumor raced across the world telling how Agamemnon brought his own daughter to her death. The terrible tragedy is now recounted by the poets and enacted on the stage so all know the story. Agamemnon sent a deceitful letter to Clytemnestra and Iphigenia bidding them to come and join him in Aulis. Why should they do so? Because, he untruly said, he intended to give Iphigenia in marriage to Achilles, who wanted her, though Achilles knew nothing of this.

Thus, commanded by their Lord and King and lured by their husband and father with false promise of marriage, Clytemnestra and Iphigenia came to Aulis. There murder disguised as a wedding awaited the young girl. Iphigenia was sacrificed and just as Calchas foretold, the wind rose. But the wind rose because a father had slain his daughter, and such a sin could not—and did not—go unpunished. Soon we heard that the great fleet had sailed from Aulis and had at last come to Troy.

Chapter 3

And as I grew older I grew more angry, and more impatient. I should be there. I should be at Troy, at a war, not dawdling at home like some cosseted and perfumed fop. I said this to my mother. She told me to be silent. My father would decide what I was to do.

In the eighth year of the war—when I was 18, a Cretan merchant ship, one of those that makes the long circuit from Crete, through the isles, to Troy and back again, trading as it went, and then when its cargo was returned to Crete made the voyage again, made port at Pylos on its way back to Troy. Its captain was a young man of aristocratic bearing, very handsome, and perhaps only five or six years older than I.

My mother commanded him to an audience so he could tell us the news, for he had been to Troy within the last few months. There were, he said, small battles and even some famous victories. What interested me most were his accounts of Achilles distinguishing himself against one invincible warrior or another. The tales of his victories enthralled me. He had taken many great cities and captured kings. He had taken the huge herds of Aeneas' cattle, which it was said made the plains of Troy black with their numbers. He had amassed vast booty from the rich storehouses of the Troadian shores. I was less pleased with the stirring tales of Achilles and Patroclus charging wildly into battle slaying their thousands. I listened to these stories of the valor of the two men with sick envy and rage.

During the audience I saw that the captain could barely keep his eyes off me. I felt a similar curiosity about him. And so I arranged that I should happen upon him in the gymnasium, for the war had relaxed social barriers considerably, and he was very attractive. I saw him, and I smiled, looked down, perhaps a bit too coquettishly. By now, just as I was eager for war I was also eager for love.

Eventually he took me several times to bed, though I hesitate to admit it, since he was, after all, not only not royal but not even noble and I am a Prince. But his heart was royal even if his blood was not, and his body was hard and lean, and he knew how to make love to me so that I came to him as a boy but left him as a man.

One night as we lay together on the hillside amongst the wild thyme, he told me the story of Troilus, son of King Priam of Troy and of Achilles, a story he had not told to my mother. Having seen the incredibly beautiful and incredibly brave Troilus day after day on the battlefield and having fought at close quarters, even hand to hand with him, and always to a draw, Achilles had begun to desire him. Desire turned to obsession and Achilles somehow got a message to Troilus to come secretly outside the walls. There they fought yet another battle, this without swords but with the lances of love, beside the rushing Scamander. (Needless to say my handsome captain's graphic description of the "battle " did not fail to arouse me.)

As they were making desperate love in the shadow of Achilles' golden chariot, the moon casting reflections from its hammered sides unto the ivory of their lithe passion, their desire became so intense that Achilles gripped Troilus in those powerful arms (my captain gripping me thus also) and delirious with ecstasy, Achilles literally crushed poor Troilus to death. Insane with love is perhaps the phrase to describe it.

By this time I too was insane with love and we were as desirous as Achilles and Troilus had been and our naked bodies were silvered, like theirs, by the watching moon. I did not die in that embrace, though at times the ecstasy of it made it seem as if I might. When we were done and lay happy and exhausted, my captain, with a kiss reminded me that prophecy assured us that Troy would be conquered if Troilus died before his twentieth year. When they met, Troilus was nineteen.

But fate laughed and seemed to confound prophecy. For as accurate dispatches were making painfully clear month after month, despite laying siege to Troy our forces had been unable to take it.

When the fleet sailed everyone believed the war would be brief. No one doubted that faced with such a vast and mighty army Troy would fall. The priests all said that the cities and peoples that Troy oppressively ruled in the Troad would welcome our coming and hail us as liberators. Kings promised that fathers and husbands, sons and lovers, would be safe again at home before harvest and justice would have been done and the world would be rid of an evil scourge and made safe at last for men who feared the Gods.

But that had not happened. All that we heard now was that the war was not going well. The glorious expedition had degenerated into a raiding party. More men were dying every day. The tales of fabulous booty and golden cities began to seem more like wishful thoughts than fact.

For me, there on the shores of Sandy Pylos, this was all dark news. Young men were growing old waiting on the shores of Troy; young men were dying there. Somehow before I too grew old I must go to lend what strength I could to a failing enterprise. I would go to Troy to fight at my father's side. And, I thought even more urgently, (I blush to mention this breach of filial loyalty) at my Achilles' side.

Chapter 4

I begged my mother to let me go.

"I am old enough now," I cried. "It is dishonor to stay when so many others have gone."

But she would not allow it unless my father would. He of course was a world away. There was nothing for it; I ran away. The young captain who brought me love took me to war. One day, even before the dawn, I slipped aboard his ship, and just as soon as the first light of dawn dappled the sea with a rosy glow, we put out into the sunrise, heading to Troy

The weather was fine, the wind strong, and in the day I helped with what needed to be done—carrying bales, shifting oil jars-- for we had agreed that no one should know of my rank, and at night I slept on deck as did all the crew, though my friend and I had cover under a tent at the stern. The crew thought I was a youth he had picked up in Pylos, and they made some jokes about us, but they were a genial lot and I found myself fond of him and knew I would be sorry to leave him.

On the day of our arrival, I was up before sunrise, standing on the forward deck of my merchant's ship, straining my eyes to see the heaven-reaching towers of Ilium. At last I saw them. Reality outran legend. Indeed the towers did seem to strain up towards the sky. Huge gates opened into broad avenues that even from my distant vantage on the ship's deck I could see. The city was splendid sight set high on its precipitous escarpment, its mighty walls rising still higher up above the cliffs. Surely such massive walls could only have been built by the gods, by Poseidon, as legends claim. Rising from out of the center of the immense circuit of walls in the heart of the citadel was the tower of the city, the great symbol of the might of Troy, its stone walls dark, smooth, well-cut, polished like obsidian. From its high vantage point generations of kings had seen their victorious armies come back from war. Was the little figure I could just barely see on the highest point of the tower Priam himself?

Below the city the plain stretched down to the beach. And there, drawn up were the galleys of the great army of the Kings of Greece. A long row of black ships snaked along the shore. The smoke from what seemed like a thousand campfires created columns etched against the glowing sunrise. The camp was stirring; I heard horses and trumpets, saw men beginning yet another day.

The ship bore swiftly in, docked, unloaded. It was time to say goodbye. I kissed my benefactor and felt a passing sadness for the loss of him. He held my hand for perhaps a moment too long and then withdrew his arm from around my shoulder. We said nothing; just smiled. I realized that in a way I had come to love him.

He went back to his ship and I turned to seek—better—to confront my fate. I knew that I should go direct to my father. But instead I wandered among the aisles of tents; overwhelmed by the sheer numbers of men, by paddocks full of horses, by dozens of campfires burning and cooking the millet for the first meal of the day. I knew that I could not seek my father until I found what I came to find. So I sought the tent of Achilles.

Everyone knew where it was and so I soon found it, a surprisingly simple tent, set far away from the others high upon the hillside overlooking the sea. I stood in front of it for a long time. Below me the sea rolled up to the beach and out again. I thought that I could just make out the merchant's ship setting out toward the horizon, its cargo, including me, unloaded and delivered. Behind me was the sea, behind me home and boyhood.

I waited, then rustled my feet in the gravel, coughed, then called. The tent flap opened. Achilles, my dream, stood there, bare-chested, wearing only a short linen skirt-like garment. He did not recognize me.

But of course why should he? For when last he saw me I was a stripling boy. He looked past me then. Now he looked at me. He raked me up and down with that javelin gaze. I became flushed, excited, desirous, but fortunately not tongue-tied. I was not without some talent for charming men and I used all I had learned: a combination of insouciant warrior nonchalance and the trace of

24

boyish seductiveness that remained. It had worked often in Pylos, and it worked with Achilles.

He questioned me as to my name and from whence I had come.

"I am Nestor's son, Antilochus. I come to fight, and to join you, if you will have me." Recognition dawned in his eyes, but his brow also furrowed and he seemed to know quickly what I had not said.

"Does your father know you are here?" he asked. I suddenly realized that I was in deep trouble for coming first to Achilles and not to my father. I was no longer fluent of speech and I guess I became quite panicky and stammered out a plea to Achilles to intercede between me and what would surely be my father's towering wrath.

No man to let things lie, he took me by the arm and dragged me to my father's tent. I cannot describe the shock that registered in my father's face when he saw me, or the shock in mine when I saw how old he had become. I shall not repeat the recriminations, nor my father's angry lecture and threat to send me home. I am sure that would have happened had not Achilles taken my father aside and after a lengthy conversation that I was not allowed to hear, miraculously made things right. And— joy beyond belief—he arranged for me to be a squire and orderly for himself and Patroclus.

I presumed—hoped—there would be more, a price for all of this. There was. Not long after I arrived, with Patroclus out on a raid, Achilles came upon me polishing brasses in the tent. It was a hot afternoon, the dust lay heavy, the heat was palpable. We were alone. There was no preamble. No courtship gesture. It was quick. He was—as I had heard—brutal. I didn't care. Whatever he wanted, I did.

Patroclus returned three days later. Each one of those days I was with Achilles; each night I was in his arms. He did not crush me to death, nor was he cruel again. Indeed, after him I have wanted no other man. When Patroclus came back, we had been up for barely an hour. I was terrified and exultant and as well dreadfully embarrassed when Patroclus came into the tent, hot, dirty, filled with the joy of a battle won. I had to help him undress, rub him down, wash his body, while Achilles sat next to him, reaching out fondly to touch him, talking the talk of lovers reunited. I seemed never to have existed. I then saw the difference between what Achilles had with me and what Achilles and Patroclus had together. I had to leave the tent to hide my tears.

But it was soon clear that fidelity was not a part of their relationship. Patroclus, I discovered, had a sweet eye for his charioteer Automedon, and I got the distinct impression as I massaged his smoothly muscled body with oil that if he had not been tired and Achilles not there I might have been another trophy of battle. If I say that I eventually became that trophy for Patroclus, would it hurt Achilles? And was my moment with Patroclus only his way of making things equal with Achilles between them?

Often, when the three of us had eaten well and drunk well, I could see that it occurred to them to make me a third party in their sex, but it never happened. And so, after an evening with them, after affectionate exchanges, a little anticipatory tension, the moment never came and I would return alone to my tent. Once—once only—I lingered outside the tent and heard them make love. I heard the passion and the sex, but I also heard Achilles say, in that voice: "I love you."

Oh, the javelin in the heart.

Sometimes as I sat in my tent, alone, wondering where it all would end and what it meant, I thought back on the war stories I heard when I was young. In the great hall in Pylos far away, at feasts given to honor the courageous living, I loved to hear the singers tell of the battles of the ancient days and of the glorious dead. Ever since I could remember I had heard my father's tales of old victories, of hard fought campaigns, of the glittering triumphs of those days when he was young and men were heroes. I have my own war stories too, and some may one day be in the songs, though others are best forgotten. The best ones are about Achilles.

Book Two
Chryseis: Daughter of Apollo

*We sacked the place, choosing Chryseis of the lovely cheeks as
a gift for Agamemnon.*
        --Iliad 2. 328-330.

From: Dionysos of Tenedos, A History of the War at Troy

Though watchers from Troy's walls saw in the distance the vast and splendid and seemingly invincible army of the invaders, yet could they come and more closely survey the Achaean army, they would see a less invincible horde. Looking down on the camp from one of the fifty wooden watch towers that rise from the high earthworks erected years ago to defend the camp and the access to the ships, the disarray that distance conceals is all too clear. The tents, seemingly numberless to the distant eye, are patched, many lacking clothe to repair or pine-pitch to secure the mend. They are torn and open to the night. The towers themselves, built with wood despoiled from the surrounding low hills, are rimed now with sea salt carried in by the incoming wind that rusts the spikes that fasten the planks and rots the rope that secures the timbers of the towers.

The ships rest upon the beach, but close examination would reveal that the sails are tattered, the ropes waterlogged, and the planking of the decks beginning to rot. Both towers and ships need urgent repairs, but there is little wood left for that. The hills are barren and what wood there is, is needed to fuel the cooking fires, which as time has gone by have been ordered by the king to be made smaller and to be shared, no longer a fire for each cohort, but one for two or even three.

And if there is little wood, it does not matter much since there is little food to cook and rations are strictly controlled. Not anticipating a long war and believing they would be welcomed with rejoicing as liberators, the Achaean High Command planned to fight as they had done in other campaigns and forage for food from the countryside. Thus, so as to make room in the ships for men and chariots and precious horses, the Achaeans brought only small herds of cattle and few provisions, thinking that what was needed could taken, and quickly, for the war would be short.

But they were wrong. Food grew daily more and more scarce. The army's stock of cattle had little to graze upon save the coarse brush that grows on the sandy plain, and they become thin, and fewer calves were born each year. So meals of meat-- ox ribs and the thighs of cattle rich with fat and dripping blood, flavored with sea salt and rosemary and roasted over a cheery fire-- were seldom to be had. What grain remained was rotten, and with all the native farmers dead, there was no harvest. And thus despite larger numbers, the Achaeans were weak, and did not have enough fighting strength to mount a full attack upon Troy. The massive force had set out in search of glory and the honors of battle, but such things, so often celebrated in the songs of poets, are reduced to meaninglessness by empty cooking pots.

After nine years of inconclusive battle, the giddy optimism, the expectation of easy victory, and everyone's hope to seize a fortune in Troy's treasure for themselves that had so intoxicated the invading forces in the first years of the invasion, had evaporated like rainwater on a dry rock under the blazing sun. As the years dragged on the war--if war it could now be called-- had come to a standstill. It had become all too clear that the Achaeans were not going to walk through the land of the womanish Trojans quite so easily as their first awe-inspiring strikes might have suggested. Instead of welcoming them the local population rose up against them, engaging in lightning acts of harassment and sabotage, attacking wherever and whenever they could. No soldier dared go beyond the camp walls alone lest some small band of farmers—sometimes only two or three—might surprise him, stun him with a stone flung from a sling, and, as they did to one poor soldier who stupidly ventured out in search of a missing horse, hack him into pieces with their scythes.

Like the insurgent peasant farmers in the countryside, the Trojan army came out from behind the city walls to harry the Achaeans too. Every now and again a war party sallied out from Troy's high gates in their huge war chariots, followed at a swift jog by a cohort or so of men at arms, all looking fit and well fed, armor polished and smart. They came swiftly across the plain, usually no more than a dozen chariots and a hundred or so men, and raced to within a short distance of the Greek camp. The men at arms halt with a crash of weapons and form a smart defensive line, shields up, spears poised. The chariots wheel with a rush and as they pass the walls; the drivers taunt the Achaeans, the soldiers in the chariots not even bothering to leap out to fight. Sometimes the Achaeans respond by sending out a cohort to engage them. They fight; someone is killed or maimed or wounded. Then it ends. It is never decisive. Day after day it is only a skirmish and never a battle and never a victory for either side.

Indeed, these encounters had become battles of lesser men, for it soon became clear that the Trojans did not send out to these small confrontations the men whose names were known by all the world as heroes, and soon neither did the Achaeans. Certainly there was no Hector in these raids, nor did Paris, who started it all by kidnapping Helen, ever ride forth. Polydamas once was sent out, perhaps because he is not of Trojan royal blood. But mostly it was cohorts of hoplites, men at arms commanded by some lieutenant or by some younger royal son of one of Priam's secondary concubines thirsting for glory, who, having only seen battle in cattle raids, hoped to find it in a fight with the Achaeans. What are these skirmishes? They are like dances in which everyone knows the steps.

For both sides time passed like single grains of sand moving through the smallest aperture of the inverted glass. Everything is at a standstill. Each morning King Priam went to the highest tower of Troy to stare at the Achaean army. Agamemnon spent his days in his tent with his brother and Odysseus, plotting ways to storm the walls. He sent out spies with instructions to seek out weaknesses in the defenses. But they come back to report what he already knows: Troy bravely flies its banners, trumpets sound from its towers, guards change and detachments march ten abreast on the battlements, and the walls rise black as obsidian and featureless, with no handhold to seize, no foothold on which to climb, no obvious weakness of which to take advantage. The great gates, bronze-bound and iron-clad seem as impregnable as the walls.

As each futile mission reported back to Agamemnon with no good news, or with no news at all, the army became restive and the ranks thinned as men disappeared. The king seemed paralyzed. He withdrew more unto himself, talking only with his brother, who never argued with him, or with Odysseus who flattered him for his own purposes. He ceased to hold councils, for he refused to listen to Achilles who urged a swift frontal attack and damn the consequences. He barely paid lip service to Nestor's age and the wisdom of his sage advice. He dismissed Aias as a bullying fool and since Diomedes and Idomeneus, able soldiers that they were, differed heatedly both with Odysseus and with Achilles on strategy, the king threw up his hands and refused to call a Council that could not agree amongst itself and could come up with no plan of any kind. Calchas, the priest who read the omens, daily brought news to the king garnered from the entrails of birds or the movement of eagles against the sky, insisting that this sign or that-- surely from one god or another—augured to the good.

The king's anger exploded: "I have had enough of gods and their omens," he shouted, and threw the golden wine cup across the room, its dark contents spilling across the floor like black blood. He was never without his wine cup, at all hours.

"Look where the gods have gotten us," and with his arm made a sweeping gesture that took in his shabby camp, his hungry men, and the distant, forbidding walls of Troy, dark, unscathed, un-breached. Yet Agamemnon did nothing.

In the ninth year of the war Achilles, sick of inaction, furious with the incompetence of his king, set out to find glory and plunder for himself and his band of men. In a series of swift raids Achilles captured Lyrnessus. Then with bloodshed and wanton ferocity he sacked Thebe, east of Mount Ida, killing Eetion its King and father of Andromache, Hector's wife. At this time along with gold Achilles took hostages, some for slavery, others for ransom. Among them was Briseis, the wife of a rich merchant of Thebe whose treasure he took also, and more significantly, Chryseis, daughter of Chryses, Priest of Apollo. That Chryseis was under King Eetion's protection was of no concern to Achilles' conquering hordes. That she was also under the God Apollo's protection did not seem to concern them either, though it should have.

Chapter 5

It is now a full year since I came here, nine years after the war began. The glorious battles have ceased, but the sordid minor skirmishes continue. Men still die. Everyday some Trojan force sallies out from behind their still un-captured walls, trumpets blaring. Across the plain they come in clouds of dust, chariots thundering, cohorts of Trojan soldiers jogging behind. We sound our alarms. We sally forth. We engage them. We kill some of them. They kill some of us. We drag our wounded or our dead back into the safety of the stockade walls the surround the camp. The dead we burn, the wounded we hope will heal. Every day Trojan forces return victorious to their city from the day's fighting. We are losing the war. The priests say that the gods have turned against us, that Apollo is protecting Troy and defeating us. They offer prayers to Zeus, endless sacrifices, yet he ignores them. And the Trojans attack, attack again, and win, and win again. In our camp, power wars with pride: Agamemnon's power, Achilles' pride, for there is animosity between them and we all wait with anxiety for some spark to ignite their hatred into a quarrel. What its end will be no man can tell.

We look to Achilles for help. And wait for him.

I wait for him too, as I have always done. But after that first and passionate encounter, Achilles has been all business, as one could say. I am his squire because that is the arrangement Achilles made with my father. I serve him at table, polish his armor, water and groom and walk the horses, keep the chariot well oiled to protect it against the salt sea air. And thus far the only taste of battle I had had was watching the pitiful excursions of a cohort or a chariot band of our men as they sallied forth from our camp in pursuit of some small Trojan force that had come racing out of Troy's gates, but which seemingly had only come to mock us, for they never stayed to fight. This I saw as stood at my lookout post on the camp walls. But I was deemed too inexperienced to fight, though I protested to my father that I was not. But to no avail.

"You are Achilles' squire. That is what you wanted. He will send you to battle when he thinks you are ready," my father said.

"Now go back to his tent; do as he commands you."

Oh, that he would command me, I thought, to do anything. But he does not command me. Thus I stayed at my post, as every soldier was required to do, and watched. So I was overjoyed and excited one day as I pottered around Achilles' tent, grinding some grain for bread, when he came up to me and tousled my hair.

"Enough of women's work. Get your sword. You, little lady, you must learn to fight like a man—like a Myrmidon."

I saw that he indeed had his own sword in hand. I grabbed mine that lay nearby. Then without warning and laughing, he lunged toward me. I tried to parry his thrust but failed, and with a swift and expert move he knocked my sword from my hand. I had thought myself good at arms, agile with the sword, strong at casting a spear, but Achilles showed that I was not, even as he taught me how to fight.

In the beginning our practice would usually end with me exhausted, knocked to the ground and out of breath, my sword lying on the sand nearby, and Achilles standing above me, his sword at my throat. I always hoped something would happen when we are out there, far from the camp, alone on the windswept shore. But we go for swordplay not love-play.

"Run, boy run," he shouted as he cast spears at me as I raced across the sand, trying to side step the oncoming missile. We practiced closer infighting so that I could master the lightning thrust of the long bronze-tipped ashen spear that could impale a man upon it. These exercises always ended in the same way, no matter how much I leapt and landed on the balls of my feet, or thrust hard toward Achilles. He always managed, with a graceful whirling pirouette like a bull dancer leaping over the oncoming beast, to knock the spear out of my hand and send it flying far away even as he tripped me and sent me reeling down on the sand. Then he would be upon me, kneeling over me, his spear across my shoulders, pinning me down.

"Be pleased that it is me, here, boy. Otherwise you would be dead."

I would lie there breathless and look up into his grey eyes, feel his breath on my face, the drops of his sweat falling on my naked chest—we always practiced naked just as we exercised naked in the gymnasium. If I could have freed myself I longed to throw my arms around him, pull him to me, kiss him, and let him do what he wanted, pierce me with a better sword. Once in a while he seemed to stay a moment too long on top of me, looked at me too intensely, and I sensed that there was some inward battle there, desire warring with his soldier's sense of duty. In his eyes I saw passion, but I also saw Patroclus.

As the days and weeks went by, and the war remained at a stalemate, there was not much else to do but learn from Achilles his warrior craft. From hand-to-hand battle on the ground it graduated to the war chariot. Racing along the ocean's edge, hanging on to the rails for dear life as Achilles drove us at breakneck speed, the water splashing on the horses flanks and on us, I grew to love it, the sheer mad exhilaration of it.

One day, Achilles said, "You drive."

Drive I did. Achilles threw spear after spear from a dozen in a case tied to the inner rail of the chariot, impaling as we careened past them the straw men we had set up as targets. That too I learned to do along with my less warlike chores.

My routine was to rise at dawn, and go to their tent, start a cook fire, mix some honey and wine, take it and bread and cheese into the tent for their breakfast. Achilles and Patroclus of course slept together, and ate together, fought together. And then of course, there was love. That too they did together.

Sometimes they were awake when I came, up and dressed in the simple short tunics they both wore. Sometimes though, they had not yet dressed, and they lay naked together on their bed when I brought the food, or the water I had taken from the stream nearby for them to wash. Those moments were not easy ones for me. They

34

are both so beautiful. And by now, as I have said, I had known them both. But no acknowledgment of that fact ever glimmered in any eye. I went about my duties, but I felt them watching me. And I wondered.

Then one morning Achilles roused me before the dawn.
"We march today, he said. Ready the chariot."
I leapt out of bed.
"I'm sorry my lord, I should have been up."
"No," Achilles said, "you should not have been; you did not know. I decide just this morning. But you know, my Antilochus, I think you have trained enough. It's time to put it into practice. Patroclus, on order of the king, goes out with a hunting party. They will be gone for a week to try to find food. Why should we sit here idle?

Within the hour two cohorts of his Myrmidons stood at ease before his tent and with them two units of horsemen. One cohort and horse would go with Patroclus, the others with Achilles and me. Achilles and me! I thrilled at the sound of that. In the tent I helped each of them to dress and to arm. Then we were ready.

Outside the soldiers came to smart attention. Achilles and Patroclus stood together before them, their armor glittering. Oh so beautiful. Then they embraced. The soldiers cheered, for they loved them too. Patroclus mounted his chariot, Automedon, the driver lightly flicked his whip against the horses. With a clatter and a cheer they went toward the main camp.

"Well, get up," he said, leaping in. "Drive."
Drive! I was to be Achilles' charioteer. Off we went.
"Do we go to the king for orders, my lord," I asked.
"No," he said. "Patroclus has orders. He must obey them. We have none. Head south."

I called to the horses as he had shown me how to do and off they went at a canter, quickly, but slow enough for the soldiers to come jogging along behind. I knew they could keep up this pace for hours. The chariot swayed as we moved forward; I held the reins loosely in one hand. With the other I steadied myself against the rail. Achilles stood next to me bareheaded, his golden hair gleaming in the rising sun. He did not hold the rail; he held in spear in one hand and in his face I could see adventure. He looked at me and grinned and quite suddenly threw his other arm around my shoulder; pulled me too him. I have never again been so happy.

And so after weeks of mock warfare with Achilles, now I felt ready. But I was not, for I had never seen war. We marched for three more days, camping at night, sleeping rough in small tents big enough to just squeeze in two men each. Two men were always on watch for we were far away from the area our forces controlled. True, the land was mostly empty, much of it burned and fallow, and where there were farms or small villages, these had often been despoiled in the early years of the war. But roving bands of peasants—insurgents we called them-- still lurked in the outlands.

We marched south toward Lyrnessus and Thebe that lies beyond Mount Ida. So we watched at night and moved fast during the day and came eventually in sight of Lyrnessus, a large settlement and still garrisoned by a small Trojan force. We could see it in the valley below, near the sea. We kept our distance, camped that night without fires. At dawn, we attacked, careening down the hillside, Achilles ready with his cache of spears in chariot, I driving like fury, his soldiers fully armed and wearing their fearsome helmets with long horsehair plumes, dark slits for the eyes that made them look inhuman. We fell upon the city just as the gates were opening at the first flush of dawn. It was total surprise. They had no time to close the gates before we raced through them, cutting and slashing as we passed.

I was not prepared for what happened. But the other soldiers were. This was the business they signed up to do. We coursed through the narrow streets, killing as we went, our chariot in the lead.

"Don't stop," Achilles said, as we headed straight toward a Trojan soldier, still half-undressed from his bed, trying to fit an arrow in his bow. I didn't stop because he might have been able to shoot it. I felt his body slam against the chariot wheels as we passed and heard his scream fading as we rushed ahead. Around us mayhem: fire arrows lighted the straw of a house roof; a band of men forced open a door and in high good humor tasted first blood, took what they could find, bits of gold or bronze, had quick and brutal sex with some woman handed laughingly around from man to man and followed by the swift flash of the sword as they cut her throat. I saw a poor lad shoved up against a wall and taken hard and left for dead. Pots were smashed when no gold was found, old men murdered by a blow to the head with a mace, old women too slow to avoid them run down by careening horses as riders spurred them on without a pause, babies snatched from mother's arms and tossed up to land on spear points. Houses burned. The screams and shouts: screams of the dying, the shouts of the looting soldiers caught up in the heady excitement that goes with war, spurring them on to do with dispatch and efficiency and with rivers of blood and the screams of the dying what armies are meant to do.

And I? I drove. I drove Achilles my lord and love. But I noticed that amidst all the carnage, he had thrown no spear. Later, after it was done, and I had been sick, and lay trembling by the fire. He sat beside me, bathing my forehead. I could not speak.

"That, Antilochus, is war," he said. "You'll get used to it."

I looked at him, at the cold grey eyes, the grimy face, the dust covered golden hair.

I had to say it: "but you did not kill today."

"This was for the men," he answered. "They needed it. I did not. I kill when there is a worthy enemy."

And so we kept on moving south towards our primary objective, Thebe, one of the largest of Trojan cities. Its king is Eetion, and he is the brother of Andromache Prince Hector's wife.

"We will do the same thing there, "Achilles said. "But with a difference. There we will take captives if we find them. They are worth their weight in gold."

Thebe is—was--a beautiful city. Its temple and acropolis rise above its walls; it is obviously ancient and obviously rich. Our strategy was indeed the same: barely at the break of dawn, just as the gates of the city had been opened to admit the farmers bringing goods to the market, without warning and before anyone knew what was happening, some farmers—our soldiers--threw off ragged cloaks to reveal armor. From the covered wagons—taken from Lyrnessus--usually full of produce, foot soldiers suddenly leapt and from out of the copse of trees that bordered the river our chariots and horsemen thundered toward the gates. The guards tried desperately to close them, but were overpowered by the sword-wielding foot soldiers, and almost without resistance the chariots swept through. The alarm bells sounded, but the sound was overpowered by the clatter of chariots and the horrid shouts of the triumphant invaders as they poured into the streets and into the market square that was already teeming with buyers waiting to secure the best of the day's provisions.

Our chariots rushed into the square followed by our horse and foot soldiers. I saw that many spears were already bloodied. Running by the sides of the chariot the soldiers, shouting horribly, brutally. I saw one soldier thrust with his spear and spit an old woman like a chicken. She sank into the dust as the soldier ran on without a second glance. All around, in the square, in the side streets, soldiers were cutting down the masses of people, swords flashing, blood spurting over baskets of carrots and cabbages fallen from lifeless hands.

The alarm bell had roused the garrison and it now began to pour into the streets. Behind us, King Eetion—it must surely have been he-- himself appeared, terrible in his armor, with a brace of spears. One he threw with unerring aim and downed a passing charioteer. Behind him arrayed in battle armor too were his seven sons. The king and his sons leapt with bloodcurdling cries down the steps of the palace and into the melee. The appearance of the king and his sons and his soldiers—but far outnumbered by our hordes still pouring through the gates--seemed to halt the onrushing tide of men, but only for a moment. Then I saw about thirty of our men fall upon the King and his sons and they disappeared into the battling throng.

The horsemen now formed a dizzying circle speeding around the square. The foot soldiers meanwhile were on the outside of the circle, spearing a body if it still writhed on the ground, cutting a throat that called for help, pushing women or boys against the walls and raping them quickly, and as quickly killing them. I could see flames begin to curl around the houses. A quartet of Theban soldiers started toward our chariot with rage in their eyes.

"Quick dismount," Achilles shouted to me. We leapt down and with our back to the chariot. The four attacked. Achilles and I fought side by side. As we cut and thrust, suddenly it came upon me, what I was to learn to call the rage of battle—excitement, exhilaration—and dare I say—the lust to kill. Two of the soldiers, thinking me an easy prey ran toward me. I caught the first soldier with my sword. I felt it enter his body and hit hard bone. With satisfaction I wrenched it free and saw him spit up black blood. The next one, scrambling up the palace steps, was upon me. I ducked as he swung, and then with full force brought my blade down on his shoulder. He crumpled and fell screaming. I grasped a spear from the dead hand of one I had slain. I ran it with all my strength between the shoulder blades of the soldier nearest me. I heard the voice of Achilles—"Well fought! Antilochus." Then he was gone, back into the savage mass of fighting men.

Then I saw what I had not seen before. Cowering behind a column was a girl. By her clothes I could see she was no peasant. A golden filet about her head and fine linen told of high birth. I heard Achilles voice in memory: "We will take captives. They are worth their weight in gold." I started toward her. Two Theban soldiers—perhaps protecting her--appeared out of nowhere, one moved toward her as if to pull her away, the other one toward me. I grappled with that one, but he was strong. The other began to pull her away.

Suddenly a chariot veered out of the melee and made straight for the place where I was trying to impale my attacker. For a moment the apparition of the onrushing chariot distracted the soldier, just enough for me to do what Achilles had so well taught me and I rushed my attacker, gathered my last strength and drove my sword into his throat, his blood spurted out and bathed me in the baptism of war. On came the chariot. As the chariot rushed towards us our soldiers shouted: "Achilles, Achilles, Achilles!"

The chariot seemed to pause in mid-flight and Achilles shouted to me: "Take the girl!"

She was still there where I had last seen her. I raced to her and seized her arm as the chariot came closer to us. With one hand holding the chariot rail Achilles swung himself out, precariously balancing on the lip of the chariot and with a loud shout to the me— "Get in, damn it, get in!"-- in a single movement he snatched the girl around the waist and pulled her, screaming, to him. I vaulted into the chariot and we wheeled away into the dust of slaughter. Achilles drove and I held the girl.

I remember nothing till I awoke the next morning in a small tent, lying on a pallet on the ground. Someone had covered me with a woolen blanket, but I was stiff and sore from the hard ground and the cold; there were dark bruises on my arm. It all came back. I remembered the attack on the city, and I remembered how much I liked it, how much I liked driving my sword into that unknown soldier's throat. Should I be ashamed to say it? No, I am not. I am soldier. This is what I do. And he was a worthy enemy. But the girl. Where was the girl?

I stooped through the low tent flap and came out into the sun. As I came out of the tent, the guard saluted.

"Lord Antilochus, Lord Achilles said not to wake you. But there is water and some bread if you want it."

"No, not now, thank you," I said. Plumes of smoke rose into the sky and distant and even darker clouds that hung like a pall over what I knew to be direction of the city. The sky was black with death. I walked toward what I knew were funeral pyres.

The flames crackled as the flesh caught fire and the fat burned from the bones. Before them a priest—a Theban priest--was saying prayers for the dead. Along the edge of the field soldiers in battle gear were drawn up. At the head of them, standing bareheaded was Achilles.

"Who are the dead?" I asked the guard.

"Ours. And theirs."

I watched the burning from my vantage there on the little hillock, surrounded by a score of campaign tents. Horses were all around, hobbled so as not to stray, and near them Achilles' chariot, still dusty and covered with mud. On it I could see dark stains dried almost black, the blood of innocents on the weapons of war. For all this slaughter Achilles had been responsible. He commanded death. Yet now he honored the dead, the same that he had slain. For such honor to the dead how could I not respect him, how could I not love him more?

Later, after the pyres had burned and the rites were done, Achilles came to me. He saluted when he saw me. I saw respect in his eyes.

"Well fought, young Prince," he said. Then: "Make yourself ready, for we must go. The girl is in the large tent, will you bring her."

I went to the tent. It was in fact Achilles' command tent. He and I had slept in a squad tent so that this girl could have the relative comfort of the larger one. She was there, not bound, and dressed as she was yesterday in simple linen. But over her clothes she wore a heavy woolen cloak; it was Achilles' cloak. About her head she still wore the golden filet, a narrow band of beaten gold inscribed with stars and symbols—symbols, I saw with a start, of Apollo, the archer God. I hesitated and knew that she was no ordinary girl. Despite her disheveled appearance she was invested with a quiet dignity--almost an aura of sanctity. I had seen that aura before—when my mother donned her robes as priestess of the goddess. I simply said, with a bow: "Will you come, my lady."

Tents were stowed into packs, fires stamped out, and the small army waited the order to march. In the chariot it was a tight fit, me as driver, Achilles, and the girl. She was not tied, I noted. He wrapped a blanket around her shoulders and told her to hold on to the chariot rails to steady her.

We set out, but set no swiftly careering pace, but moved at such a speed that the men who jogged behind would not tire too soon, nor would the hostages that some of the soldiers had taken, some boys for slaves as well as some woman, among them one named Briseis. Of her I thought nothing. But she would come to cause us grief.

As we passed the field where the pyres still smoked Achilles raised his hand to signal a halt. At his command, the column presented arms, an honor from soldier to soldier, from the living one last time to the dead.

41

We rode on in silence. He did not look at me. He did not speak. I realized he was exhausted as was I. As we moved ahead, the chariot bumping over the stony ground, the girl was jostled and nearly slumped down to the deck of the chariot. Achilles saw that and gently helped her slip down so that she could curl herself at his feet. He took a wine skin from his side and offered it to her.

"Drink," he said. "Have no fear. I know who you are. I honor the Archer God, as I know you do."

Then he turned to me.

"You too, Antilochus, drink." And handed me the wineskin.

Three days we traveled. We camped each night and each night the girl—her name we now knew was Chryseis—was given the larger tent, while Achilles and I bunked in the smaller. On the third night, the night before we would arrive back at camp, and--- as I well knew --the last night before he would arrive back to Patroclus, we had sex—no, not that—we made love. It was that simple. There was little preamble. I did not expect it. We were lying in the tent—there was not much room to do anything else other than lie together. It was late, the camp slept around us; the only sound was the horses and the distant clink of the arms of the sentries.

"You did well," Antilochus, he said. "You fought well. And you treated her well, as befitting her rank. Do you know who she is?"

"She is not ordinary," I said.

"Your instincts are good, then, for she is worthy and she is holy. But I fear she will bring us sorrow." Then he said: "How did you feel when you killed."

I knew what I wanted to answer, but hesitated to say it. Then I said: "I ... I liked it. But I would not do it unless I had to."

"You will make a worthy soldier then," he said. "You cannot hate killing; you are a soldier; it is what you must do. If you hate it you may fear to do it when you most need to—to save yourself. But do not like it enough to do it without reason."

Then he took my hand and pulled me to him, held me, kissed me, and made love to me. This was not the brutal Achilles I knew that first time. This was a man making love to a man, sharing himself with the other.

42

And as our bodies, naked now and gleaming in the guttering firelight joined together, as hands explored and touched and caressed, as lips sought lips, as at last we joined, we rose up into that mystic world where the two become one at last, where identity vanishes and life and care have no meaning and love is blessed, whole, and divine and ecstasy is shared and returned, again and again.

Afterward, we lay there together, hands grazing one another, close in the confine of our little tent. I looked at him, wondered if after this, after what we had shared, if he felt Patroclus out there someplace, watching him. I got my answer when, suddenly overwhelmed with the wonder of what had happened I said—I could not help myself from saying it—"I love you."

He turned his head toward me, his grey eyes shrouded in the darkness, his gold hair glowing softly in the firelight. I waited, hoping to hear what I most wanted him to say. For long time he kept silent, then looking away from me and out into the night as if he sensed that someone else was there, waiting, he said: "Don't love me. It will only bring you grief."

I could say nothing, could not stop the tears. And so I let them fall as I watched him fall asleep, lying there, one arm flung out over my chest, his hair falling into his eyes, his head cradled by his other arm, a light blanket barely covering him, riding low on his hips, his body covered with a fine down of glinting golden hair that glowed in the wash of moonlight that shone through the open tent door so that he seemed to float on a silver cloud. It is as everyone says. He is the most beautiful man in the world, and the most tragic—for who does not know what is foretold. I love him; we have loved. It is said that he who loves is more worthy than the beloved. I will be worthy.

At the end of the fourth day we came down into flat lands. I could see the ocean glinting, smell the sea. It was not long till in the distance I saw Troy's high tower rising above the horizon, then gradually the city itself same into view. We turned toward the sea and as the sun was setting we came to the high wall of our camp. From wooden watchtowers a challenge came. But no one doubted who it was awaiting entrance at the gates. No one need be told that

Achilles, slayer of men, had come back with plunder and with captives.

We entered the camp. Men ran up to unyoke the horses. The tired soldiers dropped their heavy packs and, dismissed by Achilles, disappeared into the forest of tents. Achilles helped Chryseis from the chariot. A slave waited nearby.

"Take her to Agamemnon's tent," he said. He bowed to her. "My Lady Chryseis," he said, "forgive me. Though I have captured you, you belong to Agamemnon. I have no choice."

Chapter 6

Spoils of war we call them—gold, jewels, horses, weapons, women, boys—anything taken by the victor from the vanquished. All of it is the property of the king, our lord and master. He decides who will be given what trinket or what treasure as a reward for fighting well or killing many so as to fill the king's coffers with loot or his bed with women. Thus it was only a few days after we-- Achilles and I--brought the Trojan captives to the camp that we were commanded to come to king for the sharing of the spoils.

Agamemnon lounged in a low chair, a goblet by his side. We stood to one side of him as the captives were brought in. A brace of soldiers herded them into the tent. There were six of them: two boys in their teens and four women-- two peasant women, another captive, a dark haired woman whose name I had learned was Briseis and who must have been captured by a cohort of Achilles' men for I had not seen her till now. And of course the beautiful young woman with long golden hair whose head was hidden with a hood, but who Achilles and I knew was called Chryseis. They stood with heads bowed.

They dared not look up for they were in the presence of Agamemnon, the man whose name had for so long now struck terror into Trojan hearts. I wondered what must be passing through their minds as they stood there, their captivity come about and their daily lives destroyed because we Greeks had swarmed ashore from our thousand ships, brutally attacking their villages and towns, despoiling their countryside, pillaging, raping, burning, leaving nothing in our wake but ruin. Now they were in the midst of the enemy—their enemy—in the camp where our huge army waited outside of Troy's walls like patient spiders lying in wait for the prey to make one false move.

"Well Achilles," the king said, "what have you brought me?"

A scribe sat at the king's right. Achilles signed to the scribe who began to read from a list.

"Twelve bronze cauldrons, three bags of gold, fourteen bags of copper coins, fourteen golden cups, a cache of swords, bows, and spears, seven amber necklaces, three coffers of assorted jewels, eight amphorae, three of wine, four of oil, one of vinegar, a cartload of grain, twelve cows, three newborn lambs and four ewes, two horses, and six captives, who you see before you sire."

"Not a bad haul, Achilles." the King said. "I accept it. Since you brought this, you and your men, take the weapons and a bag of gold. Give the copper to your men. Take one—no I will be generous-- take two of the cups for yourself and if you want the boys, they are yours."

Turning to the scribe he said: "Put that all down as the Lord Achilles' share. Now let's break open some of that wine and kill one of the lambs for my dinner. Its time to inspect the livestock."

Then he rose and came to where the captives were standing in a row. He stood at the head of the line and gave them all a look, then began to walk slowly along the row. He came to the boys, who were first in line. The first of them, the older of the two, almost a man, perhaps 17, with dark glossy hair and dark-set eyes, with high cheekbones and olive skin, was exceptionally handsome. The king lifted his head, felt the muscles in his arm and them moved to the next one, shorter, younger, barely 14 summers I judged, but even prettier. They must have been brothers.

"So Achilles, which boy do you want? Perhaps both?" The king asked. I heard a note of mockery in his voice.

"Neither my lord. I do not need boys." Achilles—very coldly—replied.

"Neither? Neither?" the king said, "well what use are they to me? I do not want boys, and they will take too long to train as soldiers. That will be too much trouble. We need no more Trojan rats. Scribe, mark it down, kill them in the morning. Now what next?"

"My lord, let us reconsider." Odysseus, standing just behind the king's chair spoke up.

"Yes, Odysseus," the King said, "Do you want them? I did not know you liked pretty boys."

"I am faithful to my wife Penelope, Lord King," Odysseus said, "but it is a shame to kill two perfectly healthy and perfectly useful boys who can be perfectly useful slaves. If my lord Achilles has no, uh –use-- for them I can find a place for them in my service." He looked at Achilles, who merely nodded agreement.

"Well good that is settled then," the king said. Moving on until he came to the next two captives, one a girl, the other an older woman, dressed in the tatters. The king casually forced his fingers into old woman's mouth to look at her teeth, as if he were appraising cattle at market. He grimaced. "Old crone," I heard him say.

Then turning to the girl he ran his hands slowly across her body, lingering on her breasts, running his hand beneath her tattered and skimpy dress and then, between her legs. She whimpered and cringed as he touched her. I could see the older woman's face go white with fear and with rage. She was certainly the girl's mother.

"Ah, a sweet tender child," the king said, as he continued to caress her. "She will soon be sweeter. Scribe make a note: Take her to the woman's tent, put her to work, but do not fail to remind me that she is there. Oh yes, find out if the old woman can be ransomed. If not, kill her."

It was then the turn of the dark-haired girl. The king looked her up and down, just as with the girl, touched her, ran his hands over her body, cupping her breasts in his hands, probing her stomach."

"A bit flabby there, he said, "what is your name?".

She stammered, "It is Hyppodomia, but they call me Briseis."

"And your father, Briseis, is he rich?

" He is dead my lord."

"But then a husband, surely you have a husband?"

"He is dead too," she said, through tears.

"Oh dear," the King said, "dead father, dead husband, not a virgin, no money I suppose either. And not too pretty, a bit old for my bed. What can you do, can you cook?"

" No Lord, but I can read and I can write."

With an incredulous look, he said: "A woman? Read and write? You must be mad--or a liar. No women can read or write;

47

they do not have the brain for it. I am sure you can carry water and wash clothes."

Last in the line was Chryseis. Through all the terrible interrogations she had stood silent, unmoving. The king went to her and pulled back the hood. I could hear a gasp in the room and the king said, "Well, this is a different filly altogether."

She was—is—beautiful. Ivory, flawless skin, deep grey blue eyes, hair like flax or spun gold. Raising her head she looked directly at the King. I could not see her eyes, but I could see his, and for moment he seemed taken aback, almost frightened by her unflinching stare. He reached out his hand as if to touch her as he had the rest of the women. But with a sudden movement she stepped back and raised her hand in a commanding gesture

"Touch me at your peril," she said, her voice melodious but commanding, ringing a cross the room.

I could see the rage mount in the king's face. Then he stepped back. I was sure he would have her killed on the spot. But instead he stood looking at her for moment.

"Who is she?" he asked to the room. "Who is she?" he shouted. No one replied.

Then she answered: "I am Chryseis, daughter of Chryses priest of Apollo Smintheus. I am given to the god and I am sacred and no man can touch me."

The king smiled a slow cold smile.

"A different filly indeed and spirited one. Perhaps you are right, lady. You need no mere man, you need a king to break you."

At that point Achilles stepped forward.

"I protest. I claim her as mine. I won her in battle and she is mine by right."

"Oh yes, Achilles, you would not take pretty boys who bring no ransom and would only be good for fun, but now that you hear that she night bring gold you leap forward to claim her. No she is mine. I will keep her. I am king. Take this other woman if you want a prize. Though what you will do with her I don't know. She is a damaged goods. You should have taken the boys when you had the chance. That is my decision."

Achilles went white "I debase myself staying here," he said.

He walked to Chrysies and bowing said, "Lady, you will need companionship for what is to come; take this woman Briseis, she will serve you well."

He turned to the king.

"And that, my lord, is *my* decision."

With no bow to the king, he left the tent.

The king stood just in front of me so I could see rage mingled with—with fear perhaps-- in his eyes. This was Achilles after all, who they call slayer of men, the most fearsome of all the Greeks. Perhaps not even a king would dare to do other than what this man had commanded.

"Oh no matter," the king said, "She is no prize. Antilochus do take the *Lady* Chryseis"--he emphasized the title mockingly— and all these slaves away." I saluted and escorted them all out of the tent. The boys I sent to the stables, the two women to the cooking tents and Chryseis and Briseis I escorted to the tent where Chryseis was now to be quartered and where Briseis would be her slave—a slave to a slave, as fate had ironically decided. A slave in the Greek camp. A slave meant for Agamemnon as all women are meant for Agamemnon, as all are his slaves and toys of his desire.

Despite his words—"she is no prize"—I could see it in his eyes that he thought she was one indeed. And it would come to pass that the King became nearly besotted with her—though it may have been the madness of lust—and from the lust of a single man there came great harm to all of us.

Chapter 7

When the king's storyteller lets it be known that he has composed a new tale or another version of the old familiar stories, the army is often called together to hear what he has made. The event is an entertainment; it relieves the boredom of the camp and the stories inspire us all for they praise the prowess of Greek arms in battle, retail our victories and remind us of the tales of gods and men that we have all known since we were young.

On this instance I was detailed to bring the Trojan captives—the two women Chryseis and Briseis, and the two pretty boys, the older of whom I had come to know better perhaps than anyone imagined, and so I asked that he and his brother be assigned to me as grooms for my two horses. Why waste such strong boys I thought, and Odysseus agreed and he gave them to me.

I led them from the slave tent pitched a short distance from that of the king, along the narrow path, trodden smooth now over the years, that runs to the place of assembly. As we walk I hear the eerie sounds of the night birds, the plaintive and musical cry of the cuckoo, the mournful calling of the owl; small creatures in the grass scurry away as we come. From someplace in the camp a horse whinnies; something is dropped with a clatter; a low hubbub sounds from the assembly field toward which we walk; someone in a tent curses as we pass; I smell millet and onions cooking. In the distance the waves break against the beach where the long ships have been pulled far up on the sand, the sound a slow steady rolling beat almost more felt than heard. I cannot see them, but I know that the wine dark waves rush in from some distant world in steady procession, propelled across the lengths of the sea until they come roiling and crashing against the hulls of the black ships where their smooth fluid darkness is broken into moonlit spray and sea foam. Then, their force spent for a moment; they retreat back again out into the night, down the beach and dissolve, only to return again to make another assault on the land. The sound calls me home to the land of my father and mother and I wonder if I will ever see it again.

50

The firelight casts strange shadows against the tents, small gray canvas ones for most of the men, larger ones in regimental colors for captains, spacious ones for great lords and allied kings, the largest, striped, its poles gilded and with pennants flying, for Agamemnon. The walls of the camp, looming at a distance in darkness, seem to rise higher in the shadows the firelight casts. We come to where the men are gathered, the camp parade ground. The men are not, as they would be at a review, armored and standing at stiff attention. Instead they lounge in groups, or sit around small fires, talking with one another, throwing dice, or passing leather cups of wine and water, sharing flat loaves of bread and red clay dishes of lentils and onions. We move around the edge of the field; no one notices us as we come to one side of the dais where Agamemnon sits with Menelaus by his side. At the center of the circle of men stands the man we have come to hear.

He wears a long robe, somewhat soiled, and a cape of some dark equally untidy material, which is, in odd contrast, clasped at the shoulder with a brooch of rich and intricate workmanship, set with carnelians, and filigreed in gold. His face is lined and sunburned, set off by white hair flowing over his shoulders. He seems to stare into the firelight as if finding there dancing images with which to people his songs, though of course he sees nothing, since he is blind.

I wonder what tales he will tell tonight. To recall the men to faith in deity, perhaps he will revive old songs of the birth of the gods and the foundation of the world. To sober them and remind them of their duty to gods and kings, he may tell terrible tales of vengeance and humiliation, warning songs about how that dread Goddess Nemesis punishes those who walk with too much pride.

Or he might amuse the men with lewd accounts of Pan and how he pursues young women and sweet boys into glades and groves and has his way with them, frolicking naked with them in the leafy moonlight, a golden-haired girl taken in a frenzy of goatish passion as they lie on a rock at midnight by a murmuring stream, or a dark- haired black-eyed boy held in wild embrace as they consummate their desire. The men will like these stories.

But perhaps to steel their resolve and inflame their warrior hearts, he will tell the deeds of Ares, God of War, who loves battle

51

for its own sake and delights in slaughter and the sacking of towns, or of Jason and the brave Argonauts who captured at great peril the Golden Fleece. I am sure that Agamemnon will have ordered him to tell that tale to remind his men that Troy is their Golden Fleece.

But tonight he tells no old tales. Instead he has verses from a new story, the one that all the world knows that he has long been making. Agamemnon must have commanded this. Slowly he begins, voice like a clarion, surprisingly strong in a man so old. It carries to the furthest reaches of the field, and its echoes return from the encampment walls. He tells the story of the outrage committed against the ancient house of Atreus--the terrible wrong done to the noble Menelaus and the dishonor this has brought upon Agamemnon his brother, all men's lord. At this the soldiers raise a hearty cheer and they cheer even more loudly when he recites a catalogue of Trojan vices. Soon he has them worked to frenzy, booing and hissing at any mention of the scheming and vicious people whose sole aim is to rule the world and destroy the cities and rape the wives of decent god-fearing men. "Thus our heroes have come to Troy," he loudly intones, "to make the Trojan warriors drink dark blood and bring their walls crumbling to dust."

The men are in a thoroughly good mood now, hanging on his words. Lowering his voice and leaning intimately toward the troops who strain to hear him, he begins verses describing Helen, Menelaus' queen. In his rich, deep, and hypnotic voice he chants the honorifics that he has written about Helen--"Praise her, White-armed Helen, that noble, devoted, and ever-faithful wife." A keen ear can hear from the ranks a muffled burst of knowing laughter. Menelaus hears it too and his eyes darken and his brow furrows.

The men listen eagerly as the tale progresses: upstart Paris, son of the Trojan king steals Helen away; he seduces her. Some of the men give their mates jabs in the ribs, winks of complicity, and others snicker. At this Menelaus and Agamemnon adopt suitably outraged glares. The commanders, standing at the head of their cohorts, shoot dark looks in the general direction of their men. Those in the front ranks quickly compose themselves, but from the rear rank the snickers and a voice: She had it coming because she wanted it."

Our poet tells stories for men: tales of war and plunder. of battle and death, and about how men win and break the hearts of women; how women betray good men and do them wrong. Nothing pleases a man more than to hear that women cannot be trusted and that they deserve the treatment men mete out to them. He has no laments for women taken in battle, for young girls raped or old women slain, for mothers who have lost a daughter, for women who are captives and slaves.

He pauses a moment and looks into the firelight with sightless eyes. I wonder: does he see visions there, sometimes brilliant and detailed, sometimes vague, fleeting, difficult to discern? Did he look into the future when this terrible war began to see what the end might be? As if in answer to my unspoken question, he raises his hand again, signaling for silence.

"Now my Lord," he says bowing to the king, "and all you brave soldiers of Greece. Hear now my new song for it foretells the days of glory that will soon come to all of you."

His voice begins softly and then rises to a stronger note as he speaks the mixed half-spoken half-chanted verses of his tale. The fire blazes up as if a magician had repeatedly thrown his magic powders on a flame as they do when they conjure incandescence out of night, and I—all of us—are transfixed by sound of the poet's voice. The world around me seems to disappear and as he conjures a vision of what will come, his keening voice is hypnotic as if he has cast a spell upon us—upon me— and I can see—actually see—what I hear him sing.

Everything around is lit with unnatural light. In the lightening flashes I see horrors. Black ships with water like white teeth foaming at their prow fly upon the beach—they are our ships, ships of our proud Greek army. Men pour over the sides. A beacon flashes from one of Troy's towers. They march, flowing across the plain like a silent and deadly tide creeping toward the sleeping town. They are at the walls. The gates open. Men pour through. Still the city sleeps.

From a dozen points along the walls flames begin to rise. Then, in an instant Troy's walls are a ring of fire and with a shout and a clash of arms that shakes the heavens, the Achaeans attack and at last in the city an alarm is sounded. Trojan soldiers pour out of the barracks, but like ants swarming from a broken nest that is stamped upon and killed by the feet of their destroyer, they cannot stand and fall back overcome and are finally overwhelmed by the on-rushing Greek forces swarming through the gates and through the broad streets of Troy.

Towers sprout bright bouquets of fire, the flames shooting up like beacons lighting the carnage: ranks of grim Greek soldiers march shield to shield across the square, like reapers their swords are scythes cutting living grain, spreading a carpet of black blood upon the pavement. Nothing stands against them. They do not stop but move inexorably, their boots crush the bodies they have slain and as they pass they skewer any who seem to cling life. A screaming woman runs from a burning house. A soldier purses her. With a stroke her head is lopped off and with a shout of triumph he scoops up the bloodied golden goblet she was cradling in her arms.

In the lurid light of the burning city soldiers run from house to house forcing barricaded doors and windows, tossing burning torches through them and rushing in even as the flames begin to crackle. Then they are out, herding frightened people. A flash of a sword, a thrust of spear, they fall—an old woman, a mother clinging to her child, someone's aged grandfather—or an arrow hisses as an archer picks them off as they stumble out through the rising smoke. From house to house they go, from palace to palace, and the heaps of treasure grow and grow as warriors return with sacks bulging with gold and gems, with arms laden with treasures that have come to Troy from all the world, amassed for a thousand years.

In the square soldiers rush toward the palace and mount the broad steps that lead to its great bronze doors. As they run they cut down the royal guards who stand, and die, vainly to protect them. The attackers are at the head of the stairs before the doors. Someone shouts, "Batter them down! Take the king!" But then the doors slowly open. The attacking soldiers stop, wait, to see if some larger force will issue out.

The doors are open wide now. There, in the door, standing in the center, is a man, old and alone. It is Priam. The sacred Lord of Troy, High King of Ilium, son of a thousand kings. He waits, robed and crowned, with his sword in his hand and around him a corona of light seems to glow. Who could not be stunned and stirred by that? The ancient majesty of Troy, descended from the blood of Zeus, has come out to defend his realm. The soldiers stare in awe at what they see. They falter; they begin to fall back.

Then their commander leaps in front of them and races up the steps to where Priam stands. He shouts: "We did not come here to let him live," and with a single stroke his sword like a whirling silver arc slashes through Priam's neck and the body falls in a shower of blood. The commander stoops to retrieve the crown, fallen to the ground. He raises it and the soldiers, their faces mirroring at once horror and triumph, race up the palace steps. and soon the cries of the dying horribly resound from inside the ancient halls.

Dreadful sights flash by my eyes without respite. The city burns. Its people die. Hecabe, Troy's Queen is taken in fetters, cursing, to Odysseus' ship. The palace is put to the torch. And from its heights I hear screams, terrible screams. A woman struggles, her face a mask of horror. It is Andromache, wife of Hector. She shrieks a curse at the soldier who turns from the parapet over which he has just hurled her child, Astynax, heir of Troy. The child seems to float on air for a moment like a bird—then falls, falls, plunging toward the rocks, strikes them, and like a pomegranate that splits wide open when it plummets from its tree, stains the pavement upon which it falls a rich dark red. With a satisfied smile the soldier makes a sign. Guards bind her, and drag her screaming away. Her scream echoes, and in it I hear the agony of all the ages and the prophecy of the end.

And then as suddenly as it came, all is now calm and silent. My head is full of inchoate images, meaning nothing. The silver moon, full and glittering sends a beam, like a path to heaven. Time readjusts itself and I return to the moment, beside the dying fire. The bard stands, immobile, as is still in his holy trance, and all around the ranks of the men, as stunned and hypnotized as was I, ponder the vision they have been given.

Then the full import of the tale hits home and the men raise a cheer and roused to patriotic frenzy by the perfidy of the Trojans and to militant pride by the nobility of the Achaeans and by the promise of victory to come, they settle down to drink, as men do when they have nothing else to occupy them and few women to share.

I escort my charges back to the tents, our little procession passing close by to the dais where Agamemnon and Menelaus sit, now drinking with the storyteller. As we pass the king sees us out of the corner of his eye.

"Look, there she goes," he shouted. "Isn't she a beauty? That's Chryseis. You should tell her story some day," he said loudly. "I took her from her father. That would make a good story. And I've got some other stories that would spice it up, if you know what I mean."

Laughing he clapped his brother on the shoulder and drained his cup. I see a flush of shame cover the Lady Chryseis' face and she breaks free from me and runs back to her tent.

I could hear the king shouting after her: "Run all you want, I know where you are. Better get ready. By the Gods I want her," he says to Menelaus. His raucous laughter follows as I ran after her through the twisting narrow aisles between the tents. My men lopping along by my side I pass her and reach the tent before she does and hold the tent flap open for her.

"Sleep, my lady," I say. "He may be too drunk to remember that you were even there. Do not be afraid, I will wait awhile here at your door."

But drunk though he was, he did remember her. Sometime later as I stand with my guards outside the tent, I hear shouts coming from the parade ground, the sound a crowd makes as it leaves a building or a stadium, a disorderly sound, nothing comprehensible, people talking or laughing, the noise rising and falling as hundreds of people walk or run, hurrying somewhere.

56

The men are returning to their quarters. And coming along the same path is Agamemnon, alone.

"Dismissed!" he shouts at my men. " I salute and begin to leave.

"No, Prince Antilochus," he says, "you stay." There is rage in his voice. My men march away. He enters the tent.

"Follow Me," he brusquely says. I follow him in. At a table with a single lamp burning before her sits the Lady Chryseis. She should rise when the king enters. She does not.

He unlooses his cloak, undoes the sword belt and lets his sword drop to the ground.

"Help me," he commands me, gesturing to the breastplate he wears. I am no servant, I think, but nevertheless go to him, unlace it; that too falls to earth. He throws himself on the bed.

"Bring me drink," he commands.

I look around. Briseis, the women Achilles gave Chryseis, cowers in the corner, her face a mask of fear. I pour some wine from a bronze pitcher into a goblet. The king takes it without thanks and drinks it down and holds it out for more. I fill the cup again. He drains the cup and throws it to the ground.

"Watch, soldier" he says, "See how a king takes his pleasure."

He advances to where Chryseis sits.

"So fair-cheeked Chryseis," he says, his voice low and menacing, "did you enjoy the tale our bard has to tell? Tell me, slut, did you like it? Did you think of your father?"

Suddenly he pulls her to her feet and slaps her. She staggers back. He advances and takes her arm, pulling her to the bed and forces her down and with both hands pinions her shoulders to the mattress. Then he is astride her his knees pressing into her sides. His fingers grip her shoulders. She struggles, but he is too strong.

"Tell me," and his voice now is low and menacing, "Tell me, whore, do you want your father? Or will I do just as well?"

He frantically pulls at the brooch that holds her gown.

She screams.

He hits her again.

"Tell me! Tell me!" he shouts and rips the garment from her shoulder, baring her breasts.

"Tell me!" he shouts again. "Will I do just as well as your father?"

I can bear it no longer. I must stop him. His back is to me and I leap at him, grappling him from behind in a fury, and pull him from her, putting my hands around his shoulders, holding him in a wrestling grip. I think: what am I doing? I am laying hands on the king. Treason, sacrilege, I will die for this.

I do not care. He breaks free and turns to face me. I see rage and madness in his eyes and smell the sour wine on his breath. He shoots his fist out and catches me on the side of the cheek. I stagger back from the blow that sends me reeling. I taste blood – my blood. But anger drives me and I return the blow catching him on the shoulder. He staggers back now. His eyes are dark and his face is red with wine and anger. I have no choice and I rush at him again, knocking the wind out of him with my charge. Then he goes limp and like a discarded rag doll falls heavily upon the ground. As he falls I hear him say, to Chryseis, "I am not your father. I have no daughter now." And he begins to sob and slumps to the earth.

We stand, Chryseis and I, staring down at him. All my anger drains away. I am filled with strength. The king has slipped heavily to the floor and is snoring now, unconscious. I watch him there, this King of Kings, this Lord of Men, this drunken, broken, despicable sot. All I feel is contempt. I despise this man. I hate him for what he has done to her, to all of us. But what will it matter I think. I have attacked the king. My life is forfeit.

Chryseis reaches out a hand to me and I am sure that she must see in my eyes that I am shaken, breathless and fearful—fearful for my life.

She bends over the unconscious king, kneels beside him, passes her hands over his face, touches his closed eyes with her finger tips and I can just hear her as she softly croons low indistinct words—strange, foreign as if it were an incantation. It almost seems to me that around her kneeling figure the light gathers into a hazy aura. I rub my eyes. The light is gone.

She rises and looks at me. She smiles and says: "You need have no fear, he will remember nothing of this night."

She makes another gesture. And as if he were a puppet on strings controlled by Chryseis, Agamemnon struggles to his knees, and unsteadily rises. He stands, stares at us, but it is clear he sees nothing. And then like a man in a trance he stumbles out of the tent and into the night.

Book Three
The Priest of the Archer God

Chryses, priest of the Archer–God Apollo, came to the ships of the bronze clad Achaeans to set free his daughter. He said: "Agamemnon, you hope to sack King Priams's city. The gods will grant that wish but only if you reverence Apollo and set my daughter free."
--Iliad 1.10-12; 18-20

From: Dionysos of Tenedos,
A History of the War at Troy

It was thus in the ninth year of the seemingly endless and futile war and soon after the capture of Chryseis, that another person also came. This was Chryses, Priest of Apollo, father of Chryseis who Agamemnon held as a slave, and he brought a glittering ransom to convince Agamemnon to let him take his daughter home.

And who was this Chryses who came to confront earth's greatest king? A simple priest? How could he dare challenge a king? But Chryses was not just any priest. He served Apollo the Archer-God, slayer of men. Through Chryses Apollo spoke when, knife in hand, wrapped in the robes of his calling, Chryses subdued the poor struggling creatures that had been brought to the temple to be sacrificed. It was then that the God was made manifest, and if he deigned to speak to men, it would be Chryses who heard him.

Daily he served at the altar as priest of Apollo, hierophant of His sacred mysteries. Daily he conducted the rituals appointed since time began and celebrated the great festivals in the God's name, there in Chrysa, at the temple that all men call the Smintheum, for Apollo is also named Smintheus—plague bearer. There Chrsyes prayed: "Hear me, Apollo, great Lord of the Silver Bow, you who rule above Chrysa, you who are sacred in Cilla and Lord over Tenedos, Lord Smintheus, god of Pestilence and slayer of men, hear my prayers."

I have seen this temple. It is small and simple: six columns simply capped support the pediment and ten march down each side, some showing just a trace of color. Though when Chryses served there it must have been gorgeous with red and ochre and blue. The large central room in which people gather, not only for holy things but also for fellowship and safety, is paved with huge ancient stones, worn by the passing of untold numbers over untold years. In the sanctuary the altar is raised on a low stone platform at the end. The image of the god was washed with color so long ago that now it is more a suggestion than an actuality. The long belted robe, which

61

somehow the sculptor didn't quite finish at the base, falls in straight folds; the arms are tight at his sides. His face is worn, impassive, and on his lips there is the hint of an odd, almost knowing smile. His blank eyes, once no doubt painted to look like life, stare out across the room, past the temple porch and toward the distant sea. Both the image and the temple are of an age beyond the memory of any man.

I placed a garland on the altar for Apollo and left grain for the mice that played about it, for as all men know, mice—sminthios in the old tongue--are sacred to this God, and carry his messages and sometimes his wrath—the pestilence before which evens strong men, helpless, fall. When I was there I could not help but feel that I was being watched. Was it by the spirit of Chrsyes, who served at that altar so very long ago? Ah, Chryses, would that I had known you, instead of trying to imagine you so as too make you real in my story of that terrible and unjust war.

Chapter 8

I had been on lookout duty in the south watchtower when the ship came into view. Its sail, yellowish ochre with a device in dark blue hard to make out emblazoned on it, hung lank and hollow, since there was no wind. And so the painted oars rose and fell, rose and fell, glinting silver in the sun, with every sweep driving the ship in, closer to the shore.

The ship is not a big one, one deck only and a single bank of about ten oars on each side. But it is luxurious; painted a rich royal blue, and picked out with a long red line running along the length of it. On the high deck in the stern there was a stripped canopy—red and blue also-- raised to shield whoever might be carried there from the sun. The prow rose high, carved into the head of some sea creature not easy to see from where I stood, and the great eye, painted just above the water line so as to allow the ship to see its way, stared watchful and unblinking into a vague distance, seeing things no doubt hidden to mere men.

I watched the ship drive straight in to the beach, moving with a white rush of foam across the mirror that was the sea. By its side as if in escort, dolphins leapt and dove and gamboled, affable messengers from Poseidon I had been told in school, meant to keep ships company and show a sign of Poseidon's good will.

I could just hear, echoing across the water, the thud, thud, thud, thud of the oar-master's drum keeping his men in even stroke. Then the beat stopped, and like a forest suddenly appearing, the oars were raised and with a flash of foam the ship drove straight into the beach, slowing as it came, until ever so gently it came to berth, a neat and elegant piece of seamanship, I have to say. It landed at the far end of the line of our ships, which put it some way down the beach, since the Achaean vessels were drawn up in a line nearly a league in length.

I rang the watch bell three times and three times again—an alert that said that something was occurring but that there seemed to be no obvious danger-- and shouted down to the guard at the base to hotfoot it to Menelaus, who was in conference, or perhaps just drinking with the king. The ship was berthed now, and its crew, not a large one so far as I could see and looking like miniatures from this distance, were swarming down the ladders that had been dropped over the side and were shoring up the prow with stout timbers that had been tossed off, along with the anchor stones, by some still on board.

Since no ship, none at all, had come near us for more than a year, this was an event. And it was no surprise that the sound of running feet heralded the arrival of Menelaus himself and close behind him Calchas, robes flapping, panting, his chaplet askew. Menelaus clambered up the steep ladder to the tower and pulled himself up through the trap. I threw a salute and without a word pointed to the beach.

"Well, well," he said. "Can you see if they are armed? "

"I don't think so sir," I said. "It's hard to see from here, but the ship is no warship and the crew can't number any more than thirty all told including the oarsmen."

By this time Calchas pulled himself on to the platform just in time to see the distant sail with it's vague blazon lowered and furled. Calchas stared into the distance, his black eyes narrowed, and it seemed to me that just before the sail was hidden from view I heard him make a sharp intake of breath. Then he looked at us from under his bushy eyebrows with that dark staring look, full of meaning and mystery, with which he manages to convince everyone that his every utterance is fraught with eternal significance.

Calchas said sharply: "Inform the king. This is a holy person. He must be received with honor." He clambered back down with no further word.

"Well," said Menelaus, "I guess we've been told."

He leaned over the tower railing and shouted to his aide who was waiting below:

"Rouse Talthybius, I want a general quarters sounded. And get someone up here to take Lord Antilochus' watch."

Turning back to me: "Go rouse your father. I'll go tell the king."

I stand just to the side of my father, on the dais on the right hand of the king, the place of honor always reserved for my father and for Menelaus, the king's younger brother. The king is not sitting, but impatiently paces, talking in low tones to Odysseus and to Calchas. Sometimes he stops and calls for a report from the lookout in the near tower. We all wait the arrival of the stranger whose ship was sighted this morning and which has now berthed itself at the end of the long line of our ships, about a league or so away. A herald was sent to meet him, but he has not returned because he will accompany the stranger to the king. Thus no one yet knows who our visitor might be. But he is someone of consequence, that is of no doubt, and thus the army waits on parade.

We are gathered under an awning of heavy sailcloth that seems to keep the heat in and whatever breeze there might be out. The rank and file are drawn up in the full sun. It is not possible from where I stand to see the figures around the ship, but the lookout in the near tower calls down to say that they appear to be waiting for someone to disembark. There are just a handful he says, and he can see no arms. Eventually he calls again to say that someone has at last left the ship and has been installed in a carrying chair, that our herald has greeted him, and that now the stranger is being carried, followed by an entourage in procession, from his ship toward the camp.

We wait the arrival of the visitor. We wait to learn the purpose of this unusual event, to see what news it may bring us, for we never hear news from home. It seems that all we ever do now is wait. Indeed, it is a year? Two? More? —that I have waited here. I have become a man and a hardened soldier, though a bitter one as well, for all we have done is engage in endless inconclusive skirmishes with the Trojans. Instead of battle and glory and plunder that I had hoped to find, the days have dragged on into months and into years, and the air of discontent and boredom has foully ripened into dissatisfaction. Back-biting quarrels erupt over nothing so much as miscast dice, and anxiety and anger lie heavy on everyone. Minor plots and intrigues are rife among the men and even among the high command. Daily, complaints about the conduct and the point of the war make their almost constant and poisonous appearance about the campfires. At least the arrival of this stranger will break the monotony, provide a little relief to boredom, or maybe even bring us some long-awaited news from home.

I feel a line of sweat trickling down on to my lip from under the nosepiece of my helmet. The flies are everywhere, buzzing about in swarms like the Furies. There is no breeze to dispel them, though they are not as bad as the sand gnats that work their way up under the greaves that cover your legs and bite like the jabbing of sharp little pins. The dead air can do nothing to dispel the trace of a strange sweet decaying odor that has hung over and permeated the camp for some days now. No one can locate its cause. My father flips the flies away with a horsetail whisk, and kindly, seeing that a couple have lighted on my hand, flips them away too.

The king is impervious to such small discomforts and so must we be too. He is in full armor, his tall helmet with the lion's head crest and the long horsetail plume, a battle breastplate of embossed gilded leather worked with writhing snakes, a jerkin beneath it of ringed chain mail that reaches to his knees, and greaves of leather with bronze facings, and heavy boots as well, a purple cloak fastened with a heavy jeweled brooch over his shoulders. He bears no arms save the long sword at his side, that too gold-encrusted, but with a wicked blade, that has come down to him from Atreus, his father. His squire stands next to the throne with the king's shield and spear and a large cup of wine, one of which the king seems to require to be at hand at all times of late.

The king is still huddled with Calchas and Odysseus. Chalchas has been speaking, but I cannot overhear what he has to say. Whatever it is, the king looks annoyed and is visibly upset. Chalchas is trying to calm him, speaking in comforting tones and raising his hand in a gesture that says "Trust me, I know all." He does this sort of thing well, appearing cool and possessed in his white chalmys and the heavy embroidered cloak denoting his priestly rank, the diadem that bespeaks his role as our chief augur circling his brow. But then he must look the part of the comforter--it is his stock in trade always to seem to know everything.

Odysseus nods sagely and appears to be wisely pondering whatever it is that Calchas has said. He has a reputation for cunning and wile and wisdom; he is, next to Menelaus, the King's closest

66

advisor. But neither he nor anyone has yet been able to find a way out of this hellish campaign and it makes you wonder sometimes if his cunning and honeyed ways are a pose he assumes when he has no more idea what to do about a thing than does anyone else. Yes, I suppose he is clever. He is only king of little Ithaca, half a world away from Troy, one of the smaller of the isles, and far from Achaea, and yet he has managed to parlay that small eminence into a spot at the right hand of the throne, so I should not underestimate him.

The others on the dais are Talthybius, the chief herald, whose voice can carry across all the ranks when need be. The three kings are there too: Diomedes, King of Argos, young and brawny, ready always with a quip, and curiously gentle despite his alarming prowess in battle. Menelaus, who is King of Sparta, of course is there, and Idomeneus, Deucalion's son, now, after his father's death, become Great King of Crete. In the last year or so, Diomedes and Menelaus have become inseparable, so much so that the men in the ranks joke that Menelaus should give up Helen for Diomedes. And as everyone almost daily says, Helen has been lost to Menelaus for so long, why bother. She was once a great beauty, but who knows now? But of course she is a prize because she is—well, because she is Helen--- celebrated in legend and rich beyond measure, heiress to a hundred islands, a queen in her own right. From her father Tyndareus she inherited Sparta and brought it to Menelaus, thus making him its king. So despite her dubious past and her alleged "abduction" by Paris, she is something valuable to retrieve, not only as a matter of honor but as a matter of politics and cash.

Nestor, my father, High King of Pylos, of course is there because he is accorded a place as the oldest and wisest among us; I am there as both a captain and as my father's squire for I am no longer Achilles' squire. I was almost too old to be that when I came, but Achilles knew what he wanted. But perhaps finding me too obedient, or too willing, Achilles made no argument when my father commanded that I must return to serve with our troops, as second-in-command of the cohorts of Pylos, a command I could hardly refuse.

That now seems an eternity ago. I loved Achilles when I came, and I love him still, but he is a strange and moody man. I still dream of him, but it is in dreams that I see more of him than in life. He is correct when he sees me, but he keeps a distance. It is as if he had never held me, though sometimes when we meet, as meet we always must in this crowded camp, after the salute I must give him and his acknowledgement in return, there is always a moment of odd tension, especially if Patroclus is not there. Just yesterday I came upon him as he rested after running laps around the track on the parade ground. As I came around the corner of the ordinance tent, I saw him. He was stripped nearly naked, glistening with sweat. In the mid-day sun he seemed to glitter as if he had been washed in gold. He knelt in the dust breathing hard, catching his breath as he wiped the sweat from his forehead and with a careless gesture tossed his golden hair back from his brow. Oh, Gods, he was beautiful. He saw me and slowly rose, negligently stretching. I saluted. He just waved, said nothing. I paused a fraction of heartbeat in hope that he might want to say something, anything to me. He did not. I turned and walked away. Then, I could not help it. I looked back. I caught him looking at me with those cool gray eyes, then he turned and started to run again. My heart broke. Oh, I thought, the lovesick boy that I was still lurks in the heart of the man I have become.

From my vantage by my father's chair I can see that our men, ranked in front of the dais are already suffering from the heat. They are restive too. From this close you can see that many men have dented and unpolished armor, shields are missing bosses, some do not wear helmets and all the men look worn and tired. While most of the men stand at something like attention, others actually rest on their shields that they have grounded, and a few even squat or lie on the ground. In the beginning such lapse of discipline would have been unthinkable, but now no one seems to bother with such things.

The king has taken his seat, and sits morose and slumped in his chair and seems not to see or care about that evidence of military laxity before his eyes. If it can only be called laxity it might not be so bad, but in fact it is a sign of the general malaise that hangs over the camp, so thick that you can almost breathe it in, like that sweet sickly odor of disease or decay. Here with our backs to the sea and behind our walls, getting hungrier by the day, for us there is no glory.

Ah, I hear a trumpet. At last he's arrived, the person we've been waiting for all this time. Everyone is standing at attention now—the heralds have sounded the "Present arms." There it is now, the procession—coming up the causeway -- only a handful of people, and a closed sedan chair, curtained, but in cloth of gold, carried by four men, and about a dozen others with trunks and baskets are following. I can't see who is inside.

The shouts of the captains echo over the field. Spears are grounded with a crash. The king though is not on his feet. Very rude. The stranger's attendants lower the sedan chair and as they do so all the rest in his entourage kneel. One of them starts shaking one of those little bell-like things the priests use when something really holy is happening, and another has lighted incense and the smoke billows up. They begin to chant. Very impressive. Yes, there. He's getting out of his chair. There he is. As he descends from his chair, helped out by a slave, the kneeling men in his procession now prostrate themselves in the dust before him.

I glance at my father. He is talking to himself as he often does. I hear him say: "Oh dear, I know who this man is. This isn't going to end well at all."

Chapter 9

The heat is unbearable. There is no wind and so the dust clouds that were kicked up when the men assembled hang in the air and slowly descend, coating everything, armor, skin, face, irritating the eyes. The ever-present sweet sickly smell seems to be getting worse. The flies and sand gnats are everywhere. The priest—for everyone knows that he is one--stands silent. The king does nothing. He seems deliberately to avoid looking at his guest. The priest must be my father's age, an imposing man, with deep-set blue eyes, and a strong face, lined with age, but once handsome. His snow-white hair is carefully combed and falls to his shoulders and on his head he wears a golden band in the center of which is a single huge moonstone. From the back of this hang long golden ribbons. Despite his age he stands very straight; he is in fact quite tall and very dignified. There is something about him that says he is someone to be reckoned with. He does not look down as one might expect someone to do who stands before the High King of Achaea. He stares at the king with as much intensity as the king seems to be trying not to look at him.

Around him his attendants kneel and clouds of incense rise. The priest turns slightly and nods to one of the attendants kneeling closest to him, who rises, bows, and backs away as one does from royalty. He goes to the sedan chair from which he brings an object, wrapped in glittering golden silk, long as a spear. He goes back, kneels, and carefully unwraps the thing, and presents it to his master. It is a staff. The priest takes it, but does not lean on it as a man of his age might. Instead he holds it at arm's length like a scepter, and extends it, not imperiously like a king might do with a scepter, but simply to let everyone see it, in a gesture that says, "Look at this, you know what it is."

It is a gorgeous thing, elaborately and curiously worked, gilded or perhaps even made of gold. Flowing from it are long ribbons worked in gold, and at its head, centered upon crossed arrows, the disc of the sun gleams. There can be no doubt what it is: For all men know about it even if none have seen it. It is the staff of Apollo kept in the secret treasury of Apollo's temple, an object so old and so sacred and so full of power that men must avert their eyes from it. Calchas, I can see out of the corner of my eye, is staring at the old man with considerable hostility and not a little alarm. A priest bearing the staff of the Archer God stands in front of the King. Apollo has come to Agamemnon.

The priest nods again and the dozen slaves who have come with him rise from their knees and bring forth the gilded boxes and leather trunks trimmed with silver and painted with swirling blue and red designs that they had carried in procession behind the priest's chair. With a sudden billowing gesture like the opening of a cape, four other slaves shake out a huge cloth of gold and it settles like a glittering cloud slowly to the ground. From out of their horde of boxes and baskets and trunks they bring out bales of cloth—cloth of gold, purple-stained silk from Tyre, fine white linens from Egypt-- and glittering objects—figurines, armlets of snakes with garnet eyes, bracelets of figured gold with electrum inlaid upon them, necklaces of amber and lapis lazuli, daggers richly worked with ebony and ivory pommels, chalices and beakers of silver and of gold chased with figures from ancient legends. They lay these on the golden ground in front of the King. Box after box yields some new and breathtaking treasure, trunk after trunk adds more and more to the horde.

The soldiers crane their heads to see, the ranks surge forward, a buzz of wonder rises into a swelling chorus of amazement. The officers bark commands for attention, but they too are as curious as the ranks. Everyone is staggered at the riches displayed there. In this dreary camp it is long since we have seen such color and elegance and richness. It is long since anyone among us, paid mostly in millet meal and an occasional piece of meat, has seen what so many men who had signed on to this endless war have come to find: riches, loot, plunder, gold, the ransom of a King. We all stare astonished and we are astonished too that the king still does not extend his hand as would have been proper in the face of such munificence that is so obviously meant to be a gift. But he does not raise the old man unto the dais, give him a chair, bid attendants bath his feet.

The moment seems to be frozen in time like a picture painted on a wall. I think of the picture of the sacrificial procession painted on the walls of my father's dining hall, priests and people, animals bedecked for the sacrifice, always unchangingly there. Everyone stares. No one moves. Sounds carried from the distance punctuate the heaviness of the air—a distant command from the distant walls, water slapping against the sides of the ships, ropes and vessels creaking, a wheeling hawk high above the parade ground sounds a hunting cry, dogs bark; horses neigh.

The king rises. He walks to the edge of the dais, and for one moment stares out across the ranks at the men, and his look is dark and menacing. Beneath his gaze men look away, for they know all too well what the wrath of Agamemnon can bring.

Below the king, standing in the dust, an old man stands, leaning on a staff. Around him kneel servants, before him on the ground is spread a staggering treasure

The king inclines his head to the priest.

"Speak," he says.

And speak he does

"Lord of Mycenae, King of the Achaeans, Overlord of the Thousand Isles, Son of Atreus, hear me!"

His voice is strong and echoes across the camp that is preternaturally silent now.

"I am Chrsyes, Priest of Apollo the Archer-God. I am he through whom Apollo speaks and I call upon you in his name to hear me. You, Agamemnon, you have come to this Trojan shore to avenge a wrong. You, Menelaus, come to regain a beloved wife. Both of you come for vengeance. I too come to you to redress a wrong. Know you this. With the power of the god I serve I could have come in fury and with the Archer at my back and no man could stand against me should I call down his wrath upon those who wronged me. The god at my call would swoop down upon you and bring you low in the dust, for such is his power.

"But I do not come to threaten you with the power of the Archer. Instead I come as a father and a supplicant and beg you to

72

return my daughter who you wrongly took. And for this I bring ransom richer than any man has seen. And hear me more. As Priest of Apollo I make this prophecy. You come here to take Holy Troy and level its walls and sack its palaces of its ancient treasures. And I say first you must return my daughter to me. Let her go. Restore a daughter to a father, reverence Apollo, son of Zeus, and if you do, Troy will be yours. This I vow by the scared staff of the god that I hold here now before you."

His words are passed quickly from rank to rank of the troops, and as the gist of his message becomes clear to all, the soldiers break out into a cheer in a wild cacophony of approbation. The pandemonium increases. Agamemnon signals to the heralds. The trumpet brings the men to silent attention

"Priest," Agamemnon said, "Priest, I hear your words." His eyes are dark with fury. I can see his hands working by his side, as if were he able he would actually strike the priest, an act that would be worse than blasphemy had he done so. "I hear your words, but now you hear mine. Chryseis is mine. When I took her I did not do so merely to use her and give her back. I want her." Slowly he says it again, almost obscenely savoring the words: "I want her." Some of the men in the front ranks, who could easiest hear this, gasp in horror.

"Old man." The king says, "you can ask all you want, demand all you want, lay whatever treasure you will before me. I will not set your daughter free."

He turns and gestures. Two guards appear, holding between them Chryseis. The men gasp at her beauty, for none have as yet seen her. Though bound she stands like a queen.

Agamemnon stares at her for a moment. Then he turns back to the priest.

"There she is, old man" he says, "and here she stays. She will grow old in Argos, far from her home that she will never see again. I will put her at the loom where she will weave cloth for me and I will take her to my bed and she will give me pleasure there. That is why I took her, your girl with the golden hair, and that is why I will keep her. Now, old man, don't anger me more. If you want to save your skin, if you want to live. Go. Now."

Chapter 10

I can feel the palpable shock that runs through the entire company. But no man dares remonstrate. The steely cold rage in the king's voice and the dark and level menace of his look quells everyone who sees it. The priest stands for one moment more. All the earth seems to hold its breath. Then he dismissively gestures toward the splendid hoard as if to say, "Take it, it is nothing to me." Without a bow to the king the priest turns his back full upon him. His entourage turns also, all of them, backs to Agamemnon.

The priest now faces the army drawn up before him. He raises the glittering staff of Apollo high and with it makes a gesture that encompasses the entire parade ground. A gasp of horror, of naked fear, runs through the multitude.

Then lowering the staff and leaning on it he enters his sedan chair. The curtains are drawn. His bearers lift it high upon their shoulders and to the sound of the tinkling cistrum and in a cloud of incense he is carried off toward his ship. As he passes in front of the ranks many of the men make the sign to ward off the evil eye.

Agamemnon watches him pass, and I can see that there is evil in his eye as well. As the priest's procession moves toward the ship, I think I see out of the corner of my eye, coming from the heap of treasure perhaps, a little mouse scurrying across the long expanse between the king and the army.

In the distance we can still hear the jingling of the bells as the priest's litter carries him away. Odysseus fiddles with the clasp of his cloak; Calchas has pulled his cowl over his head and turned away. Agamemnon looks out across the assembled troops, his face impassive, but I can see that he is closing his right hand so tightly that his nails must bite deep into the flesh of his palm. I know that gesture. It means his rage is bubbling near the surface and he is fighting for control. His hand clenches and unclenches, as if in that strong grip he holds the old priest's throat and is squeezing the life out of it.

But then the fixed attention of everyone is broken by a terrible screeching cry. A bird—an owl I think and oddly so for they fly at night and never in the day--swoops down right in front of the dais and unpleasantly if triumphantly shrieks as it catches in its claws the same mouse that had come out of the pile of trunks and boxes and across the open space toward the dais.

With the little creature struggling in its claws the bird lifts high up above the army. But then suddenly, the bird screeches as if in pain, and swoops back down and inexplicably releases the mouse, which falls at the feet of the king. Pausing for a moment as if to celebrate its own triumph, the mouse disappears into the midst of the assembled men.

The men are shaken. So am I. What is the meaning of this omen, for omen it must surely be? What does it mean, this owl from out of the night, Athena's bird, dropping that easy catch like a hot coal as if contact with the creature had singed its iron claws.

I do not want to think further. But I cannot help it. I know, as does everyone there, that the mouse is sacred to Apollo, whose priest our King has sent away in shame.

This spectacle is too much for the men in the ranks, superstitious at the best of times. Such occurrences, the priests tell us, are no accident. They bring us messages that we should heed. A murmur goes through the ranks. The omen, for omen it has to be, seems to everyone to be a judgment on the king's refusal to acknowledge the man who has presented such incredible treasures. The murmuring becomes louder, swells, and the sound is ugly.

Someone, or perhaps many men independently, begin to drum on their shields with the staves of the spears, bringing the wooden spear hard against the leather-covered shield, which produces a low, hollow, flat, and ominous boom. At first it is random and erratic, the beating of spears against shields an inchoate un-rhythmic rumble coming from no one place in particular. But then as more men join it, the deep booming becomes louder; it increases in intensity and in depth and soon all the men are striking their shields in unison in a steady, alarming thunder as if a giant oars-master was beating a huge drum to keep a thousand oarsmen in steady stroke. There is in my experience little that is so unnerving to a commander as this sound, for it is the sound of an army showing its displeasure, a slow rhythmic thunder like the sound of a thousand boots marching toward revolt.

Cohort commanders look to their captains for instruction. The captains look to the generals on the dais. They looked at the king. Such things must not be allowed to go on, for in the midst of such a thunderous steady protest, the control of armies has been known to shift on an instant from commanders to commanded. The deep and steady drumming gets, if possible, even louder and the sonorous boom must have sounded across the plain to the foot of Troy's walls, risen and given hope to the defenders in those cloud-capped towers, for this sound was the ancient and universal sound of an angry army in distress.

It seemed as if the fearsome drumming of the spears on shield would never stop. Finally Odysseus who had several times looked toward the king as if awaiting a signal, impatiently shrugs his shoulders and without so much as consulting the king, pulls Menelaus by the arm and together, without a word but obviously in agreement, the two of them advance toward the ranks. Menelaus signals the heralds to sound the call to attention.

As the silver-tongued trumpets blare above the thunder, Odysseus makes a hand sign to Achilles, who turns and raises his hand to his Myrmidons. Superbly trained as they are, used to instant obedience, they stop instantly. Achilles gives another command. His men smartly wheel around, spears raised, shields up and using the shields like a wall, begin a slow even pacing right into the ranks behind them. Step by step they force the men behind them back, and in turn the men behind them, thus forcing them to cease their infernal drumming.

Again the heralds sound the call, this time from the surrounding watch towers, and the captains and generals now move along and into the ranks, shouting commands at the troops for silence, Odysseus even threatening some with his staff. Gradually the clamor lessens and finally stops, leaving an almost breathless silence in the air.

From where I stand I can see that even Achilles, usually so cool and calm, is shaken. Unusual for him when on parade, he turns and looks at Patroclus next to him and Patroclus looks back at him, his face ashen. Achilles reaches out and places his hand on Patroclus' shoulder. Then looking at Agamemnon, standing on the dais, hands on his hips, Achilles shakes his head, as if to say, this man is mad.

Agamemnon goes to the edge of the dais—facing his men, facing them down. Before the king's unflinching gaze, his sheer brutal majesty, the men slowly begin to quiet. Finally there is silence.

The air is heavy with apprehension and fear, and with that smell, sweet, sickish, a little nauseating, that in the stifling heat seems to intensify and to fill the nostrils with its sickening odor, a stench, I thought, like death. The king raises his hand. The commanders break the tension by shouting an order to stand at attention. The soldiers, as if of one accord, hesitate for just a moment before obeying, but then, though with what sounded like a low obstinate growl that passed from rank to rank, they come to attention, grounding the hafts of their spears in the dusty ground.

"At ease boys, at ease," Agamemnon shouts in his best parade-ground bellow. "Now lads," he went on, "we all know who we are and why we're here. We're all Achaeans, lads. And just who is that old fool? Have you ever heard of him? I'll tell you who he is, boys. He's a Trojan. Who have we come to fight? Trojans. I pay him no mind and neither should you. All that hocus-pocus doesn't go far in my book. He says he wants his daughter back. Well, you know what I said to that. Now let me ask you this. How many of you would give up a good looking girl who's already warmed your bed just because someone said you should? I can bet that you wouldn't just hand her over. And neither will I. She's a Trojan too and what's more she's a prize of war. This is war, lads, and I took her fair and square. You all know that, so why should I give her up?"

I could see a look of disgust pass between Achilles and Patroclus. Everyone knew that the king had nothing to do with capturing that girl. But no one said a word.

Agamemnon went on: "You know why we're here?" He gestured to the gleaming treasure spread out before him. "Gold is why we're here, lads; treasure brought right to our doorstep and we didn't even have to throw spear. They're afraid of us, boys, don't you see it? Don't you worry about that miserable priest's so-called signs. Forget it, lads, I say forget it. Here's a sign, right here. A king's ransom, by the gods, enough for a king and for all of you too. Don't you see it boys, the gods are smiling on us."

At this incredible utterance Calchas pulled his cowl even further over his head and sank down into a chair; he seemed to by trying to catch his breath. The commanders on the platform gave each other uneasy looks. I couldn't believe what I was hearing. I just closed my eyes. "Fool," I thought, "arrogant fool. You'll be the death of us all."

The king, not noticing what was happening on the platform in back of him, seeming to be oblivious of the obvious unease of the men, many of who looked at their king with incredulity, blustered on.

"Here it is, boys, what's on the ground is what we came to get. I intend to take it, since he was fool enough to leave it behind. There's enough here for all of us, lads. Every man of you will get your share, believe you me."

He paused, as if waiting for some response, a cheer, some kind of hip hip-hooray for good old Agamemnon. But nothing came. Only silence.

"Commanders," he shouted, as if trying to quickly fill the soundless breach, "send out some men to help divide this up. Lets do it now."

There had been precious little plunder for a very long time, but no one stepped forward. The tension was like the silent moment between a lighting strike and the crash of thunder. All apprehension. Agamemnon stared at his men. His men stared back. The king shrugged his shoulders.

"No takers boys," he said. "Well, maybe later then."

As he turned from them, I heard him say to Odysseus: "Maybe later, and maybe not."

He shot a look at his brother Menelaus. "Pick it up."

At a sign from Menelaus, slaves quickly began to gather up the glittering loot. I looked out across the parade ground, the men waited, still silent. It was clear to me that this was a flash point ready to explode into flame, into mutiny, or worse. Agamemnon ignored it.

Throwing one more dark look at the men, he shouted in exasperation: "For god's sake, dismissed."

He and left the dais and headed toward his tent

.

"Oh yes, and her," turning to Chryseis held by two soldiers. "Take that baggage back to my tent. I will come to you later, lady."

His laughter is cruel and terrible.

The moment for rebellion passed. The men dispersed, some going toward the tents, others to their posts, still others to kindle a cooking fire, they passed by the laboring slaves packing up the glittering fortune, a fortune that they had, to a man, rejected. They wanted nothing to do with it now. It had a curse upon it. As they passed, some making a sign to ward off evil, I could see their purpose in their eyes: by taking none of this stupendous plunder they hoped that they would be spared the terrible threat of Apollo's wrath that all the men, except for the king it seems, knew was certain soon to fall hard upon them.

When I walked out to try to take some air because that sickly smell seemed to be getting worse—it smelled like rotting meat—I saw soldiers talking in pairs or in groups. They broke off their whispering and walked away, trying to look busy or innocent if they saw me coming.

But I knew well what they were talking about. All the old discontent started to bubble up to the surface: a large part of the army and even some of the commanders had lost confidence in the king and no amount of treasure could change that fact. I could see the situation was getting serious.

And what was most serious of all was this: Achilles and Agamemnon. It was no secret that they hated one another. No secret that Achilles thought the king both arrogant and unfit to rule. No secret either that the king hated Achilles because he feared him, feared him because he knew that if it came to the test he, Agamemnon, would lose.

But as the days went by and the discontent mounted, the army forgot about Apollo and his priest and began to blame the king. As it turns out, Apollo hadn't forgotten about them.

Book Four
The Arrows of Apollo

Chryses prayed fervently to Apollo… Let them pay for my tears with your arrows…Apollo came down in fury from the heights of Olympus with his bow and quiver slung over his back. His decent was like the nightfall. Not far from the ships he knelt down and shot an arrow, and dreadful was the sound of his silver bow. He attacked the mules and the dogs and then aimed his arrows at the men themselves and struck again and again. Day and night the pyres consumed the dead.
--Iliad 1. 36-42; 43-53.

From: Dionysos Of Tenedos, A History of the War at Troy

But what of Chryses, shamed before the vast army of his enemies, insulted by Agamemnon, his priesthood reviled, his God blasphemed by the arrogance of Agamemnon, lord of men? As he sailed back to Chrysa did he summon up the last image he saw of Agamemnon standing on the dais, his face black and twisted in anger, his eyes furious, almost it seemed, mad. Did he hear, again and again, the king's voice: "Now, old man, provoke me no more. If you want to save your skin, get you gone!" The memory of that terrible dismissal must have echoed repeatedly through his mind and struck deep into his heart. The outrage of it summoning him to courage and to revenge.

All the world knows what terrible revenge the God took upon the Greeks. But how did that recompense come about? I can only imagine it. But imagination is as good as truth. I see him now, in his temple, taking the knife of sacrifice, still covered with its flaxen cloth, and going to the bull docilely waiting. He uncovers the knife, raises it and shows it to the people assembled there. All of his people are assembled there. All are silent as if they have all ceased to breath. From behind the bull he lifts the mane that falls over the animal's forehead and cuts a few strands of his hair. Then he bends to the bull and whispers into his ear "Forgive me," and as he does so he grasps the tether around the bull's muzzle, pulls back his head and in a swift movement, so long practiced, so many times repeated, with a single slashing stroke cuts his throat, deeply, cleanly. Amazingly, the bull makes no sound--the best of omens for it means that the animal has assented to his own sacrifice.

The dark blood sprays like a pent-up fountain, spurting across the barley covered floor, soaking Chryses in the stream of dying life, and so strong is the force it sprays as well those most closely assembled around the altar. All this is in an instant, and from the

83

people simultaneously there is a loud expulsion of breath, as if anxiety was suddenly released, or fear assuaged, a sound almost like the release of sex. Then the village women, as they have done for age after age when the sacrifice is done, cry out, a terrible keening shriek, mixed of joy, terror, and ecstasy. The blood is shed; the god drinks his fill. The bull slumps to his knees, falls, and then lies silent on the blood-soaked ground. Chryses is covered in blood and the people are shouting, laughing, the tension broken. Joy seizes them all as if they had drunk deep of some intoxicating wine or breathed the fumes of some forbidden drug.

Chryses begins the last of the rites, slitting open the bull's stomach and extracting the hot and smoking entrails, the huge heart, that seems almost still to beat, the lungs, so short a time ago filled with the incense of his own sacrifice, the dark liver and the kidneys. He hands them to the eldest woman who waits by his side as the eldest always have and she quickly and expertly skewers them and places them on the fire burning in one of the cauldrons. He cuts off the tail and removes the gall-bladder and thigh-bones which are wrapped in layers of the bull's rich thick fat and carries this precious offering to the altar and places it on the altar flame.

As the fat sizzles and the smell of burning flesh rises to the nostrils of the god, Chryses raises his arms before the god and in a loud voice invokes him: "Hear me, Apollo, great Lord of the Silver Bow, you who rule above Chrysa, you who are sacred in Cilla and Lord over Tenedos, Lord Smintheus, god of Pestilence and slayer of men, if it has pleased you that here I have rebuilt your temple and always faithfully burnt the rich thighs of bull at your altar, I call upon you give me this one thing in return for all my fidelity and bring this wish to pass for which I pray: Loose your arrows upon all the Achaeans and make them pay bitterly for the tears I have shed."

Chapter 11

That night I had a dream. Perhaps even a vision. I saw myself moving through a thick blue mist. I could see nothing else around me. There was an unpleasant odor of decay. Then the mist began to clear and I saw—not with the dim sight of dreams but with the clarity of foreknowing. A doorway to another world opened.

What I see is terrible. From the darkening clouds, their edges touched with flame, I see the god descend, terrible in his wrath. He comes like the night, for the darkness swiftly falls and the moon breaks out from behind the clouds and glitters on his silver bow. Somehow solid and transparent all at once, he kneels, whips an arrow from his shoulder and fits it to his bow and lets it fly. One after another, so fast his movements blur, and like stabbing shafts of summer lightning the arrows fly. The sound of his bow is horrible to hear, a steady whistling hum, the swift passage of arrows like the hiss of thousand snakes as they find their way home to flesh. Nothing escapes. Mules writhe on ground; dogs, who had howled at his coming are slain in mid-alarm, and then, soldiers, aroused by the shrieks of animal pain, pour out of their tents unto the parade ground where they too fall like mown wheat. Arrows flash into chests, cleave between their eyes, plunge horribly into throats, and men collapse on the ground coughing up black blood. There is Agamemnon sitting in his tent, slumped in his chair, his eyes blank, face white with horror, despair rides upon his shoulders. Outside dead men lie. I see funeral pyres, hundreds and hundreds of them, bodies burn and flesh sizzles, sputters, explodes, and the stench of death and pestilence arises everywhere.

I awake in terror, sweat covering my body. I rise and go out into the night. But was it a dream? No breeze stirs the heat, and the sickly nauseating smell, like rotting meat and spoiled milk, is everywhere, lying upon the camp like a smothering blanket. I walk from my tent through the compound of the kings and commanders. Rows of tents stretch into the darkness, separated from the

85

encampment of the ranks by the huge expanse of the parade ground. The larger tents of allied kings, with devices painted on them or flying pennants to identify their occupants, are pitched with the smaller ones of their officers around them. At the center is the huge tent of Agamemnon, stripped in blue and gold. Many are dark, but from others dim lights shone and I can hear men talking. Sounds of raucous laughter come from the king's tent and someone is singing a bawdy song. A woman cries out; more laughter. I see Menelaus stagger out of the royal tent. Agamemnon comes to the tent flap and shouts something after him. Menelaus turns and unsteadily makes a stiff-armed gesture of offensive and unmistakable import. Agamemnon laughs and disappears back inside and Menelaus lurches away into the night. I walk away. I don't want to know.

I cross the parade ground toward the camp of the ranks, rows of smaller tents, each with a tripod in front to hold a cook pot, stretched into the darkness. Here too lights shine through the tent flaps and though it is well past midnight, small groups of men sit outside by the cold cooking fires and speak quietly, urgently. They fall silent as I approach. I continue through the tents and toward the beach where the ships lay, prow outward as if looking into the distance toward home. As I go, underfoot mice and even rats scurry away at my coming. So many of them. I pass the great storage tents where grain and supplies are kept and I fancy I can hear them gnawing at the grain hordes, at the barrels of salted meat, even at the tent pegs, at anything they can reach.

At the edge of the camp near the sandy expanse of the beach, are the corrals where the horses and mules are picketed and the hunting dogs kenneled. In the distance the ocean spreads out before me, but unlike most nights there is no sparkling silver furrow of the waves breaking on the shore. The water is smooth, glassy, almost oily, its surface dark. No moonlight is reflected in it. But in the distance on the horizon a huge cloudbank, dark, almost purple, the color of a blood engorged bruise, looms up obscuring the stars. It rushes toward the shore like an avenging Fury and as it comes vapors rises from the ocean to increase its size and engorge it further. A dank noxious fog, it rolls swiftly toward the beach. In its ominous and shifting mass I think that I see a giant figure, striding

86

across the heavens toward the camp. Am I awake? Is this still my terrible dream?

But awake I was, and overcome with fear; panic rose in my throat. I turned and ran, arousing the dogs that set up a cacophony of howling and barking. As I ran the terrible fog closed in around me, and the stench was overpowering. The dogs were howling now, not to raise an alarm, but in abject fear and pain. I raced past the horse pickets, careened around the edge of corral, stumbled and went flying, panting and breathless, face down in the mud. Panic mastered me. I pushed myself up to my knees, and as I made the final effort to rise I saw before me, lying inertly on the ground, the body of a mule, its eyes wide with horror, its stomach bloated. Its black and swollen tongue lolled out of its mouth; its muzzle was covered with thick bloody foam. I raced blindly back to my tent and threw myself into my bed, shaking with fear.

The next morning I struggled out of sleep, fighting off the smothering grip of my dream, but also trying both to comprehend and not to believe I knew to be no dream but reality. I sat bolt upright, my face sweaty, my heart racing. As I became fully awake from outside the tent I could hear someone speaking in a low but agitated voice. I got out of bed and opened the tent flap. In the half-darkness of early morning, in front of my father's tent pitched next to mine, I saw Calchas with my father, who, apparently awakened by the excited priest, listened bleary-eyed as Calchas spoke.

I could hear snatches of his talk: "a vision," "the punishment of the god." "The mules are dead and the dogs," he was saying as I hurried up to them.

"I tell you its come." Calchas was trembling; his voice was hoarse with fear.

"What's come? Get a hold of yourself, man." my father said.

"Apollo has come. The punishment is on us. For Agamemnon." the priest said, almost sobbing.

I came up in back of him and putting my hand on the priest's shoulder I said, "Reverend sir, please take a seat," and pulled up a stool for him.

Calchas breathed deeply for a moment in an effort to regain control and began to tell us how, last night after he had seen us, he walked down to the sea to "commune with the gods" as he put it—he was pompous even in his fear—and had come upon dead animals at the horse corrals.

"Horrible, horrible," he said. " It will come to us, mark me!"

"Does anyone know of this?" my father asked sharply, now fully awake.

"No," Calchas said. "No one was awake when I came back to my tent. I came here directly after I took precautions and consulted with the gods."

I said: "Father, I saw it too. I have seen the dead."

My father turned to me, "Get Machaon," he said.

Machaon, Ascalepios' son, is our chief healer. His father taught him everything and taught it well, and so he knows all the spells of healing, and how to use herbs and potions to protect men against sickness. He has cured many a wound in this long terrible war, and when no cures were to be found, comforted the dying with soothing drinks to make them forget their pain.

I soon returned with Machaon. He carried his staff entwined with double-headed snakes, and carrying his bag of herbs and medicines.

"What is it, Nestor, that gout acting up again?" he said as he approached, for I had told him nothing. He glanced at Calchas, and gave him a formal bow and nod. There was little love lost between these two. Machaon thought Calchas was a charlatan and Calchas was always at pains to point out to anyone who would listen that he had the ear of the gods while Machaon gathered herbs under the moonlight and brewed up noxious potions like some village witch. Professional jealousy, I suppose.

"Tell him," my father said to Calchas, and the priest recounted again what he had told us. Machaon's brow furrowed.

"You must destroy the bodies immediately," he said. "They must be burned, along with anything they have touched. Even the ground on which the bodies have lain must be dug up and thrown into the sea."

We looked at him.

"But…" Calchas began,

"Now!" Machaon said.

Someone must tell Agamemnon, Calchas said.

We looked at Calchas.

"Should it be you?" my father asked.

"I? No not I," the priest said, alarm in his face. "I will find no favor in his eyes if I bring this news."

My father stared at Calchas with ill-concealed contempt and said curtly. "I will do it." He put aside his cane and rose from his chair and I could see the old man give way to the king.

"Machaon, give Calchas a potion to help him sleep; he has done enough for today."

All of us but Calchas could see that my father's command had a double edge. Turning to me: "Antilochus, find Nikon and send him here. Then send to King Agamemnon to say that I must speak with him by sunrise."

Machaon and I took Calchas to his tent, supporting him, one on either side. The arrogant priest, self-appointed advisor to the king, who always positioned himself conspicuously by the king's side ready so as to be seen seeming to offer sage wisdom, had suddenly become a fearful old man. He muttered to himself as we went.

"Why did I not know/" he kept saying, "Why did I not know? I should have known so as to tell the king."

We almost had to carry him into his tent. Unlike the simply furnished soldier's tent of my father this was richly appointed with a carved Egyptian bed, gilded stools, hangings of silk and linen, and on a large table lay all the material of his calling as an augur and soothsayer, clay images of animals, dried herbs, bay leaves to induce visions, claws, feet, heads and wings of dead creatures, ancient tablets on which spells and curses were scratched in the clay. Machaon looked at it all with the bemused disdain of the practical healer. The tent was filled with bluish smoke from a brazier aromatic with burning herbs, angelica, and verbena.

"Well, at least that's right." Machaon said. "This is what we must do throughout the camp."

We took Calchas to his bed. Machaon rummaged in his satchel and drew forth a small bag; taking a cup from the beside table he poured some powder into it and filled it with wine and said to the priest.

"Take this, it will help you rest."

Turning to me: "Come, we have little time."

When we returned to my father's tent I found him with Nikon, the horse master, who he commanded to detail soldiers to collect the bodies of dead soldiers, and of the mules, now bloated and stinking, and the lithe hunting dogs now a mess of putrefaction, and burn them and make sure that the living livestock—fortunately most of it survived--was well-watered and separated from the dead.

"But at all costs," Machaon cautioned, "your men must not touch them. Grasp them with hooks to pull them to the pyres or burn them where they lay. Wrap your faces in cloths soaked in the preparation I will give you, it may protect you from the scourge."

Nikon saluted and turned to go.

"One more thing Nikon," my father said.

" Sir?"

"Treat them with dignity; they have died though no fault of their own."

I went myself to the king's tent. The guards stood stiffly at the door. All was silent inside.

"I must see the king," I said to the captain in command.

"Lord Antilochus, we can not disturb him, the feast went into the night."

"Then leave word that it is a weighty and urgent matter and that King Nestor must attend upon him," I said. The captain saluted smartly, but I could see that he dared not disturb the king.

The dead beasts were burned on the beach and the smoke billowed over the camp, the ever-present stench of decay mixed with

90

the smell of burning flesh. My father sent again to the king—for there was no reply to my message and he had not left his tent during all the chaos—to ask his orders, urging him to call a council of the commanders to assess what this might mean. But the messenger came back without answer. The next morning the sickening smell still hung over the camp; it was as hot and airless as it had been the night before. The pyres still burned and the sky was black with the smoke. It must have seemed to the Trojans watching from their walls that we were offering especially huge sacrifices to the gods. And may be we should have.

That was the first day and the least of the horror. On the second it was worse. Despite our efforts, men began to die. It seemed that the sickness had fallen mostly on the camp of the rank and file, and among them some died, others were spared. Two men to a tent, one would lie gasping, cough blood and die. The other would amazingly live. There was no reason behind it, only the horrible awareness that we could do nothing; that our fate lay---lay where? In the workings of blind chance, or with the will of some malevolent god? Was it indeed the vengeance of that now departed priest that was striking us down?

Somehow I was spared. My father was spared. Was the sickness kept from us in the officer's tents, which were separated from the camp of the army by the huge parade ground? At first we thought that, but then we lost a captain, and a cohort commander. Young Diotheles, an orderly to King Odysseus died horribly. Three men from our guard were stricken; their comrades, their faces covered, pulled their bodies to a pyre and fed it with its dreadful fuel. We knew that no one was safe.

For five days more the horror continued. Calchas, keeping to his tent, sent warnings that we must placate the gods by sacrifice. Machaon walked fearlessly among the dying, giving help where he could. But when he returned to us at night, his look said that it was hopeless. And still the king did not appear.

Nor did the Trojans. We were vulnerable, but Troy sent out no war parties to take advantage of our weakness, for by now they must have known what had befallen us. Were they rejoicing that we were being stuck down by divine vengeance, or were they too living in terror that it would spread to them? Above Troy we could see clouds of blue-black smoke rising. They too must be igniting huge fires, burning aromatic wood and herbs to purify and protect themselves, just as we were doing in the camp, though to no use.

On the evening of the seventh day, Machaon slumped exhausted in a chair by my father's tent, his face still wrapped in the protective cloth that he had prescribed for those going among the dead and dying. I sat on the ground, toying with a cup of wine, bread and olives lay untouched before me. My father seemed to doze in his chair. We were exhausted from doing nothing, for there was nothing to be done. Thus all day we had waited, but for what? Machaon had given us strict instructions to stay by our tent, and not to go among the dead.

"We need you alive," he said. "You must not be exposed to this."

Occasionally a messenger would report, telling of more losses, for news had traveled about the camp that the king had not appeared and Nestor had taken charge. As dusk fell we sat staring out across the parade ground, toward the grey ocean beyond it, and the darkening horizon. The furious banks of clouds that had accompanied the onset of the plague had gone now, and the sky was tinged with a dim and sickly grey–green light that was slowly fading as the night came on, cast against which was the ever-present glow of the funeral pyres and with the plumes of acrid smoke. Out of the gloom three men strode toward us, Diomedes and Idomeneus, and Menestheus of Athens.

Wakened by the clank of their weapons, my father looked up. I arose to salute them as did Machaon. They bowed to my father, for of all the kings he is most senior.

"What will King Nestor have us do," Idomeneus asked without preamble. "There must be something."

"What would you do that has not been done, young Lord?" my father replied, wearily. " We must wait for the king to decide."

The three men gave each other quick glances compounded of helplessness and frustration.

"But sir," Diomedes said, interrupting, "the king is not deciding. He keeps to his tent; no one is allowed to see him. He sends away the messengers. He and Menelaus..."--he paused for a moment, took a breath, and nearly spat out his next words--"they *cower* there, afraid to show themselves."

"Then we must wait for him," my father said. "He is king. What would you have me do, send soldiers to pull him out by force?"

Then Menestheus spoke: "But it is surely Agamemnon who has angered Apollo when he defied Apollo's priest."

"And," my father said, "it is Agamemnon to whom we have all sworn oaths of loyalty and obedience before the altars of the gods. Would you have us all be foresworn and break that sacred oath? What punishment from on high would fall on us then?"

"Then what must we do to appease the gods?" Diomedes asked.

Machaon rose and walked away. I heard him say to himself "Gods! Are there gods? What god would do a thing like this?'"

Then he turned to us. " There is no help for this sickness; but one thing I do know; it will end. I have seen it before. It will run its course. But it is the morale of this army that is sick and that must be cured and we can only trust in men to remedy this. I say call for Achilles."

That night, exhausted beyond measure I fell on my bed and dropped into a restless and dream-crazed sleep. I dreamt about dying animals; I saw myself wandering through the camp. All around me men, faces black, eyes glazed, tongues lolling, reached out to me and pulled me down to them. I thought I heard the hiss of arrows and the cries of men mortally wounded as the sharp barbs tore into their flesh.

I jumped up, shaking, and shook off the sleep that still held me and went outside. The sky was black, no stars could be seen. The silent airless night of all the past evenings was now stirred by a strong hot wind blowing stinging sand from the beach toward the tents of the men. Just as in my dream I could hear cries, though this time real, drifting on the wind. I felt myself drawn to the edge of the parade ground even though Machaon had urged that I go no nearer to the afflicted camp. As I approached, by the light of the weak moon I picked out two figures standing, looking up at the lowering sky. It was Patroclus and Achilles.

Achilles and Patroclus. They are legends, these strong and handsome men. They are the world's most famous lovers and they well know it. One can see not only that they adore one another but why. That is part of their legend—their devotion. All admire it, and poets have even made songs about them, comparing them to Zeus and the beautiful boy Ganymede who the King of the Gods so loved that he took him to Olympus where they love eternally. Or to Orpheus, who when his Eurydice died, could not bear to look at another woman and turned instead to the love of men and sought solace in the arms of the beautiful youth Calais.

When Achilles and Patroclus stand together on the parade ground in the front rank of their soldiers, wearing as they sometimes do matching golden armor, it is a vision: Achilles' golden hair glowing like a halo in the sun and Patroclus beside him, his long black hair framing his finely-chiseled face, and those famous dark eyes seem to discern every man's secret. Behind them are their men, armor polished and the plumes of their helmets combed out, eyes staring out from the narrow slits on either side of the long nosepiece of the sinister helmets they wear, their tanned skin and shapely legs show beneath the short but armored *chitons* falling briefly just below the curve of the breastplates that are shaped like the well-muscled chests of athletes. In precise measured lines they stand, ready at any moment to go to war, ready to change in an instant from a static image of militancy on parade into a savage killing machine, plunging spears brutally into men's breasts, thrusting swords deep into stomachs, or coolly winging an arrow between the eyes.

When men look at them, at Achilles and Patroclus they see the so obvious love of the one man for another and the so obvious heroism of the two. In them soldiers sense all that moves the deepest well-springs of their souls—courage and bonding--the necessary love of brave men for brave men. For these soldiers Achilles and Patroclus are legend embodied in life. In them they see the hero

Hercules who loved Hylas and Apollo, Lord of the World, who loved Hycinthus, about whose passionate love for the god and tragic death boys learn in school

They turned as I came toward them and separated to allow me to stand between them. Achilles put his hand on my shoulder. With that touch past memories stirred. Patroclus placed his on my other shoulder and we stood for a moment, living men united as one in the face of all that death.

"What is it?" I said.

"You know as well as I," Achilles said, in that low level voice. And I did.

"The god will have his way," I said. "We can do nothing."

Achilles looked at me unsmiling.

Then he said: "I can."

Book Five
The Wrath of Achilles

Achilles was torn by fury and indecision as he considered whether it were best to control his rage or to draw his sharp sword and cut down Agamemnon on the spot.
--Iliad 1.188-191

From: Dionysos Of Tenedos, A History of the War at Troy

The point of war is plunder—to take by force something that belongs to someone else. Though our poets like to claim that at Troy men fought for glory and honor, land and gold always come to the victors, though sometimes at a cost so great in lives and treasure that in the final accounting, the spoils of war may not outweigh the cost of war. But soldiers and even kings rarely think of this when the lust for blood and battle and plunder is upon them. For the men in ranks a handful of coins, a golden statue, maybe a sheep or goat to slaughter for food, or a scrawny boy or a pitiful whimpering girl is the reward of battle.

But to the great—the princes and the kings—out of the division of the plunder come cartloads of treasure and ownership of the defeated—strong and handsome lads or the highest born and most beautiful of the women, for not only are women taken as prizes for men's pleasure, but if high-born enough they can bring a huge ransom from their grieving kin. And too, what greater revenge is there on the defeated then for the victor to command the vanquished -- a woman, perhaps a princess in her own land--to serve on her knees at his table and submit to his desire in his bed? Such human prizes are trophies for a warrior.

When Achilles returned to the Achaean camp with gold and hostages—among them the women Briseis and Chryseis--and with a long list of conquered cities to add to his already huge roster of victories, the rivalry between Achilles and Agamemnon that had begun even before the fleet had sailed, erupted again. It came as no surprise that Agamemnon took Chryseis and a lion's share of the gold as the king's part of the division of the spoils. He took her as his right, though all the world knows that he had won her through no valor of his own. This was a canny choice for she was the daughter of Chryses, who was priest of the richest temple outside the walls of Troy and so could command a ransom worthy of a king.

Everyone knew that Agamemnon wanted the beautiful Chryseis for more than her value as a hostage—he wanted her for sex. He then proposed that Achilles take the other woman Briseis, though she had no value as a hostage and everyone knew that Briseis was not to Achilles' taste. But from the spoils Achilles had in fact asked nothing for himself. But to give him Briseis was an insult, especially since he did not want her.

It is said that the king, ever on the lookout for ways to belittle Achilles, laughingly whispered to Menelaus--and loud enough so Achilles could hear: "I guess none of the boys were pretty enough. Now whatever would he do with her anyway? Make her wash his toy boy Patroclus' laundry?"

All men knew that Achilles would stand no one making a mockery of his passion for Patroclus. Thus when the king made his sneering remark how could anyone be surprised that it would set Achilles aflame with rage?

The insult was not forgotten.

But there was more. Though Achilles did not care for gold or women he did care for honor. The king boasted incessantly about Chryseis and when he was in his cups with a captive audience for his drunken ramblings, he would shout that he took her right from under her father's nose.

"I grabbed her by the hair from the old fool's arms," he would shout. "Right off the temple steps."

No one dared comment. Everyone knew it was not true and only the pitiful boasting of a drunken man, for the king had taken no part in the raids, leaving that work to "lesser kings" as Odysseus advised him to do. Agamemnon's embroidering of history enraged Achilles even more.

"Better than my wife," he bragged. "Tired of that old bag anyway. Think I'll keep this one for a while. Screw her good I do every night."

Agamemnon treated Chryseis like a slave, kept her at the loom, made her wait upon all the officers at the table, bragged that she was wild in bed. Then he would burst out into peals of raucous *laughter, which sometimes, unaccountably, would end up in bone-wrenching sobs. Any who were present would turn their heads away. It is unseemly to see a King in tears. At such times Achilles would look at the king in disgust, and without so much as a bow, leave the room with his Patroclus in tow.*

Like many among the ancient royal families of Hellas, Achilles believed the House of Atreus to be upstarts and Agamemnon king not by sacred right but by devious manipulation. Not only was Achilles royal, he was young. Like the young he was rigid. He believed that honor must never be besmirched and that dignity and valor must never give way to compromise. He also believed that excess is weakness and that when weakness threatens the strong, like a gangrenous limb it must be hacked away. That he thought Agamemnon was such a diseased limb seems beyond doubt. That he valued his pride and honor even more than he valued victory was his tragedy.

All those who were present on that fatal day when the Agamemnon's obduracy and Achilles' pride finally collided knew one thing beyond doubt: that just as surely as the sun shone down upon them, without Achilles they had no chance of winning the war in which they had been for so long and interminably engaged and that had brought them no glory and no closer to capturing Troy so as to take its treasure.

Chapter 12

On the eighth day just as dawn broke, I awakened to hear Mecisteus, my orderly, calling my name.

"Sir, there is to be a council of the officers; Lord Achilles has called it."

Ah, I thought, he has taken matters into his hands.

"Has the king agreed?"

"No one knows."

"When?"

"Within the hour," he said. "Let me help you arm, sir."

Mecisteus is a handsome youth and noble; his father, Talaus, holds a small island kingdom, and Mecisteus has been my orderly for two years now. If I were not his commander I could easily find him more than interesting. He knows that, and has let me know by a glance or a lingering touch as he bathes me and helps me arm that he would be willing. I sometimes wonder why I do not proceed with it. There is no hope for me, ever, to be with Achilles so long as Patroclus fills his mind and heart. Mecisteus is the age I was when I came here. He is honest and brave; I like him more than a little. He would be a perfect lover. My father would approve for he is forever impatient with what he always calls my "eternal sighing" over Achilles. And it is so; all my life up to now has been fixed on Achilles, and to no avail, and so, save for occasional hours of pleasure with a handful of handsome men, I have been alone. Soon, when this terrible war is over, I must marry. My father and mother already have some Argive princess picked out for me, I am sure. But before I take a wife and begin a family, which as prince and my father's heir I am bound to do, I should know the joy of having a faithful companion to stand by my side and love me as I love him. And if I should die here, he as my sworn companion would gather my ashes and say the prayers for my soul, just as Achilles and

Patroclus have surely vowed to do for one another, should one or the other not survive.

Mecisteus drew me back from my reverie.

"Sir? Are you unwell?"

I looked at him for a long moment and almost began to speak my thoughts, then thought better if it. Now is not the time.

" No, I am well," I said. "Go and awake my father."

I rose from my cot, splashed my face with water, and ate some stale bread and cheese and olives left from the night before, dressed and buckled on my breastplate. Taking my helmet and sword. I went out of the tent. My father was already there. I embraced him and together we walked toward the king's tent where officer's councils were held. We were soon joined by Machaon, the healer, and then by Diomedes of Argos and Idomeneos of Crete. They saluted my father.

"Lord Nestor, what is this about?"

"You know as much as I do," my father said. "Achilles sent a messenger before dawn. That's all I know."

We walked in silence, each man deep in his own thoughts. And silent it was indeed. The usual noise and bustle of the camp-- men shouting, dishes rattling from the cook tents, chariot wheels crunching across the gravel—could not be heard. No dogs barked, no horses whinnied nor mules brayed from the distant horse corrals. There were no birds singing, no hoarse calls of crows or shriek of a hawk as it wheeled and then dove upon its prey. Even the constant wash of the waves from on the beach, crashing and retiring, again and over again, a sound become so familiar that after all these years we no longer heard it, seemed to be absent on the morning air. Its absence made the silence even more ominous. It was as if the entire world waited to hear what Achilles had to say.

The king's tent stands at the center of the officer's compound, surrounded by those of the other kings, princes, and officers, though in no order of rank. In front of it a large open space is used for councils of the commanders. From this four wide pathways radiate, one leads to the parade ground, another to the beach, the others to the northern and southern gates. In front of the tent a group of men were gathered talking among themselves. I counted most of the great officers of the army there: Idomeneus of Crete, Diomedes, King of Argos, Aias of Salamis, Menetheus, Prince of Athens, Meriones, nephew of Idomeneus, Peneleos of Boetia, Phoenix of Dolopes, and the great bowman Teucer, all waiting before Agamemnon's tent, some standing, others sitting on chairs and stools that ringed the council ground. I brought a chair for my father. Before the tent Talthybios, Agamemnon's herald, stood next to the gilded chair of the king. The royal standard, fixed to a pole next to the throne, hung limply in the dead air. A dozen royal guards stood at attention. I could not see Achilles anywhere. Nor the king.

But we did not wait long. From the far end of the grassy causeway that led in a straight line from the tents near the southern end of the officer's compound past the parade ground and to the council space in front of the king's tent, we saw him come, Achilles in full battle armor and with him Patroclus. Between them walked a third. It was Calchas. The three approached up the wide path. Achilles looked neither right nor left, his face hidden by the fearsome Myrmidon helmet, his beautiful body encased above the torso in the tight gilded iron armor he favored. His legs were bare save for gilded graves and boots, boots specially made it was said, and especially protected from harm at the heel. Patroclus was in light parade armor and helmet-less. He supported Calchas who seemed to be walking unwillingly with them. Calchas was a sight; his hair disheveled, his eyes frightened, his cloak askew. He leaned heavily on a staff and the laurel wreath of the priest tilted lopsidedly on his brow.

They approached the assembled officers. Patroclus saluted the superior officers as he passed them. Achilles, seeing my father, bowed and saluted him and motioned Patroclus to escort Calchas to a place next to my father and me. He removed his helmet and handed it to Patroclus, and strode to the spot before the king's tent reserved for speakers. A young herald stood at attention holding the speaker's staff--a long wooden branch cut from an olive tree, highly polished and painted, decorated with golden studs--which must be held by whoever would address the council. Achilles motioned to the herald to hand him the staff.

He took it and as he did he shouted, "Agamemnon! I want you!"

Talthybius, the King's herald, brawny and broad shouldered, with a voice that could carry across the parade ground, stepped forward, his hand on his sword.

"What do you want with the king?" he said. Though he used the timeworn formula heralds use to respond to supplicants who come before the king, it was clear that he was ready if need be for a fight.

"You won't need that sword, Talthybios," Achilles said, not shouting now, but his voice menacing. "I call for the king to come out and lead his army as he should."

There was an indrawn breath from among the officers. Achilles' demand was not only a condemnation of the king's leadership, but a challenge to his authority.

"Go," Achilles said imperiously, "and summon him."

"The king comes at his will," Talthybios replied, adding after a moment, "Lord Achilles."

"There is no time for waiting, even upon the whim of kings," Achilles answered. "Men are dying. *His* men are dying. I demand...we demand"-- and here he made a great circular motion with his arm to include all who stood there—"we demand that he come out. Now!"

The royal guards shifted uneasily. You could see that they sympathized with what Achilles said. Perhaps even as did Talthybios.

"But Lord Achilles..." Talthybios had just begun to speak when the tent flap parted. Agamemnon appeared. He was not in armor as he should be for a council, but wore a long robe, richly embroidered, as if he had just come from a feast. Behind him followed his brother, Menelaus, and Odysseus. The guards stood to attention and all the officers saluted. But Achilles did not move.

"What do you want from me, Achilles?" Agamemnon asked. His voice sounded strained and tired. His eyes were hooded and darkly circled. He sank into his chair.

"Agamemnon," Achilles said, "for eight days now-- eight days! -- men are dying, their reeking bodies food for the vultures. But you remain hidden in your tent."

I looked around to see how the officers took Achilles' words. There were nods of agreement. "He is right," someone quietly said. A dreadful silence had fallen upon the assembled officers. An eternity seemed to pass. The king said nothing, only stared at Achilles. But I could see that his faced had reddened.

When at last the king spoke his tone was contemptuous. "What do you want me to do? If you're so afraid of dying then run away, board your ships and sail home." The king spat on the ground.

"I don't run, Agamemnon. And I don't fear death," Achilles said, his voice cold with rage. "But what do you fear? Have *you* walked among the dead, have you tended them like we have done. Have you lit the pyres to honor them? Have *you* stopped counting your gold and toying with your women long enough to come out of your tent to see the horror with your own eyes? No you have not. Or are you afraid even to do that?"

The two men stared at each other across the assembly ground. On one side stood the king, his face almost purple, his eyes flashing with hatred and with his guard at his back; in back of him Odysseus and Menelaus stood, tensed and ready. Menelaus had half drawn his sword. On the other side Achilles, still as a sentinel, his face stony and composed. Around them, in a tight circle, the great officers of the coalition—lords, princes and kings--watched like spectators at a wrestling match. Or I thought, perhaps like nothing so noble as that. More like hungry animals circling at the edge of a clearing as two wild beasts fought for supremacy, eagerly waiting for one of the combatants to fall so that they could rush in to eat their fill of the still quivering flesh.

Then from somewhere in the rear of the crowd someone shouted, "Give the girl back!"

"Yes, give her back," another voiced echoed. "She has caused the plague."

And then a third, and then another: "Give her back!"

I could smell rebellion in the air. So apparently could the king. He stepped back and away from Achilles and looked around him.

104

His guards were a good twenty paces away. Agamemnon is a cunning man and no fool. I could see his instinct to survive mastering his rage. He stood for a moment, listening to the shouting men. Then, turning slowly, with a slight almost quizzical smile, he nonchalantly walked back to the space before his tent, stood for a long moment as if deep in thought, and turned and faced us. The anger was gone from his face. He opened his arms in an expansive gesture as if to include all the officers assembled in front of him in a huge embrace.

"Give her back, you say. Well let's talk about this then, my lords. You know I always listen to your advice. Come, gather round; we are all friends here. Let's discuss this."

Here he gestured to an orderly standing nearby—" bring chairs for those who do not have them, and bring wine for everyone. No sense in talking with a dry mouth."

Servants brought wine, cups, and water for mixing with the strong dark wine. For the king a richly gilded cup was placed on a table next to his chair. The cups were filled and passed around. Everyone drank. I noticed that the king did not dilute his wine and drained his cup before he spoke again.

"Now maybe I've been a little hasty," he said. "I see that you all have a point, and maybe the priest is right." Looking at Calchas he said, "Get up, priest, you need have no fear of your old friend."

Then to all of us he said: "Let me tell you all, I won't let some little piece of fluff come between me and my men. Though I'm not at all sure that she caused the plague as some seem to think. But you all have to admit," and here he lowered his voice and smirked as if he were about to tell an obscene story, "it's a nice thing to have a warm girl in your tent on these cold nights."

My father gasped in astonishment, and I could see some of the other officers, older ones who had lived long and faithfully with beloved wives, turn away with a look of disgust. The king did not seem to notice.

"So now you know why I don't want give her up. You wouldn't either if you were in my place. But these are bad times, you don't have to tell me, and a king has to think of his people. So if you think that I should let her go to put an end to this plague, why then she's as good as gone." He motioned to the orderly to fill his cup again.

Then he said: "Is that what you want my lords?" In answer the men began to cheer.

"Well lets drink to it then," he said, and drained the cup once more.

Wiping his lips with the back of his hand, Agamemnon, looking pleased, said: "Well that's settled then. You can never accuse me of shirking my duty."

Everyone began to talk at once; the sense of relief was palpable.

But then the king raised a hand for silence. "One more thing though" he said. "I'll give up the girl and send he back to her father. But as long as we are talking about honor, how about mine? This girl was my prize in war, earned fair and square in battle.

"Fair and square," Achilles shouted. "Your honor? There's no fair to this, no honor here, your *majesty*," Achilles said and the chill anger in his voice made an insult of the title. "I captured that girl. I captured all that gold. I did it all. And everyone knows that. You have the girl, raped in your bed I imagine."

The atmosphere crackled with tension. "And the gold? What about the treasure her father brought? Its all still locked away in your treasury. Have any of us seen a share of it?"

I could see the rage in Agamemnon's face. He strode to where Achilles stood and the two men faced one another, hatred in their eyes.

Then he stepped back and raising his arm pointed an accusing finger at Achilles. "How dare you challenge your king? What other gods do you want to offend?"

He looked around to see what effect that would have. Some of the men nodded and made the sign against evil. The king had scored a point. As if to celebrate his small victory, the king took a long draught from his cup.

Achilles seemed about to speak, but the king pushed past him and spoke directly to the officers.

"But, men," he said, "let's not worry now about such trifles." His voice was thick and I realized that he had drunk too much.

"You know that I can be trusted and that I can be reasonable. Let's not worry about who ought to be rewarded and who ought to make a sacrifice," he said, inclining his head with an exaggerated show of piety--I wondered if this gesture looked as hollow to the others as it did to me---"It is the god who we must placate."

Then thrusting out his cup to the servant in attendance, said, "You, boy, damn you, can't you keep this filled."

He drank from the now filled cup and sank back into his chair. Turning to Odysseus he said: "Will you be the one to return her, or you Lord Aias, or you Idomeneus?"

His face was flushed, his eyes gleamed with the effects of the wine.

"Ah, of course," he said, looking to where Achilles stood.

With a flutter of his fingers he motioned to Achilles: "You there, Achilles, come here. Since you want so much to have her gone maybe you ought to take her home."

I could hear Achilles' sudden sharp intake of breath at Agamemnon's gesture, summoning Achilles as if he were a servant.

Achilles stood for moment as if he did not believe what he had just seen. His eyes were hooded and dark, his mouth set in a grim line, his face drained of color. Advancing to where the king sat negligently toying with his wine cup, Achilles looked darkly down on the seated king. Agamemnon looked up at him quizzically, with an odd, twisted, almost triumphant smile. I realized with amazement that flushed with wine as he was and made careless by it, the king actually thought he had humbled Achilles. From where I stood I could see Achilles' broad back tense with readiness. His hands were clenched at his side. No one who had seen him in battle need be told how like lightening it was when Achilles drew his sword. But he did not draw it. But he advanced toward the king.

Alarmed, Agamemnon started to rise, fumbling for his sword and Achilles stepped quickly forward and roughly pushed him back into his chair. Agamemnon fell back, sheer astonishment on his face and struggled to rise but Odysseus, standing behind the king, placed a strong restraining hand on Agamemnon's shoulder. He clearly knew that if the king tried to fight Achilles that it could be the end of him. Menelaus, looking pale and alarmed, began to move back towards the tent. Odysseus flashed him an angry look and Menelaus halted.

"Oh yes, let Odysseus protect you," Achilles said scornfully, stepping back.

"It is so like you. So brave. We fight and die. You sit in your tent and drink and let braver men to bring you hostages and treasure. And you have the arrogance to threaten me! You must be mad."

Achilles spat upon the ground at the king's feet and then turning to the assembled captains he spoke directly to them.

"Why should we obey this man? He says Troy is our enemy and if we fight them here we won't have to fight them at home. Then our homeland will be secure! How secure will it be if our best men are dead? This wretched king called us to fight and die in this wretched land, but the truth is he has failed to lead us to any kind of victory. Have we even confronted the Trojans? Have we won any battle? Have any of us gotten what we came for? Is this war worth it? I don't think so. Where's the honor in following a coward for a king and filling *his* pockets and getting his cuckold brother back his slattern of a wife. It's enough! I'm sick of fighting this man's war and seeing my men die. It's over! I'm done!"

It was as if he had struck us all a strong blow to the body. On the faces of some of the officers I could see shock, and even panic. But in the eyes of most of them, I could see that they did not disagree with what Achilles had said.

In fury the king leapt up and dashed his wine cup on the ground and nearly shrieked, his voice breaking in rage. "Then go, get out, you coward. Run. Do you think I'll beg you to stay? There are plenty of brave men who can fight as well as you. Take your boyfriend and scamper away. Then you'll know who's the strongest. And all the world will see that they can't defy their king."

Achilles drew his sword and in a lightening movement leapt directly in front of the king. I was sure that he would kill him then and there. But at a sign from Odysseus the guard rushed forward and surrounded Agamemnon, just as Patroclus and I moved quickly to Achilles' side.

"No, my lord," I said urgently, "you must not."

Patroclus placed his hand firmly on Achilles' sword arm and with the other gripped his shoulder tightly. Achilles paused and looked at Patroclus and at me, and as if awakening from possession by a god, took in a deep-drawn breath, shook himself free from our grip, but also sheathed his sword.

Stepping back he said: "You pitiful drunken sot, I won't kill you; it would disgrace my sword to shed your blood. I won't fight a man who cowers behind his guard. Go hide in your tent. But you mark *my* words, king. The day will come when you will desperately need my sword. But I swear to you by this sacred staff"—here he snatched up the speaker's staff and its golden studs glittered in the sun—"I swear by this and all the gods that I will watch as the earth drinks your black blood and I will not lift my sword to defend you as you die."

With that Achilles turned his back full on the king. He stood for a moment before the assembled generals of Greece, defiant with the morning sun behind him. Its light seemed to form an aureole around him. He glittered; he looked indeed like a god, Achilles, our hero and our hope. He stared us all down, and he said nothing but his message was clear: "Choose, men of Greece. Choose me or your mad king."

I could feel the onlookers waver; I was sure that one by one and then in a rush they would go to his side, abandoning the king. The tension was unbearable. Then he turned to me.

"Antilochus?" he said. It was indeed a question.

Its answer might have been: "Yes, I am yours, I will follow you anywhere."

But I could not say that because on my answer—on my action—the entire future of this war now depended. I had become, in the eyes of all who watched, the key to what all would do. What I did they would do. I looked at my father. He was white and drawn, anger and anxiety fought in his eyes. In his lined and aged face I saw it all: years of dignity and loyalty to a king and unswerving duty to a cause. His eyes said: "Stay. Stand your ground. Do not follow Achilles." Even for my love of Achilles I could not ignore my father's will.

I turned back to Achilles. He saw the answer in my face. With a curt bow to me and with a nod of his head to Patroclus, the two of them marched away toward Achilles' tents on the far side of the camp. A sigh of frustration escaped every lip. I could feel the weight of despair settle upon us.

As the king watched Achilles disappear from view, a small cruel smile of triumph played about his lips. I felt defeated, and wondered if the world had gone truly mad.

Chapter 13

Around us groups of officers talked in whispers. I wondered if they were even now beginning to fragment into factions, some for Achilles, others loyal to the king. It was obvious that many were displeased with the conduct of the war and felt that the king's arrogance had led them into an un-winnable conflict. Should it come to it, would they cast their lot with Achilles, seeing a way to rid themselves of what they had come to think of as an incompetent king?

Who would support Agamemnon? His brother certainly, Odysseus no doubt, certain other kings who would not dare foreswear the fealty they owed him, simply because they are weak and he is strong. And if worse came to worse, if Achilles and the king came to open warfare, on what side would the army cast its dice and would the men follow their commanders? Or would it break out into internal war, faction fighting against the other, friends battling friends?

The true horror of it was that camped behind our defensive walls were all the great kings of our world. If it came to it, out of this strife between two stubborn men could grow a civil war that would throw into chaos and disarray the entire coalition that had come here in unity to bring Troy down, and thus bring all the world to open war.

And then there was Troy itself. What a perfect stroke of luck for them would our discord be. They could wait and watch as we battled among ourselves. Then, when they saw that we were so weakened from slaughtering one another that we had no will to battle any other foe, they could swoop down from their high city and finish the job, leaving the bodies of their invaders to rot on the shore of the land they had hoped to conquer.

Interrupting these dark thoughts came the king's voice, raised to attract the attention of the small groups of talking men. He motioned for them to gather before him.

111

"My lords, I see fear and concern in your eyes. And you're right to be concerned after such a display as that. But we can't let that young man's pride distract us from our duty. There is work to be done and we have to do it. I say let young Achilles sit alone in his tent and nurse his disloyalty. He'll soon come to his senses and when he does I will be magnanimous. I have said that I will send the girl back to her father and so I will, and we will lift this plague and triumph over it. Stand with me, my lords. I'm in charge; I will do what is right. Now, go back to your tents and your men."

Turning back towards the tent as he passed where we waited he said with a bow to my father, "My Lord Nestor, I have need of you. Join me. Oh yes, bring your son as well. Brother, you too, and you Odysseus. Talthybios," he said to the waiting herald, "I want you as well. Summon Calchas and Machaon the healer too." The king disappeared inside his tent and we followed.

Once inside, with what I thought was exaggerated, almost too honeyed courtesy, the king bade us all sit and motioned to a servant to bring wine, cheese, bread and olives, and some lamb marinated in oil and rosemary to break our fast. I had eaten nothing since early morning. It was now well past midday.

When we had eaten, Agamemnon said, "I hope that we all can go beyond the appalling events of this morning."

He looked around, hoping to find agreement, and found it, of course, in Calchas who, now that he had been admitted back into the good graces of the king, wanted to make it clear that he was truly sorry for having backed the wrong horse.

Calchas all too quickly said, "So true, my lord king, so true. We must surely do what we can to restore our fellowship."

Machaon looked across the room at me and raised a disdainful eyebrow.

"Yes, lets get on with it." Menelaus said. "Achilles will get over his tantrum."

Odysseus smiled to himself but kept his council.

"Brother, you're right. Achilles is hardly the most important issue before us," the king said, almost jovially. He looked around the room as if expecting each of us to voice our agreement. No one spoke.

"Good, I am glad we're agreed," he said. That our silence may have suggested that we were not all agreed seemed a fact he would rather not consider.

"Now the first thing we need to do is deal with this annoying girl—the priest's daughter, though I personally do not know what proof we have that she has any connection to the plague, nor has anyone convinced me of it."

Calchas rolled his eyes in frustration and interrupted vehemently.

"No connection! I have seen it, I tell you, it is obvious. Send her back or else Apollo will continue to punish us. You must do as I say! I have seen him shooting his arrows. I have been granted a vision…"

"Your visions come from inhaling too many of your burning herbs, Calchas," Machaon interrupted with exasperation. "Many have died; others, amazingly, have been spared. I've seen such plagues before. They rage for a time and run their course. Their course can be long or it can be brief. But this I know and I will stake my reputation on it: this disaster too will run its course—but precisely when it will end I can't predict. But of this I am certain; it *will* end. What does it matter whether the gods are punishing us or some foul sickness has arisen from out of the earth from who knows where? It's here and men are dying. The rest live in despair. If it will help the morale of the men to send this damnable girl back then I say send her back and lets have done with this eternal wrangling."

Odysseus, stroking his beard thoughtfully, said: "Well spoken sir. My lord king, let us carefully consider the situation. There are two paramount considerations. The first is to end this terrible plague. The second is too restoring confidence in your command and to raise the morale of the troops. If we send her back and the plague ends—either because we have placated the gods as Calchas says, or because it ends of its own accord as Machaon predicts, in either case the world will see that you have been a pious king and in obeying the gods that you have been given their favor. That will be a mighty argument against any plots that Achilles might advance against you. But if we do not send her back then we may face the most serious consequence. Let me be blunt—the consequences might well be that Achilles will have very good reason to – shall we say—to try to effect a change in the regime of the state." He let the notion of mutiny take hold for a moment.

"Anyway," Menelaus interrupted. "We don't need her now. We have the gold."

"I think what my lord Menelaus means," said Odysseus, "is that the conditions have now become such that we can well afford to give her up, since she has outlived her usefulness to the state. The king has proved who is master. Isn't that the real point of the exercise after all? Surely the girl is immaterial now."

I looked at the king. His expression was that of a man who has just been saved from falling by a helping hand from a friend.

"Yes, wise Odysseus," he said, " you do have a point."

I though to myself: the real point is that Achilles no longer stands with us. His Patroclus and his army are waiting for him to ---- to do what? Sail away into the sunset? Stir up mutiny among our men and attack us here in our camp and slay the king who insulted him? Who would stand against Achilles? Who *could* stand against Achilles? Or worst of all, would he simply sit there and do nothing? Stir the poisoned cauldron of his pride until the anger—the terrible wrath of Achilles--bursts forth to the destruction of us all.

Book Six
The Triumph of Apollo

Chryseis *of the lovely cheeks was put on board the ship and when everyone was aboard they set out along the highways of the sea to take her home."*
--*Iliad* Book 1

From: Dionysos Of Tenedos, A History of the War at Troy

It was decided. Odysseus and Antilochus were commanded by the King to take the girl-- as Agamemnon called her, though Priestess were her title and her calling and Apollo her protector— home to her father. Some say that Odysseus wandered for twenty years because he incurred the enmity of Chryseis, but those who know will not say that. He did her no harm. He wandered for other sins. Some say that Agamemnon met his terrible fate because he had inflicted pain and humiliation upon her. No one knows what the Gods plan for us, but those who know her story would not deny that among all his sins, the King's treatment of Chryseis merited his punishment. Chryseis left behind a legend and also her handmaiden Briseis, who loved her.

Chapter 14

Panic is abroad in the camp. Some of our officers have given up using their Trojan slaves for sex, neither women nor boys are called in the middle of the night to come to a tent to pleasure some drunken captain, to be raped half a dozen times by half a dozen men, or to lie shamed and tearful after a man old enough to be his father takes a boy's manhood from behind.

Though the officers put on a brave face and talk arrogantly about victory and how they will pull down those walls and slaughter everyone in sight yet anyone with eyes can see that fear governs this camp and this war.

Why? Again I say it: Achilles is gone.

All around, people—mostly slaves and servants--gather. I hear snatches of conversation as I hurry past group after group, from one to another. In one someone is hastily telling what he knows, to another someone breathlessly runs up with yet another rumor. Voices chime in. One after another says his piece, imparts a rumor he has heard.

"The king is to blame for the plague."

"The priests say that if he does not let the Lady go that Apollo will kill us all."

" Troy cannot be captured unless they let her go."

"The king has insulted Achilles."

" Achilles has quarreled with the king."

"Achilles has left the camp; he refuses to fight."

" The King has no choice, he must return the girl."

" If he doesn't we are all dead men."

I pass a group of Trojan slaves excitedly talking.

One says: "They will let her go. They will let the lady go."

The other: "How? What has happened? How do you know? "

I stop to listen. They fall silent when the see me. But I motion them to speak. The one speaking cannot contain himself and despite my presence goes on.

"I heard it myself, for I was in the cook tent serving up food to the boys who serve the king for them to take to his tent. It was just this morning. The king and his officers—Odysseus, his brother Menelaus, and the priest Chalchas. They were arguing. The boy—Calistos is his name--heard it all for the Greeks pay no attention to slaves, they barely see us at all.

Calistos says he heard them say: "'You've got to let the lady go, or we'll all die.' That's what they were saying to the king."

And now it is common news: Chryseis will be freed. Everyone talks of it. And how quickly it has happened. How quickly despair has turned to triumph.

And it is true for I was there. But this too is true. Though we die the Trojan captives live. Among the Trojans I am told it is believed that Chryseis protects them. I think I believe it too.

Because I am her guard--her jailor--and everyone knows it, everywhere I go soldiers say to me: "Ask The Lady to pray for us." They do not use her name, though all know it. She is just The Lady. The Lady of our sorrows. The Lady, they believe, of our salvation.

Yes, I believe that she will save us.

She has said this to me: "My father will save me. I will see him again. We will all live."

Chapter 15

"Prepare yourself, Lady, it is time," I said, bowing to her as I entered her tent. The king has commanded that I, as her guard, go on the voyage with Odysseus, to take Chryseis home. Chryseis stood with Briseis. I could see that she did not need to be told to be ready. She had long been prepared. She took only a white linen shift and a long mantle of wool, and bound on sandals.

"That was all I came with," she said. It is all I need to depart."

I opened the tent flap for her and we emerged into the daylight. The sky was as thick with smoke rising in the distance near to the beach, plumes of smoke from the ever-burning funeral pyres, making melancholy columns black against the sun. My small detachment of soldiers stands at attention. The priest Calchas is there as well, and Odysseus of course. A short distance from them is Nestor, my father. He comes forward, carrying a rich woolen cloak, deep blue and embroidered in threads of gold. I saw that it was Trojan work. He drapes it carefully over her shoulders and ties it snugly in front, almost as if he were tucking her in bed, just as he used to do with me. That small kind gesture brought tears to my eyes. I thought, here is an Achaean who deserves to be remembered as a noble man.

He said, "It won't do, Lady, for you to be cold on the voyage."

"My Lady Chryseis," Calchas said, with a deep bow, "King Agamemnon has magnanimously decided that you should be granted your freedom and returned to your father."

I noted that the level of deference had markedly changed from when she was known as Agamemnon's whore.

I pointedly glanced up at the sky to where the plumes of smoke drifted darkly. I knew that magnanimity had little do with this decision.

Calchas continued, somewhat uncomfortably: "The Lord Odysseus will accompany you as a token of honor, and with him he

119

brings worthy sacrifices for the Archer God. The king hopes…we all hope… that you will intercede for us when you return to your father, the Reverend and Noble Lord Chryses."

Not so noble once in this king's eyes, I thought.

"Honor Guard at the ready," Odysseus commanded. "Come, Lady, let me take you home."

Nestor gave her an encouraging smile and reached out and patted her hand. "Soon, he said, soon." I saw why my father had been spared the archer's arrows.

At that moment Briseis rushed to her mistress and fell on her knees in front of Chryseis.

"My lady, take me with you, I beg you."

Chryseis gave her a sad, almost pitying look. I knew the answer before she said it.

"I wish more than anything, my Briseis, that you could go with me and share my life in Chrysa with me and my father. As I love you like a sister he would love you like a daughter. But you cannot, for it has long been decided. There is a destiny that waits for me and one that waits for you, and I, even I, dare not try to change it. And know this too, my dear, dear friend, we will never see one another again. But this I do know: I have promised you and I say it again. You will live and you will be free."

Briseis kissed the hem of Chryseis' robe and wept—whether with joy that freedom would soon be given to her or with bitter sorrow that Chryseis would soon be lost to her.

"Do not do this," Chryseis said. "Shed no tears for me, or for you," and she softly touched Briseis' hair, in benediction.

I looked at her there, and saw what I had never seen before: Chryseis, daughter of the god indeed, but herself a goddess, terrible in vengeance, but mother of all mercies, a young and beautiful woman, but ancient as the stars, standing at the still center of the eternal universe, bathed in everlasting starlight, all women at one in her.

The two women embraced and we walked away from the officer's tents along the broad avenue that bisected the camp, toward the beach. I had expected to find all silent and empty. Silent it was, but it was not empty. Along the way soldiers lined the road, watching as we walked with Odysseus and Chryseis, and I leading with six men of the guard, six men following. Many of the men lining the road were unkempt and hollow eyed. They stared as if at some marvel. For though all had heard of Chryseis few had seen her since she had been snatched up by the king as soon as she was brought to the camp as a captive. As we walked between the ranks of men, above the tramp of the guard's marching feet I could hear voices calling out: "Save us, Lady, save us." The king was nowhere to be seen.

The way stretched down to the beach where, in the distance, I could see a ship, black hulled as our Achaean ships are, riding at anchor just a short way out in the water. Its mast was raised and its sail was ready to be unfurled. A long pennant with the king's lion device upon it floated from the mast. The oars rose straight up, ready at the oarsman's signal to be plunged into the water and with steady strokes to take Chryseis home.

I stood at the ship's rail as we got underway. A stiff breeze blew up almost as soon as we pulled in the anchor and we scudded swiftly before it. There seemed to be no need of oars. The further we got away from shore the brighter the sky became. I filled my lungs with the fresh salt air for which I had longed. As I breathed in the cold clear air a weight was lifted from my shoulders, and exhaling, I felt the fear and shame expelled. As we pulled away from the Trojan shore, I looked back at our Achaean camp. I could see the evidence of the calamity that had struck it. In the center of the camp was the huge parade ground where I had heard the bard singing, now it seemed so long ago. On this ground too the old priest had been humiliated before the army, and sent ignominiously home. Now it was filled with heaps of burning corpses. The pyres sent towers of smoke to heaven, like the black columns of some macabre temple. At the far end of the camp our ships, drawn up in neat lines, lay on the beach, prows out. Looking down on it all from its high mountain cliff stood Troy. Its towers caught the morning sunlight and from the ramparts I could just hear, carried across the Achaean camp and to the deck of the ship by some trick of the wind, the silver call of a

121

Trojan trumpet. Did they know that Chryses and his daughter had triumphed over Agamemnon?

The ship was not a large one, thirty oarsmen, fifteen to a side, for it was not a long journey, a day or two at most with good weather. The soldiers bunked on deck among the cattle, three bulls—one of them white-- five sheep and assorted other creatures, all destined as a sacrifice to Apollo to convince him to end the plague. Chryseis had a feather pallet under a small canopy rigged in the stern. I slept on deck.

We had been underway half a day already when Odysseus came to the stern where Chryseis sat looking at the waves tumble away on either side of the ship, parting and foaming at the prow. I too watched the water to see if any dolphins might swim with us. Thus far we sailed alone on the glassy sea.

Odysseus saluted. "Lady, do you require anything?" he asked.

"No, just privacy," she replied. But he did not leave.

Instead he said, almost hesitantly, "I have heard, Lady Chryseis, that you are blessed with the sight? Is that so?"

She answered, "Yes, I have been blessed, though your king's vile touch may well have ruined that gift, for few visions have come to me since I became his captive."

"Yes, but you are free now, Lady, and…well…I am glad of it. It was wrong to take you." I could see this admission cost him something to say.

"Do you really believe that, my lord, or is it matter of policy that you say so now?" she said coldly.

"This is no policy. The king was wrong and we are paying for his arrogance. I know no way to say it other than as I have done. Believe me."

When he spoke, I heard pain in his voice and saw the truth in his eyes. Then he said: " I do not know how to ask, but if it is true that you can sometimes look into the future, can you, for me…." His voice trailed off. I was amazed to see that Odysseus of the honey tongue was at a loss for words.

"Perhaps, " he said to Chryseis, "perhaps you might be able to answer a small thing for me." I could tell by his tone that it was no small thing. Chryseis said nothing, and signed for him to go on.

"I ask nothing else of you, and for it I will see that you are carried safely home."

Chryseis said: "I thought that was already your mandate from the king—to see me safely home. I cannot bargain with my gift."

"You're right," he said. "It was tactless of me to ask in that way. But you should know, my questions are not about great things, not about politics and the state, not if Troy will stand or fall, or if Achilles will prevail or the king. Nor dare I ask if Apollo will relent, for who can finally know the will of the capricious gods? No, I only ask a small question... for me... a personal one. It would comfort me if I could know. It is about...about...my wife—and my son."

As he hesitantly explained his request, I could see that here was a man, used to command and used to being obeyed, who had come to beg a favor—and from a woman. It was no easy thing for him to lower his guard, to remove the mask of command. Though he was still the shrewd and crafty Odysseus, war lord and advisor to Agamemnon, king of kings, and chief strategist of the numberless forces of Greece, yet before her—before the Lady Chryseis-- he was a husband longing for news of a beloved wife from whom he had been too long separated; he was a father who wanted to see his only son.

"What do you want to know," Chryseis asked.

"Whether they are alive and well. That is all. It has been ten years since I have seen my Penelope and my son Telemachus, who was only an infant when I went to war."

My heart went out to the father lonely for his wife and child. So my own father remembered everyday the wife he had loved, my mother, who he had for so long not seen.

"I will do it," she said, "but you must do one thing for me."

"Ask," he said.

"Protect my servant Briseis. The king no doubt hates me and because of me I fear he will harm her."

"Consider it done," he said.

"Then bring me that brazier," she said, pointing to the small three-legged dish that had been provided to warm our hands at night. At Odysseus' sign I brought the brazier and went to search for straw from the cattle stall. Coming back with the straw and some chips and scraps of wood from the wood box amidships where the cook-fire smoldered, I arranged the fuel in the brazier and lighted it with a brand from the cook-fire. Quickly it caught and blazed up and in a few moments it had settled into low flame and glowing coals.

Chryseis took sandalwood and dried Artemisia, that some call wormwood, along with some lavender, from a small bag she had tied at her waist and threw them on the flames. It burned brightly and the smoke wreathed up. She bent over the brazier and inhaled deeply. At first there was nothing. All I felt was the gentle rise and fall of the ship as it dipped into and rose on the waves, and the touch of the wind that carried with it the scent of sea salt mixed with the smell of the cattle. Other than the waves splashing on the hull, the only sound was the sail slapping against the mast, and the shriek of an occasional bird, crying out as it dove into the sea to find a juicy fish. Through the smoke I could see Odysseus watching carefully. I feared that nothing would happen.

But then behind the smoke Chryseis' features began to shift, almost to begin to fade. She inhaled deeply and her breathing became harsh, and she murmured words that I could not understand. The smoke was so dense now that I could no longer see the deck, or the cattle chewing their cud, nor the soldiers lounging aforeship, playing dice. The ship became translucent, then invisible. Around us, around Odysseus, Chryseis, and I the smoke billowed and I felt lightheaded myself.

Did I imagine it or was there etched against the white background of the smoky cloud dim forms, moving shapes, landscapes. Did I see a rocky path, running upward to the high point of a plateau—the acropolis as we Achaeans call it--of an island set in the center of the wine dark sea? Upon the heights rose a high walled citadel with a single gate of wooden and iron reinforced double doors, the cornice decorated with painted figures, and supported by thick columns painted red and adorned with blue swirling decorations running around them like snakes. The building vanished as a gust of wind stirred the smoking cloud, but dimly to be replaced with another—curious, unclear. Was it a woman sitting weaving? Was that a young boy playing with a small shield and a wooden sword? The woman, whose blonde hair was streaked with

124

grey, looked down at the boy, and could I just hear her say, "Ah Telemachus, you are your father's son."

Then the smoke cleared. I heard the ocean sounds against the ship, a cow lowed, and I saw Odysseus, face, anxious and concerned, hovering above Chryseis where she had fallen back on her bed. He held a cup of wine to her lips. She sipped gratefully. I could see the question in his eyes. Chryseis smiled. I was glad when I heard her say, "Your wife lives; and your son will be a hero. Like you."

Chapter 16

The next morning Chrysa was in sight. Around the ship hundreds of birds swooped and floated in the air, their calls seemed to be a chorus of welcome. And the dolphins, absent thus far from our voyage, leapt and tumbled before us, rising high above the waves and diving back again like acrobats performing before an audience. We entered the bay at mid-day just as the sun, Apollo's heavenly sign, reached its highest point in the sky. The gleaming rays reflected off the water, turning the foaming waves into a million diamond points breaking against the ship and shore and Chrysa's sand--fine and golden--was so washed by the sun that it seemed to be a carpet woven of fine gilt thread.

News of the coming of a ship must have spread on shore from person to person and house-to-house, for the cliff above the beach was now filling with people. I wondered if someone had gone running to the temple precincts to take the message that an Achaean ship had come to Chrysa. The people stood close together and appeared to be talking excitedly but nervously one to another, for how could they know if the ship meant well or harm. It was a dark-hulled Achaean ship after all, and such ships had brought nothing but sorrow to Ilium. But wise Odysseus, seeing this too, and wanting nothing to go wrong, shouted to the mid-ships deckhand to haul down the king's pennant and raise instead a white flag of peace, a signal that all men knew.

Seeing the flag, the people began to shout-- no, cheer-- and run toward the path that led down to the beach. And among them, indeed above them, I could see a small white-haired figure carried on a chair by four strong young men. Before him walked another carrying a staff. I didn't have to see it well to know that this was the staff of Apollo. It glittered and flashed as it caught the sun's rays, sending them out across the golden sand, across the waters, and to the horizon as if to signal that at last all was well. I stood at the deck rail and watched the little procession come down the steep path to the beach. The calling of gulls, the shouts of the people, the splashing of the waves against the hull, seemed to combine into a paean of triumph, punctuated by the steady beat of the oar-master's drum as we tacked smartly in towards the shore.

The ship rushed toward the beach; the oar-master struck a final quick tattoo; with a clatter the oars were raised and with a hiss of waves and sand we slid neatly up onto the beach; sailors leapt ashore and thrust blocks beneath the hull and with a shudder we were still. Time seemed to stop for moment. Like a frieze painted on a temple wall: a dark hulled ship drawn up on a golden beach; a young woman standing expectantly at the gangplank about to disembark; a crowd of people, among them a white-clad attendant bearing Apollo's golden staff and four strong young men who having lowered a carrying chair to the ground are in the act of reaching out to help a reverend and aging priest, white hair gleaming in the sun, face bright with joy, descending to meet her.

Then time began again. I heard the people cheering; from the ship there were cheers as well and the lowing of cattle and bleating of goats. Chryseis ran down the gangplank and into her father's arms. All around me the air was perfumed with the heady smell of lavender, wild and sweet.

I brought my men up smartly in a line on either side of the gangplank and we awaited the coming of Odysseus who was still standing on deck, waiting till the reunion was done. The soldiers came to attention, and Odysseus, a man who lived in legend, came down on to the land, and went to Chryses and his daughter of the golden hair. I followed behind.

"Chrsyes, Apollo's Priest, and Lord of Chrysa, and My Lady Chryseis," Odysseus began, using the stilted and formal language of envoys, for there are forms for such sacred things as this and language in which they must be spoken. "I, Odysseus, King of Ithaca, come from Agamemnon, King of Men and Lord of the World, to bring your daughter home. I see that you have greeted her as a loving father should do. Agamemnon my master has commanded me to bring her back to you and with her these offerings for Apollo, the Archer whose arrows have struck us all a grievous blow and left us dying in the dust. We come to humbly

127

beg you, Chryses, put aside your anger and intercede for us, beg the god to put away his anger too, and end this plague. For this we have returned your daughter of the golden hair and for this we kneel before you now." He knelt, and we all did likewise.

Chryses accepted this homage for a long moment and then bent down and taking Odysseus by the shoulders raised him up and beckoned him to come closer. Odysseus handed Chryses a bag of grain, the proper thing, and which must always be used at sacrifice.

He took it in token of acceptance and said, as formally, "Bring your offerings to the temple. I will invoke the god and make the sacrifice and then we will break bread together."

Chryses motioned to the staff bearer and said, "Ariston, help me to my chair."

Ariston, who I could not help but notice was exceptionally handsome and who seemed for a moment to catch my eye, and the four other boys helped the priest into his chair and Chryseis into another chair and they were carried up to the temple.

Behind them we had joined the procession, leading our sacrifices. Odysseus walked first, the soldiers next and behind them the priests and the cattle behind them. As we went all—Greeks and Trojans alike-- broke into a hymn to Apollo, praising his power and mercy. As the voices rose echoing mightily off the cliffs, it was good to know that in this, at least we were one, united in praise to the god and singing together in the same sacred tongue.

How must our procession have looked, climbing up the steep hillside: Chryses, white haired father in his chair, Chryseis in hers, golden hair floating in the wind chair, Ariston going before with the symbol of the god; Odysseus and my line of soldiers, armor shining, then the priests and the beribboned cattle, decorated for the sacrifice. It must have been like a scene painted on a cup, in red and black, that men have made to give to boys they love or women they adore.

We arrived at the temple courtyard. When all of the cattle had been picketed, and the soldiers given leave by Odysseus to rest, he motioned to me and together we went to the priest. Odysseus stood a head or more taller than Chryses, and was some years younger, but his hair was streaked with grey and white and he walked with slight limp. His dark eyes were shadowed by heavy brows and his face, alert and wise, was nevertheless lined and craggy. War had laid unkind hands upon him too.

"Lord Odysseus, " Chryses said, "I cannot ask you to break your fast as yet, for we—you, my daughter, and I-- must first make the sacrifice. But I will bid our people bring food for your men and water and fodder for the cattle.

"That is as it should be," Odysseus said. "I will not eat till our work is done."

"But," Chrsyes said, "we can offer you wine, for the god has no quarrel with Dionysus and the fruits of his vine. Come."

Motioning us to a seat beneath an ancient olive tree that had spread its branches here for longer then any man could remember, we all sat together in its shade. The afternoon sun washed the temple yard and colored the temple itself with ochre and gold, picking out and heightening the brightly painted frieze that wound its way below the pediment. The cicada hummed in the warm afternoon sun and the newly mown fields-- for it was near the end of summer-- perfumed the air all around us. Ariston brought some wine, sweet and chill, for they keep it in earthen bottles in the cold depths of the sacred spring as we did at home. I was glad to see that Chryses motioned Ariston to join us too, and he came and sat near to me— not too close but close enough for me to catch again a glance from his lowered eyes.

We all poured some of our wine out on the ground beneath the tree; Chryses said a prayer and we drank. A second cup and then a third made us, if not giddy then relaxed and open with one another. I felt the tension drain away; perhaps we all did. Formal manners thawed, careful and guarded speech became more free. We talked-- not about the war, not about the king, but about our lives. Odysseus told us about his wife and son and told my father about the vision Chryseis had seem, telling him that all is well with them.

"Believe her," Chryses said. But turning more serious for a moment he also said, "but do not count the days nor seek to know how long or when it all may come to pass."

Then Chryses spoke about his life before the god called him, and after; about his wife and the miraculous birth of Chryseis.

Chryseis said: "I am grateful that you have brought me home."

"I am glad to have done it," Odysseus said. "It was wrong to keep you and wrong to treat you so. But to our grief we know that now."

Chryses laid his hand, brown and mottled with age, on Odysseus arm, muscled and hard from years of battle. The hand of the priest that wields the knife of sacrifice lay on the arm of the general that wields the sword of conquest. For the moment they were not priest and general, Achaean and Trojan, but instead just two men, both getting on in years, sharing a cup of wine and having a chat and gossip, enjoying not what divided them but what they both shared, love of family. I thought, how can there be war and strife, hatred and battle, when two men can speak from the heart about the things that are dear to them.

The afternoon sun began to wane.

"Lord Odysseus," Chryses said, "it is time now. We must do what you have come for. The sacrifice must be made just before the sun sets so that the god can take its virtue with him when he sleeps. See, the people know."

Along the road from the village the people were coming, dressed in black as was right for this was a solemn sacrifice-- women in shawls drawn tight around there shoulders, men draped in dark wool cloaks. Chryses nodded to Ariston who came forward carrying a black cloak for Odysseus and Chryses' own black robe, edged with gold, the sign of Apollo embroidered upon it back and front.

"My lord," Ariston said to Odysseus, "your soldiers will be given such clothes as well. It is out of respect to the god that we do not outshine him."

He laid the cloak around Odysseus shoulders and then placed one on mine. It seemed that his hand lingered a bit longer on my back and shoulder than need be. I did not mind it.

Chryses said: "Odysseus, will you attend me at the altar?" Odysseus nodded his assent. "Come, then, the time is now."

By now a large number of people had gathered in the temple forecourt and lined both sides of the path, its stones as ancient as Troy itself, that led from the precinct gate to the steps of the temple.

They stood in silence, waiting for us to come there in procession. Ariston fell in before at the head of the procession, carrying Apollo's staff. Chryses followed with Odysseus by his side. Four young men helped Odysseus' priests to lead the cattle for the sacrifice, one brought the white bull, its horns gilded and garlanded with flowers; two of the others each led a goat, the fourth carried a cage with white doves. The priests each cradled in their arms a newborn lamb. I followed behind them and my soldiers followed me, shields slung over their backs and spears reversed, point down, and wound about with laurel and ivy.

Ariston, in his strong young voice began to sing the most sacred of the hymns to Apollo, the one that praises him for his strength and goodness and begs him to look with kindness and mercy on all his children, and to that moving chant we walked to the temple and into the presence of the god.

Once inside, all the cattle were ranged about the altar, each with its attendant who would offer the beast they attended to the god after the sacred bull had been sacrificed and his spirit sent up to heaven. Chryses began the ritual, purifying all who were there, sprinkling water and scattering grain, and especially purifying Odysseus himself, who was the supplicant. The fires before the altar burned and the smoke mingled with the incense Ariston had thrown on the flames. The air was redolent with the heady perfume that filled me both with excitement and reverence, for it signals that the god may soon come.

Ariston brought the Archer's staff. Chryses took it and turned to face Odysseus and our soldiers. Standing before them in his robes and with the staff catching the rays of the sun that were now beginning to enter level and straight through the temple door, I could not wonder that they looked at him with awe, for when they last saw him thus he had called down the curse of Apollo upon them all. Odysseus knelt and covered his head with the black cloak, and we did likewise.

"Hear me, god of the Silver Bow," Chryses intoned, "Protector of Chrysa, Lord of Tenedos, Smintheus, you heard my prayer when in distress I appealed to you and you granted my request and struck down the Achaeans who had insulted you and your priest. But now I come again, humbly, with rich sacrifice, and pray you to hear me: My daughter Chryseis, who serves your altar, has been restored and so I call upon you, Lord of the Sun, accept this sacrifice and lift the dreadful scourge from the Achaeans, who have come as suppliants and in penance, and who kneel before you and beg you, as do I, to release them from your anger."

He laid the staff upon the altar before the god, bowed three times and with Ariston purified the bull with water and grain. And then with a swift gesture the knife flashed and the bull's blood spurted out from the severed jugular, a fountain of forgiveness I was sure, covering Odysseus and me. At the same instant each of the attendants slew their beasts and Odysseus' priests released the white doves. They fluttered up to the roof the temple and then down again and circled the statue of the god.

Then we heard it: first a rustling like dry leaves blown by an autumn breeze, then, around us, from every hidden corner of the temple, mice appeared, white mice, sacred to Apollo and his charges and favored and protected by him. They can be signs of his pleasure- - or his anger, for it is they who bring the plague. They came squeaking and scurrying toward the altar, leapt upon it and in frenzy threw themselves into the altar flame and disappeared into the fire and smoke. Rather than the stench of burning hair and flesh, however an intoxicating sweet perfume rose from the fire and spread around us all, filling the room and wreathing us all in its aroma.

It was then, as if to add wonder to wonder, that the late afternoon sun struck the image full on, illuminating it in blaze of white and gold. Was it only I who thought the god smiled down at us. I cried out, "Thank You Lord Apollo." This was the sign. It meant redemption. The plague was ended. A shout went up from everyone as they all, Odysseus and the rest of us threw off our black cloaks, and the last of the afternoon light turned us all into rejoicing figures of the purest gold.

That night we all feasted; slices of beef, goat meat, and lamb, roasted with rosemary served on wooden trenchers went round among us as we all sat together in the temple forecourt. Cheese and apples were passed around, and honeycombs as well. Everyone drank till we were all giddy with wine and delight. Odysseus,

Chryses, Chryseis, Ariston and I, sat at a low table, the Achaean soldiers sat on the ground with Trojan farmers, men and women, and passed the wine jars around. My eyes met Ariston's. I knew then that I would know more of him before the night was done. We all held hands and danced to a flute that someone played and to a drum that someone found, whirling in a circle beneath the moon, soldier and farmer, Achaean and Trojan, silver dancers on a silver ground.

The next day we trooped down to the shore to bid farewell. The soldiers had boarded the ship. Odysseus stood at the foot of gangplank; Chryses with him. I between the two. They looked at one another. In Odysseus' eyes I saw the memory of the night before when, simply as two aging men, he and the aging priest had shared the intimacy of talk and wine. But now that had passed. He was again the general. The other the venerable priest.

Chryses said, "Is there no hope for an end to it all? Can we end it?"

Odysseus smiled, sadly. "No, I fear not. This play is already written; we are only the actors in it. We must read our lines, act our parts, and press on to the final scene."

I knew in my heart that he was right.

And so we went back--back to our war, back to Agamemnon, back to the endless waiting for history to complete its tale. What the finished tale would reveal, I supposed not even Chryseis' visions could foretell.

Book Seven
Sharpen Your Spears

Sharpen your spears; strengthen your shields; feed your thundering horses well and look your chariots carefully over, and think of the battle to come that will rage all the long day. We shall have no rest, not for a moment, till night falls. The straps of your shields will be wet with sweat; your arms will be weary with flinging your spears, your horses will be drenched with sweat in front of your chariots, and if I see any man shirking the fight there will be no help for him, he will be a prey to dogs and vultures.
--Iliad 2. 380-393.

From: Dionysos Of Tenedos, A History of the War at Troy

*"Raze the walls! Destroy the city." Agamemnon commanded.
And indeed he did for there is nothing now left of Troy. But then, so
those who saw it say, there was nothing like it in the world to
compare. And that is why Agamemnon wanted it. Troy was visible
even from far at sea, many-towered and gated, brooding and
impregnable behind its huge high walls, built before men reckoned
time by King Laomedon who called upon the gods to aid him. It is
said that Poseidon did the work while Apollo watched the king's
flocks and played the lyre to make music for the labor and
Laomedon's grandson Aescus aided them.*

*From a distance the roofs of the citadel—Troy's acropolis—
glittered in the sun. The citadel rose up above the city, its towers, as
poets have said; almost cloud-capped and highest of them all was
the tower of Ilios. Broad streets, lined with mansions, bisected the
city and lead to the Scaean and the Dardanian Gates.*

*The greatest mansion of all, the palace of Priam was the
wonder of the citadel with its roofs of cedar richly painted and
gilded, supported by marble colonnades fronting the polished
porticos and doors of chased and polished bronze worked in
intricate patterns. The palace was so huge that it is said that no one
had ever seen it all, for it housed vast suites reserved for the Royal
Kindred—fifty chambers it was said for Priam's fifty sons and their
wives. Endless corridors and secret places led to chamber after
chamber filled with the wealth of all the ages brought to Troy for a
thousand years.*

*In the vast throne room marble floors of deepest purple
reflected those who walked upon them like a mirrored pool, making
the expanse seem endless to one coming to an audience with the
king, as they walked weak with fear across the gleaming marble to
the foot of the throne and prostrated themselves before Priam as
protocol demanded. Majestic, richly robed and glittering, wreathed
in incense and seated on the Throne of Troy, a high backed seat
cushioned in rich fabrics of purple and red and blue, canopied with*

135

cloth of gold and wrought of silver, electrum, and precious stones, lion-armed, and raised on ten broad steps above the level of the room, Priam presided over the riches that Agamemnon came to despoil.

Upon rising from the prostration and just before they moved closer to kiss the toe of Priam's scarlet sandal, no supplicant before the throne could remain un-awed by the frescoes that covered the walls, colors like jewel tones, that told of the lineage of that ancient house. There is Zeus in majesty and Dardanos, his son, first of Troy's kin to come to the Troad. He married a daughter of Teucer, who was king there, and it was he who gave Dardanos a site for a city, called Dardania, that still stands on Mount Ida's slopes not far from Troy. He was founder of the royal line and thus Trojans call themselves Dardanians and through him their kings claim descent from Zeus and say that they are divine.

Shield in hand spear at the ready, lion skin about his shoulders, Ericthonios, Dardanos' son, strides the wall next after his father. It is he who brought riches to the city, and his herds of horses covered the plains, and ever after they have been known as horse tamers. It was this king who sent his ships filled with the rich products of Troy—pottery adorned with scenes of gods and daily life, weapons of bronze, intricate jewelry worked in gold and produce from the fields---upon all the seas of the world even so far as Egypt.

When his son Tros succeeded him, he began to build and it is from him that the name of Troy derives. Zeus favored Tros and when he saw Ganymede, Tros' son, more handsome than any boy has ever been, he loved him and swooping down from Olympus like the eagle upon the prey, took lovely Ganymede up to heaven and to his bed where he serves him for all eternity.

It was Ilus, the next king, who built the empire that is called Ilium. When he had traced the boundaries he prayed to Zeus for a sign that what he had done was good, and, as the frescoes show, the next day he found, half-buried in the earth that object— the Palladium-- so sacred it must never be described to profane ears. And to him came the voice of Apollo saying, "Guard this well, Ilus, for it bestows the favor of the Goddess and so long as you preserve *it you will preserve your city. Keep it, for it carries empire before it."*

And so near to the palace, Ilus commanded that a great temple dedicated to Pallas Athene should be built, the largest building on the citadel after the palace, and therein the Palladium was reverently placed. The temple glittered with gold, every boss and facing inlaid with it, every architrave and plinth rich with its glow, and the colors of its painted walls and columns, when the sun caught them right, cast a rich and mellow wash of red and ochre and blue upon the marble pavements surrounding the temple precincts.

While the Achaeans sat in their camp and coveted Troy, what of the Trojans? They could, for a time, afford to wait behind their walls. They had time and they had provisions: seemingly endless water from the springs that gushed within their walls; more than enough to eat, since they could draw upon the rich farms and herds of vassals loyal to them scattered throughout the Troad to the north of Troy to provision them, vassals out of the range of Achaean foraging parties and patrols. They were safe in their gleaming city. They walked their broad avenues lined with palaces full of treasure—gold, jewels, bronze axes, ancient statues of the gods that date back to the most ancient days of the race of men---inestimably valuable things that are the real objects of this war—and for which the Trojans were prepared to die and which the Achaeans had come take. It was all about gold and all knew it, for no one cared a fig about aging Helen.

Chapter 17

Even before Odysseus' returning ship grounded on the beach the king called a meeting of the Royal Council, his closest advisors—my father King Nestor, Menelaus, Diomedes, Idomeneus of Crete, Calchas, Menestheus of Athens, and of course, Odysseus and myself who came directly from landing to the king's tent. Entering, we saluted the king and even before he sat, Odysseus said, "It is done, Lords. The girl is safe; the sacrifice is made. I believe Apollo will smile." He paused a moment, weighing his next words. "In fact I believe I have seen him smile."

"He has done so already, Odysseus," the king said. "You have done well. The plague abates. The men improve. It will soon be over, Calchas assures me, for he has seen it in a vision."

"Your pardon," my father said, irritation at Calchas' obvious attempt to take the credit evident in his tone, "but Machaon, who has been going among the men bringing comfort and medicines every day assures me the same, and though he has seen no vision he has seen the men, and for this reason he says we have no more to fear."

"And so then," the king replied, "we have no time to wait. We must attack Troy. Now."

I was dumbfounded by this, and I could see that the others in the room felt the same; even Menelaus, usually compliantly obedient to anything his brother suggested, appeared surprised.

Diomedes said, "Attack? How can we attack? The army needs rest. The men are exhausted."

"If we do not attack now," the king said, almost as if he had not heard, "our chance will be lost forever."

I said: "Diomedes is right. How can we muster the army when so many men are dead, many still sick, and morale is so low among the living?"

The king seemed simply to stare through us as if he had barely heard. Then, as if he had just caught my comment he said "Morale? Well, yes, but you know as well as I, preparing for battle always

138

raises morale. A victory will be even better. I am sure that we will have a victory. Zeus has spoken to me in a dream."

I thought: has he lost his mind? "A dream, sire," I said, "I don't understand." I glanced at Calchas. He looked condescendingly back with an infuriatingly knowing smile.

"Last night just before dawn I had a dream, sent to me I am sure by god—isn't that right Calchas? You said you thought it was from Zeus."

"Oh yes, My Lord," Calchas said with a deep obeisance. "I am sure of it; I recognized the meaning of it right off. No doubt at all. It is a message, and," he said with overly solemn pomposity, "we would all do well to heed it."

"Yes, so right Calchas, right as usual," the king said. Calchas beamed self-importantly. It was clear that he was working mightily to worm his back into the king's favor after the near disaster of his temporary defection to Achilles' protection.

"I'm sure you're right," the king continued, "and can you imagine it," turning now to my father, "it was you, Nestor, who came to me in the dream. You. Looking just like you do now. Amazing isn't it?"

Now we all take stock in dreams. I would be a fool if I did not heed them. But more a fool to be ruled by them. They come in the night and are full of doubt and mystery, and who really can know what they mean? I have seen much in dreams and believe they tell secrets that were hidden to me in my waking hours. But if you have enough of them you begin to see that sometimes dreams mean something, and sometimes they are, well, simply put, nonsense. As my father has so often told me, you can't run your life on something you see in a dream, no matter what the priests say.

And you certainly can't be willing to stake the life of an army on a dream, especially a dream interpreted by that fool of a priest Calchas who is ready to tell the king anything he thinks the king wants to hear so long as he can get a leg-up in the king's favor. If it was a dream sent from Zeus, then the all-Father must be trying to delude the king. Maybe I'm wrong, but I don't think so.

I realized the king was speaking again: "I'm sure that even you don't know what you revealed to me in the dream do you Nestor?"

139

"How can he, you arrogant nitwit," I wanted to say.

I could see my father was irritated too, but he is far more diplomatic than I and he instead simply replied, "No my lord, of course I do not." But he could not resist saying, "It was, after all, your dream; not mine."

The king looked a bit displeased but pushed ahead. "He—that is, you Nestor---said that he—you—came from Zeus and that Zeus is concerned for me—for me! Agamemnon!! —and that I should prepare for battle because the time to conquer Troy has arrived. If we invade now Troy's doom is sealed. Those were the very words Nestor, 'their doom is sealed.' You can imagine I woke up and called Calchas right away. He agrees. This is the sign we need. It's what I've been looking for. We need to move ahead. Now."

Voices rose in protest, but the king raised his hand even before anyone could speak and, with a little sound of shhh, shhh, as if quieting a fretful child, the king said to my father, patronizingly

"Why Nestor, you are the one who came to me," the king said, "How can you, of all people, protest?"

My father simply stared at him incredulously.

"Sire, it was a dream. It was not me."

The king waved his hand dismissively.

"None of this matters, don't you see, what's important is action, and if the gods support it then all the better. The men have been cooling their heels here too long. They need distraction. You yourself said morale was low, Nestor. Blood and gold will distract them. They want to feel their sword arms working again. This is the best thing that could happen."

As he spoke the king walked back and forth in front if us, agitated, eager.

"I see you have your doubts, Nestor. And you Odysseus? You, my lord Diomedes? You brother?"

But before any could answer the king rushed ahead, caught up in the passion of the dream, in the obsession of the moment. It might not be blood and gold and conquest that would move his men, but it was blood and gold and glory that held the king in thrall, and who could—who would-- convince him to turn aside?

I could keep silent no longer. "I must protest this…this folly. How long can the men take this war, my lord, how long? It has all gone wrong. We—you—promised them that we would be home within a season, that Troy would fall like feather blown down by our breath. But now we know the truth. They are stronger than we thought and they snap at our heels wherever we go. Time drags on and on, Lord, and we do not meet them in battle and there is no victory. There is only frustration and anger among the men, and I see them, sick at heart and sick in body, tired and hungry, looking back across the sea toward home. My lord, ask them to fight and they may mutiny."

And mutiny they might. I could not forget the fearsome sound of an entire army striking their shields in unison in a steady, ominous thunder when the king so ignominiously sent Chryses packing. And I saw the faces of exhausted soldiers, ravaged by the plague, faces that I had seen and wracked bodies that I had helped to tend, but from which the king safe in his tent, had averted his eyes. What would happen if the king commanded them into battle now? I wasn't so sure and I wasn't so confident.

My words hung heavy in the silence of indrawn breaths; I could barely believe that I had uttered them. But it was the truth, said at last, and no one moved to contradict me, not even Calchas. But I did note that Odysseus kept his own council.

"My men mutiny!" the King exclaimed with exasperation. "I will show you that my men are loyal. They love me. You wonder if I am right? You think the men won't jump at the chance to get back into armor again, to get the kinks out of their sword arms, just because they've had a little trouble lately? I tell you, I never saw an army that wasn't ready to fight when it saw a chance to stuff their knapsacks with gold and maybe stuff something into some pliant wench as well." Here he made an obscene gesture and laughed unpleasantly at his own rude joke.

"Mark me, my Lords; they'll do what I say. They adore me and will do whatever I command. I can't blame you for doubting, but you didn't have the dream. I did. It was a dream from heaven, sent to me, the king. The gods speak to men through kings, and I am king."

He stared at us all, through us all, as if seeing some fantasy of glory beckoning from the world of dreams. Madness, I thought, madness and impiety.

I could not resist saying it: "You may be king, but we do not have Achilles."

Chapter 18

A few days after this, a guard came to me. "Follow me my lord," he said.

We made our way through the camp, past the tents where the slaves and captives were housed, past the parade ground and toward the cluster of larger tents occupied by the officers who served the king. I saw another guard bringing a veiled figure. It was a woman. Soon we fell into step together though she walked paces behind me.

We came to a tent nearest to the king's. It was one of the largest of them all, and a royal standard flew before it. The guard pointed to the entrance.

"Go in," he said.

Inside it was dim and the smoke from a brazier filled the air with sweet blue smoke. At a table at the far end Odysseus sat with his back to me, bent over what seemed to be maps and charts. I came in, stood waiting. Finally he turned.

"My Lord Antilochus, my Lady Briseis," he said—I noted the "Lady." What did it mean? He pointed to a low stool near the table. We waited for him to speak. For a few minutes he sat without speaking, looking at us both.

Then to Briseis: "You are a handsome woman, but I see that you are, may I say kindly, no longer in the precise bloom of youth. I am told that you have no kin to ransom you."

She looked at the ground.

"And" he went on, "since your mistress is gone you have no lady to serve. Of course I cannot allow you to remain in her tent; it is a bit too sumptuous to house a servant—a former servant—and at the moment you are of no interest to His Majesty, especially if you can bring no ransom. So you are of little value I fear."

He paused and looked intently at her. Was he going to suggest that she come to his tent as, as what, as a slave for sex?

He must have read those thoughts.

"No Lady Briseis, you are quite safe from me. Unlike many I am faithful to my wife. But I do need something from you. I have a duty and that is to serve the best interests of the king."

Again a silence. Again that intent stare.

"I am sure you know, for who does not know it, that Achilles and the king have quarreled. Achilles has left the camp and for all practical purposes the war, and set up his camp with his soldiers a few leagues north of here. The king is proud and angers easily. Achilles is also proud and also angers easily. Unhappily for us, he is also our most formidable weapon. The king will not admit it, but without Achilles we are at a severe, even fatal disadvantage. And, unhappily also, an angry Achilles is a danger to the king. And I— we--do not know what Achilles plans as he sits and nurses his wounded pride there in his camp, though it is barely a morning's march from ours. Will he fight against the Trojans without us, or will he turn and fight against us? Anything is possible.''

He paused and looked at each of us. Could he read our thoughts?

"Do you wonder why I tell you this, you a woman and a slave?"

He did not wait for her to answer.

"Here is why. I have arranged for you to be given to Achilles. This has two advantages, one for you and one for me. The advantage for you is that with Achilles you will be safe. For when the king realizes that you remain, though the Lady Chryseis was, in effect, taken from him, he will turn his rage toward you. And no doubt after some sexual adventuring that will surely not be pleasant for you he will quite likely kill you. Thus if you are in the camp of Achilles you will be safe from the king. Achilles, as I am sure you also know, will not touch you or harm you, for he loves his friend almost to frenzy and he is, while an alarmingly bloodthirsty killer, still a gentleman.

"The value for me? Knowledge. You can tell me what passes in Achilles' camp. You can watch and listen and discover what he intends and I will arrange a way for what you learn to be brought back to me. And thus I do my duty for the king. I believe that you can help. I say 'you can.' I probably should be direct and say 'you must.' You have no choice. And the fact is neither do I for no man can do it. Achilles would trust no man from the king's camp. But a woman, a slave, he will.

"One thing I must make clear. Honor is the key to this young man. You were his captive. Army protocol, as it were says that a captive belongs to the captor. Though Achilles has no interest in you as woman, he does as a symbol. Your mistress was his captive too, of course, and you know what the results were of the King's refusal to give her to Achilles. And so I have planted a few seeds among those in the army who love and revere Achilles and who feel that he has been insulted by the king.

"And so soon, some men will clamor that you should go to Achilles as his prize of honor, though in fact Achilles has asked for nothing for himself. He will not want to insult the good intentions of the army who love him and who he loves, and so when hears of it where he sulks in his distant tent, he will accept and we will send you to him—with a sufficient quantity of treasure from your lady's ransom to sweeten the arrangement further. You and all that gold will serve as another trophy that proves once again what no one doubts, the loyalty of the troops to Achilles.

"The king will see that too and agree, for he will hope that the gift to Achilles will end the quarrel between them. That will, I fear, be a false hope. But things are delicate between the king and his men, and he will do nothing to further discomfort the army upon whom he relies for victory over Troy which is, after all, why he—and all of us--are here."

Turning now to me he said: "And you, Prince Antilochus. You will be the emissary to conduct the lady to Achilles. Of course the king does not know that yet, but it will be so. I should imagine that your—may I say it--special relationship with the headstrong prince will make it all the more palatable for him."

I started at this and was about to speak, but he waved an impatient hand.

"Please, Prince Antilochus, spare me denials, nothing escapes me. Oh, by the way, Antilochus" he said drawing me aside, "any interesting details you may find out when you visit Achilles will be secrets of state and of course their source will be protected. But do let me remind you that as a loyal subject of the king you will be bound to share them with me."

He wanted me to spy! I gave what I hoped was a look that said there was never a chance of that and left the room without another look at Odysseus.

It was as he said. The old master of intrigue planted his seeds. In a few days Odysseus' plan took shape and then bore fruit. The king was approached by a delegation of officers demanding that Achilles should be appeased. Of course we knew what was said.

"We cannot win Troy without him," Nestor insisted.

Diomedes, bravest of the princes after Achilles, heatedly shouted: "A majority of the army believes you are wrong."

"So?" Said the king, turning away as if to dismiss them.

"I will tell you why 'so,'" Diomedes said, angrier still. "Because no king long keeps his throne if he has no army to support it."

The king went white with rage and would have struck Diomedes had not Nestor and the Calchas intervened. Odysseus finally took the King aside and after a whispered colloquy, the king, composure regained, though with a chilly and peremptory manner, addressed us.

"My only interest is victory over Troy because they present a clear danger to our wives and homes, our gods, and our way of life. Nothing must stand in the way of that."

Out of the corner of my eye I saw Odysseus nod to the king as if to say "go on."

"And this," the king said, "does bring us to the minor question of Achilles' girl Briseis."

Looking around the room with a dismissively haughty smile, he added, "though don't we all sometimes wonder what sex Achilles' 'girls' might be?"

I wanted to leap up then and there and cleave his grinning skull with my sword. My father saw my anger and signaled me to be silent.

But I could keep silent no longer and rose to speak.

"Achilles has reason to be angry. We must not anger him further. Rather than goad him, let's try to placate him. He needs to fight for us, not against us. He is formidable in battle. No man--"I paused and looked at the king with a steady and level gaze, and repeated-- "*no man* has yet stood against him and won."

The king waved his hand dismissively.

"I fear that he is already too far gone in anger, young prince," he said smoothly.

"But he is not without blame. It is he, after all, who has refused to fight. Some might call that treason. I'm sorry to say but the roles have been cast in this sad drama and we must play them out to the end. I will be gracious and send Achilles this slave Briseis. I will also send some gold, for such trinkets are more important to him than to me. I neither need nor want neither. Oh, yes, and who better than you, Prince Antilochus, to do all that for me."

"My, lord, with respect," I protested. "Achilles is a friend. Why must I be the one to do this?"

"Because I command it, Prince Antilochus, That is why," the king said coldly. "If you are indeed his *friend*," he emphasized 'friend' suggestively and I knew that Odysseus had planted this seed too, "then surely *you* can sweet-talk him into doing my will. And if you cannot—well then I will go to war, with or without Achilles, and raze the walls of Troy to the ground. Here is my message to Achilles," the king continued. "Tell him I forgive him and pardon him of any treasonable intent and as a token I send the Lady Briseis. If he will come back to fight with us another cartload of gold will soon be his. Thank you my lords. I think that will be all." And he swept out of the room leaving all amazed.

I could not believe what I heard. What a fool's errand is this I thought. Forgive him. Pardon him? I knew how Achilles would react to that.

Chapter 19

And thus, obeying the command of my king who I hated, and on an errand that I knew was futile, I made ready to go to Achilles, who I loved. The next morning, accompanied by Talthybius and Eurybates, the king's heralds, and a small company of the king's guard to watch over the cartload of gold, and with Briseis riding in it and I carrying Agamemnon's pride as a gift to Achilles, I set out. Achilles' camp was far from the main encampment, on the beach where he had brought his ships. Some said that he chose to be near the water to be close to his mother, Thetis, the sea goddess so as to seek her protection when he needed her. Who could say? Do the gods protect us? If the gods do have a hand in our lives they seem to prefer to toy with us for sport rather than to protect us. How can we revere gods who watch us die and do nothing to save us? But as I thought back on the bitter contest I had witnessed the day before, speculation about the incomprehensible purposes of the gods seemed a small thing in comparison to fathoming the human consequences of one man's pride.

As the wagon jolted across the sand I looked at the sea stretching toward the horizon and towards the land from when the Greeks had come. I sent a prayer to Apollo: "Let Achilles love me." But I knew that this prayer was not about to be answered. I wondered if the soldiers with me prayed for love as well or looked at the sea and longed for their home. Did they think how futile this war had become? But their faces were impassive as we started along the shore toward the camp of Achilles and his Myrmidons.

Their camp lay on the northernmost edge of the ridge, and a long stretch of rocky shoreline stretched from where the majority of the ships were beached at the southern end to those of Achilles that lay at the northern end. The morning was foggy, though the sun was beginning to break through as we walked. The ocean withdrew, washed back up unto the stony shore, and withdrew again taking a wash of pebbles with it which were then drawn back and flung upon the beach, the slow cadence of the advancing and retreating sea sounding a note of endlessly repeated sadness.

After a morning's march, as the sun was at its highest in the sky, we eventually reached the ships and tents of the Myrmidons. The black ships lay beached on the white sand of the shore. Unlike so many of the Greek ships, they were trim and clearly ready for sailing or for war. Achilles' soldiers were housed in neat rows of small tents, outside of which their armor and weapons hung, polished and gleaming bright in the sun. Groups of soldiers sat in front of the tents, cooking fires smoking; others exercised, naked, on the sands.

Then I saw Achilles. He was sitting on an outcropping of rock that jutted up on a rise above the sea. I was taken aback, for the warlike Achilles was not plotting strategy with an officer, or stringing his bow to send an arrow winging to bring down a passing bird so that he would be in practice when he needed to send one into the heart of an enemy. He was playing a lyre. I could hear him singing above the sound of the waves. He has a rich sweet voice and the song he sang is known to all soldiers: it is a sad one and tells of the deeds of heroes and the glory that comes to those who die in battle. Patroclus sat opposite to him. Achilles was singing to him. Both men were stripped to the waist, wearing only loincloths. The morning sun washed the two of them with a soft golden light and they looked like young gods painted on a temple wall.

I wondered how I could tell him that I came at the king's command and with a message that he would out of hand reject. The two heralds who escort me will deliver the message of the king's intention. But I am sent to enforce it. As heralds they are sacred. No man would dare to raise arms against them, no matter what message they bring when they come in pursuit of their duty. But I, I have loved him, held him, shared whispered secrets in the dark of night, felt his power and his passion overwhelm me. Now I come to do the bidding of his enemy.

But was not the king my enemy too? The king's mocking insinuation--"surely *you* can sweet-talk him into doing my will"-- echoed in my brain in rhythm with our marching steps. How dare that whoremonger demean my friendship, soiling it with his filthy words! How dare he sully Achilles' manhood with his vile insinuation: "don't we all sometimes wonder what sex Achilles' 'girls' might be?" Who but this king, so eager to aggrandize himself at Achilles' expense, would utter such filth? Who but this king, whose rape of innocent women and indecent wallowing in the arms of drunken whores has dishonored his own crown, could be so vile as to dishonor those whose deeds prove that what the poet says is true: "When an army of lovers fight at each other's side, although a few, they can overcome the world."

When Agamemnon uttered his slander I should have drawn my sword and killed him, then and there. It was for my father's sake that I did not. I bitterly regretted that I did not do it, risking all, losing all, but gaining all for honor. Had I done that, I would not now be coming to Achilles to face dishonor and even death if when, in that moment that he stares at me coldly and sees betrayal in my eyes, he tosses friendship and the past aside and draws his sword, telling me to come at him and do my best.

Patroclus caught sight of us and made a gesture to Achilles who turned to look where Patroclus pointed. His face darkened when he saw us, for of course he had no notion why we were here. He stood up and I saw then that next to his lyre his bow leaned against the rock. Patroclus was also ready; some of the soldiers nearby had risen. But it was obvious that we were no danger, a woman sitting in a cart, accompanied by four soldiers and the sacred royal heralds.

He watched us come up the rise, and soon we stood in front of him. We all saluted, as due his rank. He nodded but said nothing. Once he looked up and caught my eye. I did not know what to do but look back. I could not tell from his gaze what message it contained, if there was animosity or welcome. The cold grey eyes revealed no secret.

The silence grew and Patroclus came to stand by Achilles' side. He put his hand casually upon Achilles' shoulder. In that gesture I saw it all, and felt again the javelin in my heart. The tension increased as the silence grew longer. It was like that unbearable moment just before two sides close in battle—tense silence resonating with a terrible mixture of exhilaration, anticipation, and fear, and underscored with the almost audible beat of the hearts of a ten thousand men. I knew that Achilles would not speak; it was up to us to greet him and make our errand known.

Talthybios said, "My Lord Achilles, we come from King Agamemnon."

That was enough.

Achilles said, "I know who you come from, and you need have no fear. I have no quarrel with you"— and looking square at me— "with any of you. Come to my tent. Before we talk I will give you wine and food."

With this he led us to his tent, in front of which a tangle of blankets was spread on the ground, as if the two men had slept outside under the sky. A cook fire burned. He scooped up the blankets and disappeared into the tent. Patroclus followed and the two of them reappeared carrying cushions, a couple of low stools and tables.

"My lady" he said to Briseis, "Welcome. Rest yourself." He motioned to a stool. He was, as Odysseus said, a gentleman.

Chapter 20

Achilles' camp was not like the Greek camp where huge numbers of men were housed in countless tents and where every cohort or squad was accountable to their own lord or minor king, and he to the lord or king to whom he was vassal, and all to Agamemnon. The sheer size of the Greek army made for a certain unruliness about daily life.

But not so here. Here all was discipline and order, the men exercised twice a day on the beach; Achilles or Patroclus conducted war games among squads at least once each day. All was moderation. No drunken nights around the campfire; no slave girl or pretty boy passed from man to man for brutal fun. Up with the sun. To bed as the moon rose.

This meant that after we had eaten with Achilles and Patroclus they must go for the afternoon drill with the men. No mere embassy from the King of the Greeks could interrupt routine. The afternoon passed and dusk fell. I was left to myself and wandering near their tent I came upon a parchment scroll that Patroclus had been reading and, having little to do, settled myself by the door of the tent to read it. I must have fallen asleep, for Achilles came upon me there. I jumped up, flustered.

"I'm sorry," I said. I hastily replaced the scroll and started to go.

"No, no do not go. You have done nothing wrong. There are no secrets in that book," Achilles said, but I caught a hint of mockery in his voice. "Perhaps though you have found some others? Again that mocking tone. "Oh yes, I know what you are supposed to do. Tell Odysseus all you see and hear."

I was astonished. How did he know what I had been asked by Odysseus to do? With real anger I said, "You need have no fear of that, my lord," and turned to go.

"Antilochus, Antilochus" he said, laughing now. "It is no matter. I will fight when I am ready, not when that king commands. He will know soon enough what Achilles will do. It is already written in the stars and you have no need to tell anyone. But for tonight, perhaps we can read together. No dry history like that which Patroclus likes, but a tale of love, stories of gods and men."

Oh, how I loved him then. Oh, how I knew it was futile.

That night we ate again, a simple meal of lamb and bread and honey. It was not yet time to discuss the still unspoken topic. But I knew Achilles had made his decision.

The next day the two Heralds and I again stood in front of the tent. Achilles sat with Patroclus next to him. Talthybius relayed the king's message—the words "pardon" and "forgiveness" brought only a cold smile to Achilles' face. The offer of Briseis "as a token" was greeted with a snicker by Patroclus and the "cartload of gold' got only a raised eyebrow from Achilles.

When the herald was done Achilles began,

"You come because you are bidden to do so. He is the king and you have been given a command. I have no quarrel with an honest soldier who obeys a command. Now your task is done. You have brought Briseis to assuage my pride, as I suppose. That slight is forgotten. It is minor compared to the greater injury the king has done. So I release Briseis of my own free will. The woman means nothing to me. She is innocent, and she is also pawn in the king's game. Take her back with you. She should not be made to play a role that she does not deserve to play.

"You may also tell the king to keep his gold. I do not need it. Keeping it will accomplish nothing. Fighting for it will accomplish nothing. The king is unjust and it may be that he is mad. He will remain so, no matter what I do. My pride and honor do not depend on possessing this woman or that gold and certainly not on his *pardon* or his *forgiveness.*" He emphasized the words with heavy irony.

"If there is pardon or forgiveness it must come from him to me. My quarrel is with the king and it will be satisfied by the king and by no other man.

"Patroclus, go, bring Briseis and hand her over to these honest men. They can take her back to the king and he can do with her what he will.

"Here is the message I send back to the king and to you my Prince Antilochus I entrust it. Tell the king that I fight beside noble men, not madmen. Tell him to look to the day—and it will come-- when he needs me to save him from disaster just as I have done in the past. Let him imagine what that day will be like without Achilles there. Will I fight for him? No my lords, I will not fight for him. Tell him that, in these words. Say nothing else than that to him."

Patroclus returned with Briseis. So now, for the moment, everyone wins. The king gets another girl and keeps the gold, and so he imagines that he has humbled Achilles and wins the victory.

Achilles gives up nothing that he cares about and in the eyes of the world the king's greed and arrogance are made to seem even greater. And thus Achilles saves his pride.

What remains unspoken but evident to all, save perhaps to the king, is that when that day of reckoning comes, it will be the king who must abase himself to Achilles.

Briseis walked quietly to Achilles. She made a low bow to him. Patroclus took her hand and led her to Talthybios. "You need not bind her, "Patroclus said.

Then Achilles came to where we stood and clasped the hands of the two heralds. They gave him a smart salute. He turned to me. His eyes were without reproach. Taking me by both shoulders he pulled me too him, and held me close for a moment. I thought my heart would stop. I glanced over his shoulder at Patroclus who watched from a few paces away. There was no resentment in his eyes. I almost thought that he smiled. It had been so long since Achilles had held me. My breath caught in my throat as he whispered, "I have not forgotten you, Antilochus."

Chapter 21

I carried Achilles' message to the king. What is there to tell of this disgraceful scene? Should it even be told? Should I say that the king received the news of Achilles refusal to fight with royal dignity?

That he said, "So be it, this is what he has decided. He is free man; we will prevail then without him?"

Should I say that he then praised our labors and reassured us that our cause was just and commended us to the gods?

He did not. I came, as I had been bidden to do, directly to the king's tent, he was there with Menelaus and Calchas and Odysseus.

"I have a message from the Prince Achilles, my lord."

The king did not rise. He sat on campstool; a slave was massaging his shoulders, another stood next to him with an ewer of wine. He waved me negligently forward.

"And so Antilochus, tell me what the young puppy has said." He held out his cup for more wine. I hesitated for moment.

"Speak, damn you," he said. Menelaus smiled, Odysseus remained impassive. I was angry now, how dare this sot of king speak to a Prince of Pylos in this fashion? I hesitated no longer.

"The Prince Achilles says, my Lord, that that he fights beside noble men, not madmen. He says you should look to the day when you need him to save you from disaster just as he has done in the past. He says you should imagine what that day will be like without Achilles there. He sends back the woman and the gold. He says his quarrel is with you and it can be satisfied only by you and by no other man. He will not fight until you admit that."

Calchas took a sharp indrawn breath. Odysseus remained impassive. It seemed to me that Menelaus muttered under his breath something like "At least we have the gold." The king did not move. Then he stood up, his face almost purple with rage and shouted: "Get out you slavish whore. Did Achilles fuck you hard to get you to say that, to defy your king?"

155

And with that he hurled the wine cup at me. It fell short, spattering me with blood red wine. I started toward the king. A guard rushed forward to restrain me.

Odysseus leapt to the King's side. "Sit down my lord," he said commandingly, as if to a child in tantrum and pushed the king back into his chair. The king seemed to collapse back into his seat. Odysseus stepped forward in front of him, shielding the king from me.

To the guard: "Release the Lord Antilochus. He has done no wrong."

To me he said: "The king is under great strain. This news is troubling to him and of course to all of us. Go now, and let His Majesty him ponder this. Surely we can let this incident pass without further comment?" It was a command, not a question.

"Please send my greetings to your reverend father. You have done well. Guard, escort the Lord Antilochus out."

With that he turned back to the king. I could see that there was fury in his eyes—not at me, not at Achilles, but at his king.

I sat in front of my tent, pondering what might come of this. I idly toyed with a bowl of food--goat-cheese and olives, a piece of bread, a bit of roasted kid, sharing it with Mecisteus, ever faithful squire, who sat by my side. He offered me some wine, pouring it into a wooden cup that he had made himself, for me. So like him to do such a thing. He always saw to it that there was enough wine for me before he drank, always made sure that I got a good piece of meat from the stew that he had made, always saved the better bread for me. He helped me arm, as was his duty as my squire, when it was my lot to serve the guard duty that we all—save kings—were called upon to do, no matter what our rank. He stood at my side in assembly, and would have died with me in battle I am sure. At the end of every day he helped me disarm, unfastened the clasps on my body armor, unlaced my greaves, carefully took off my boots, brought water to wash off the day's dust, sponging me down, his hands lingering for a moment on the places I could not reach--on my back or shoulders. And late at night, after we had sat around the fire, talking or throwing dice, sometimes with other soldiers, sometimes with my father, sometimes just the two of us, he would make a warm posset of honey and wine to aid my sleep and help me settle into my bed. Attentive he always was, sweet and handsome, as much in love with me, I knew, as ever.

And I? I wished I could respond, but did not, could not. Some nights, in the flickering firelight, warmed with wine and easy and drowsy in the comfort of companionship, lolling together by the fire, or sitting on the edge of my bed while he heated the last of the wine for my late night drink, I would look at him and he at me and then for a moment it all seemed the right and the only course to take.

But always, just as I was about to make the gesture, one that might bring just a night of pleasure and release, or one that might instead change my life, just then from out of the of shadows in the corner of the tent the vision would appear: Achilles, standing with the sea at his back and the sun creating an aureole around him, godlike, and looking at me. I could hear him say: "I have not forgotten you, Antilochus."

And I would go to bed alone.

Book Eight
War Stories

Hope surged in every Trojan heart, to torch the Achaean ships.
–Iliad 15. 814-815

From: Dionysos of Tenedos, A History of the War at Troy

There are so many reasons given to fight a war: some are fought to revenge insulted honor; some are prosecuted to defend high ideals. Others happen by accident; some come about through deceit; some are simply stupid. The war at Troy can be ascribed to all of these, but of all wars it is the one wherein destiny played the clearest hand and where the victors and vanquished were only pawns in the hands of the gods. Thus great heroes like Achilles, and innocent boys like Antilochus, women touched by the divine like Chryseis, all were moved and manipulated by the dictate of fate against which there is no remedy. By this time Chryseis was safe at home and the king had forgotten the woman who brought so much strife, death and tragedy to the ranks of Greeks.

But by this time, too, Achilles, the greatest--indeed the only hope the Greeks had to win and destroy Troy if one believed the prophecy that Troy could not be won or destroyed unless he raged in battle before the walls—had left the Greek army and the arrogant king to fight without him. Achilles camped now a distance away from the Greeks, nursing his anger and wounded pride and surrounded by his men, in tents raised upon a high bluff looking out to the sea toward his home. With him of course was Patroclus.

Thus the players in the drama were upon the stage, ready to play their predestined roles. All men know the final curtain line; no one in all the world is ignorant of how the drama ended. Yet it is no less terrible for the knowing of it.

Chapter 22

The next day trumpets brayed all around the camp; the clamor and the clatter of an army arousing itself began to grow around us. And intensely, amidst the sound of running feet, shouting men, and orders given, I felt a rising almost palpable atmosphere of anxiety, for I knew what those trumpet calls meant. My father came hurrying toward us. "Come, son, quickly," he shouted, "We must attend the assembly. The king calls assembly. Don't bother to arm."

We hurried toward the assembly ground as fast as we could, I helping my father at his right side, Mecisteus on the other, for he was breathless from his hurried progress from the king's tent back to ours. I could see too that he was distressed. A fine thing, I thought with bitterness, now that the danger of plague is past the king deigns to show himself to the men.

Around us soldiers were running in the same direction, hastily pulling on doublets, or buckling up leathern half- armor. Among them were my own men, they too hurrying past us, saluting as they ran. We had been fortunate in the ranks of Pylos, more so than others; we had lost two men only, three had fallen sick but were recovering. I saluted back and they cheered us as they hurried on. But among many of those who moved toward the parade ground in a steady stream, I could not help but see that some men were being helped by fellow soldiers, by friends, or by a lover.

Some of the men I knew by sight—men from Sparta, men from Arcadia, against whom in hand-to-hand combat no one wants to come, Thracians in their outlandish garb, men from Rhodes who are fearsome spearmen, bowman from Methone. Though I knew that death had taken so many and left even more weak even though recovering, it was still shocking to see so many once strong men, once bronzed and lean and muscled with battle, now wan and sallow, leaning on the arms of their companions for support. So as to hear above the clamor I leaned close to my father to ask what he thought.

160

"Nothing but that our king is mad," he said. "He will attack Troy. He would do it tomorrow if he can."

The king and Menelaus, Calchas and Odysseus, were at the rostrum when we arrived. I helped my father to mount the platform and took him to the seat always ready for him. In front of us the disorderly mass of men, running to and fro like ants upon a swarming anthill, was beginning to form into the orderly arrangement of an army in ranks. As the crowds of men slowly became the great army of the Achaeans, I thought, what a brave sight it is, terrible and majestic, strong men massed and ready to do battle.

But the truth was clear as well. Just as I had seen when first I came, it was even more evident now that the strength of the army was not what it had been. Among the ranks of soldiers, gathered by tribes and following their kings or chiefs—small armies within the great one--among the hoplites arranged in phalanx, among the cavalry and infantry divided into units, among the spearmen and bowmen standing ready in separate squads, it was clear that ranks were thin and many units had suffered great loss. Where once a phalanx could boast full strength, now it was clear that some were much depleted, the front rows of men were full strength, the back rows less so. Over the entire throng exhaustion hung like a miasmic cloud. Agamemnon wants to attack Troy? When he sees the army he has for so long avoided as the plague raged around us, how can he imagine that he could?

A trumpet call brought the men to order. The king surveyed the troops; oddly he was not in armor as he usually was when addressing the men, but wore a soft tunic of fine woven scarlet wool and a flowing mantle dyed purple and edged with gold thread. Over his shoulder on a strap was his silver-studded sword. But he needed no martial array to show his authority and his right to kingship, for he held a long gilded staff, richly decorated. This was the golden staff of the Atreidae, the most prized possession of Agamemnon's royal house that, it was said, had been made by the god Hephaestus himself and passed from god to god, from Hephaestus to Zeus and thence to Hermes it went. From Hermes it came among mortal men when Hermes gave it to Pelops and he in turn to Atreus,

161

Agamemnon's grandfather and founder of the royal line. It was passed down in that royal house as a token that its bearer held lordship and empire over all the lands of the Achaeans. Though rarely seen save on the most high, royal, and sacred occasions, we all recognized it and for what it stood. Standing erect with the staff in one hand, his sword on his shoulder, enveloped in the flowing richness of his purple mantle, Agamemnon was indeed the very image of a king; and he knew it.

"Men," he shouted, "I congratulate you! You've been ravaged by the plague. You've come through dark times and survived, like real men should do, like Achaeans should do!"

He paused for a moment, waiting I suppose for the cheers that usually erupted when the men were complimented by the king, but he realized quickly that no cheer was to be forthcoming. From my vantage I could see some of the men looking at one another. It was not hard to read their thoughts: "And what did you have to do with our salvation, king?" I could almost hear them say.

As if suspecting their sentiment, the king quickly added, "But now lad's its over. Why? Because I've been working for you, men, right from the beginning of this disaster. The minute I heard I sent out Machaon the healer to go to you and do his best, and he did some good. And I told Calchas: offer prayers and cast the omens. And best of all, I did what you wanted, lads, I sent that girl packing. I did it for all of you. Apollo's gotten what he wanted and we've come through the worst and you're brave lads for doing so."

Now there were cheers, but still perfunctory. But the king sensed a slight change in the wind of approval and pressed on.

"Now, men, you know I've your best interest at heart. I've always said if you trust me, you'll always get the truth. Well here it is: maybe after all this time we've all had just about enough. The war isn't going well; I admit it. It's no secret. And we've been cooling our heels here for a very long time. I thought we could walk all over Troy, bring those towers down, take that gold and those women and be home to plant the next year." I looked at my father incredulously. What was he doing?

The king moved to the edge of the rostrum and leaned forward toward the men, his arms opened wide in a kind of embrace, the staff is his right hand catching the sunlight. King and father, I thought, that's the image he wants them to see. I couldn't help but admire his skill. He was a spellbinder still. Loudly enough for all to hear, but still as if sharing a secret with them all, he spoke again.

"Now I know some of you think that Troy may never fall and all that gold may never be ours. I wouldn't blame you if you weren't sick of the whole thing. But here's one thing we better not forget. No matter what's happened to us here, we are still stronger than they are. We have a bigger army, and you are the best fighting men in the world, and so what a scandal it would be if we turned tail before the job was finished, left all that gold, all those women, and never got the Lady Helen back out of the hands of that namby-pamby Paris and those Trojan butchers. But it's your choice lads; we can stay and fight or we can take our ships and sail for home."

We all waited. Was he so sure that they would rally to him and demand to continue the war that he made this dangerous gamble? I was not so sure. I knew these men. An army can only take so much—so much waiting, so many deaths, so much hardship, so much doubt and fear--before they began to wonder about the wisdom of the cause and of their leaders too. I wondered if the king man have overplayed his hand.

"What's in it for you if we stay?" a voice shouted from the midst of the ranks. "I see your trick. You profit whether we stay or go. Your treasury is full of gold; you've gotten the first pick of anything from any town we've sacked, you've got all the women you want. Anyway, what are we going to do without Achilles? He's holed up in bed with his boyfriend, and the king wants us to stay and fight. I say lets go home, boys, see how the king gets on without us."

I knew the voice, we all did, it was Thersites, an Aetolian soldier who everyone disliked. Bandy-legged and short, he was reputed to be the ugliest soldier in the ranks, and certainly the nastiest. But he could be a fearsome fighter and his scurrilous quips, usually at the expense of his betters, amused the troops. So he was left alone, though several times Agamemnon had considered having him hanged.

But his comments did not simply amuse the men; instead I could see that they had struck a chord. I felt again the same groundswell of rising anger that had once before overtaken the army, but this time instead of striking spear on shield, I saw that some had actually dropped their shields to the ground and thrown down their spears. As if a breeze that had sent mere ripples across the waters of a lake suddenly picks up and becomes a stormy wind turning ripples into waves and waves into breakers, the army began to stir and erupt into a cacophony of sound. Men began to shout, discipline dissolved and as if someone had shouted "fire" in a tightly packed arena, the men began to rush toward the seaward gate that led to the ocean where ships were beached.

On the dais we were struck dumb. The king, seeing that his gamble had failed, seemed stunned and sank into a chair. Menelaus simply stared onto space, and Calchas, robes flapping was climbing down the rear of the dais, intending I surmised to rush back to the comparative safety of his tent. As the din became even louder on the parade ground I could see Thersites, not running to the ships at all, but doubled up with laughter, sitting on the ground amidst the running men.

Then, from the edge of the platform Odysseus leapt. Incredibly, he had in his hand the Royal staff, and was running full tilt toward the seaward gate toward which the men were streaming as if they would board the ships immediately and set sail for home. Some of them had already gone through, but because of the crush of men, most were still within the parade-ground enclosure. As he ran Odysseus shouted, "Antilochus, Idomeneus, captains, to me, now!"

Odysseus rushed into the midst of the melee, shouting as he went, and began laying about him with the golden staff. We—myself, Idomeneus, and now some of the other captains, including, at last, Menelaus--saw what to do and like Odysseus ran to the seaward gate. Above the noise I heard the trumpets of the heralds sounding quarters, and in a voice that carried like a thunderclap, Odysseus commanding them back to their post.

Seeing him, and the staff he wielded, and feeling his blows, and beginning to feel the pressure of the captains who were now marching in rank, swords drawn, toward the mutinous men, slowly the tumult began to subside and slowly the men turned and went back to the field and began to form into rough bedraggled ranks,

164

heads down, eyes staring at the ground. It was not lost on anyone that what they had done could be punished by death. But it was lost on no one too, especially the king, that it was almost the entire army that joined in the rush to the sea.

Once quiet was established, Odysseus, the staff still in hand, rose up and addressed the men.

"I'll make this short and quick, boys. You know what you've just done and what the penalty for it could be. I wouldn't blame His Majesty if he ordered the ringleader in this affair hanged right here and now."

Here he walked over to Thersites and with the staff, forced him down on his knees. Thersites began to whimper.

"But I'll tell you, my lads, the king won't do that because he himself has said that he knows what you've been through. You heard him say that didn't you?"

He looked around at the men, pointing first at one, then at another with the staff, getting hangdog but grudging assent from each man he pointed to.

"And another thing: the king himself admits this war is a hard one and that its not going well and that we've been cooped up here nine long years. Isn't that right? Didn't he say that?"

Again he pointed with the staff and again the men he indicated agreed.

"Louder." Odysseus said, "Say it so all can hear it."

A ragged chorus of assent rose from the ranks

"So I say who can blame you for wanting to take those ships and go back home? But the king is right about another thing. How shameful would it be to do that? Are you the men who want to go down in the poet's stories as the Achaeans who cut and run and leave Troy stronger than ever? We could all go home, back to our farms and easy life. But if we do, sooner or later, men, our lives won't be so easy because we'll be fighting for our lives in our own homeland—in our streets, even in our homes."

Then Odysseus strode over to where Thersites knelt in the dust.

"This is how we deal with those who give comfort to the enemy by speaking against our king and our rightful fight against Troy."

He struck Thersites viciously across the back and shoulders with the king's staff. The heavy blows felled him to the ground and the sharp golden studs raised welts that spouted dark blood. Thersites lay cringing in the dust, his hands over his eyes, whimpering.

I looked at my father. He shrugged his shoulders as if to say,

"Odysseus and the king have the upper hand. Ready or not war it will be."

Odysseus, still standing amidst the men, had one last argument ready.

"Now, men, you complain that its nine years we've been here, and nine long years it is. But what about this number nine? Let me tell you. You seem to forget that Calchas prophesied years ago that it would be nine years before we took Troy? You know that, but you chose to forget it even though Calchas is always right."

Odysseus had found the key to appeal to the superstition of the men—armies are always superstitious and grasp at omens and prophecies to alleviate the difficulty and uncertainty of military life. And so even as he began to speak again I knew that the battle was already won. I was pretty sure what would be coming next. I was right.

Odysseus continued. "The king didn't tell you this—but he told me and all of us in council just this morning. He had a dream. And this is the best part, men, it came from Zeus—Calchas says so. And what's the message in it? Now is the time to march against Troy and take the city. What more do we need than that, men? It's the voice of god! So. All of you, soldiers, countrymen, heroes, now is the time for battle! Don't back down now when victory is in sight. Stay the course, as the king says. Soon the spoils will be ours—the city, gold, jewels, spices, horses, women and boys, the ransom of kings, the treasure of all the ages so long stored there, soon rightfully ours. Bring down Troy and with it the tyrants who want to destroy our homeland and our way of life."

The army was now in state of wild excitement. Cheers broke out. "Troy, Troy, Troy," men began to chant. "Down with Troy."

Odysseus returned to the dais and handed the staff to the king, a look of satisfied complicity passed between them. As he took the staff from Odysseus I heard the king say, "Thersites. Hang him." Odysseus replied in the assured tone of one who knows that he is in control because he holds the debt of another in his hand.

"No my lord, I think not. Let the men see how merciful a king you are." I noticed that the slangy soldier's brogue had now been replaced by the smooth tongue of the courtier.

The troops continued to chant their defiance of Troy, their faces flushed with excitement. I knew it was a dangerous moment for the army's mood had changed from sullen near mutiny to wild and bloodthirsty exaltation. In whatever mood they were, I knew that it could soon become an army out of control. Odysseus sensed this too and looking toward us all—at the captains ranged in front of the army--began another chant, his voice rising above the cacophony of the men. We, hearing him, solidly and in unison joined in more and more loudly. Ag-a-mem-non! Ag-a-mem- non! Ag-a-mem-non, we chanted and soon those in the front ranks heard us and began to take it up. Like the tramp of marching feet, thunderously echoing across a battleground, the army shouted its allegiance to their king. They were his to do with what he would. The king moved to the front of the platform and signaled the heralds to sound the call to attention. The shouting subsided. He raised his staff before them, and the sun just then broke out of the clouds and enveloped him in an aureole of gold.

"I hear you lads," he shouted. "I know what you want. Who can argue when brave men command? If its Troy you want, its Troy you'll get. Its war, my lads, its war at last!"

The cheers were deafening and as they grew even more clamorous the king leapt down from the rostrum and waded into the front ranks, clapping this men on the shoulder, seizing another in a bear hug embrace, straightening a tunic or joking with an entire rank of men and laughing with them when they broke out in guffaws at what was certainly an off-color joke. And thus the king went through the ranks, from man to man, from cohort to cohort, from company to company, from tribe to tribe.

I watched it all from the rostrum. It was a brilliant display, the king among his army, a soldier among soldiers, man to man. And as Agamemnon passed through the ranks I could see the men straighten to attention as he came, broad smiles breaking out on their weathered faces. What had been a nearly disorganized rabble just a short time before had become an army again, strong, fearsome, armed and eager for war, with slaughter in their hearts.

But as I surveyed the line of battle and the vast and warlike display, there was one terrible thing: not a presence but an absence.

To the right of the king was the place of honor where at stiff attention in glittering armor and fearsome slit-eyed helms, the sharp tips of their long and deadly spears catching the swift gleam of the morning sunlight like murderous beacons, had always stood the most fearsome of all our force. Here in every battle until now, standing ready-at-arms were the Myrmidons, warrior-killers from Thessalian Pythia.

Now the space was empty. On either side surrounding ranks stood, but none moved to fill the gap, as if in unspoken agreement that such a space was sacred to heroes and to their god-like lord and leader, Achilles, slayer of men.

No doubt Agamemnon saw this broken rank. But of course, how could he acknowledge it? Leaping back unto the rostrum and raising the royal staff high for all to see, he signaled and around the parade ground the nine royal heralds raised their trumpets, and high on the morning air the silver call to battle rang out. Sounding against the camp walls and from the sides of our black ships, it mounted up to the heavens and with the voice of echo rebounded a thousand times from the surrounding mountainside and was carried thus to the walls and watchtowers of Troy, putting them on notice that the Achaeans were ready to go to war. But did Troy know that the man they feared the most would not march today?

Chapter 23

In the early dawn again the trumpet call sounded. But this was different. No call to assembly this, but the call to arms, the call to battle. At last it had come. I came out of my tent, which is raised on a higher vantage than most of the others. From it I can look toward Troy across the plain. The sun was beginning to gild the high towers, the deep purple of the night shadow dissipated, and I could hear the silver sound of Trojan trumpets too, carried to us on the wind.

What must it be like there in that beleaguered city? I try to imagine it. Does King Priam stand on his high tower of Ilios, looking toward our camp? From his high vantage point does the sound of our war trumpets cut through the sighing wind and the shriek of the hawks circling overhead and the soft conversation among the courtiers who wait for King Priam to have his fill of looking across the plain, toward the sea and the mouth of the Scamander, toward the Achaean camp—our camp, our army?

I picture them there, King Priam, robed in purple and wearing his diadem, carried in a chair, and wearing the glittering mask that a Trojan King wears so as to hide his face from the irreverent gaze of the common. But these trappings do not conceal his frailty. Does his hand tremble as it grips the lion head of the arm of his chair?

Around him is ranged his court and his family and all the pomp and panoply of that ancient throne: the Master of Ceremonies self-important as he makes sure no item of ritual is ignored even at this time of crisis, the court chamberlains, guards, fan bearers and boys with incense. Is that an unsmiling Hector and his Andromache—one day to be king and queen? Perhaps they will. Perhaps not. Who now can tell?

They all stand frozen in place, everyone silently staring out toward the bay. The king's guard stands stiffly at attention, but beneath their helmets their eyes flicker towards the distance, eager to know what is happening. Is that Hector rushing to the parapet? Is that Andromache clutching her cloak tightly around herself, as if a gust of chill morning wind had whipped around her? Is Helen there, the cause of it all? What must she be thinking? Does she see freedom at hand, or retribution from her cuckolded husband? The king, the better to see, has half risen from his chair, supporting himself on the chair arms—a servant has rushed forward to help him rise. Does fear grip them all, fear that the threat was now upon them, or is it relief that finally, after all this time, reckoning has come?

The sun was high enough so that I could see clearly across the plain to the high barrier ridge that encloses and protects the bay of Troy on the seaward side and extends like a long arm reaching almost to the Strait of Helle. At the landward end of the bay facing the city—on the side where the mouth of the Scamander opens into the bay after it completes its journey from Ida--an uncountable mass of tiny figures like angry ants swarmed. The Trojans had heard our trumpets and knew what they meant. Already they swarm out of the city. The dust thrown up by hordes of men on the march, by chariots and horses moving into position, obscured the details of the advance. It is so far away that I cannot hear what I know to be the din and the shouting of men, but I can hear, dully, the throb of their war drums beating a fast marching cadence.

Our trumpets continued to sound the assembly to arms. Men were hurrying, struggling into armor as they ran and I could see the cohort captains on the run as well, hotfooting it across the huge expanse of the camp toward the assembly ground where the army would be drawn up to hear the king give us his orders. Soon—remarkably so for such a huge force--the men were assembled, the parade ground packed with men in armor, shields on their arms, swords slung over their shoulders, a formidable host bristling with spears. The king stood on the rostrum.

"Men," he began without preamble, "you've guessed it by now. The Trojans are massing their forces on the other side of the Scamander and some have already crossed it at the ford. This is what we've been waiting for. Now here's the plan. We'll sally out and pull our front line up along Sigeum Ridge. Its a good defensive position and high enough to see them come—we can see the ford

170

from there--and the thorn brakes are thick and will slow them down if they try a frontal assault. I'll take the center and Menelaus will take my right; Odysseus and our charioteers the left. We must keep the camp at our back, and the gates will be manned if we have to retreat. But by Apollo know this: I am Agamemnon King of Kings, I don't retreat."

The army gave a thunderous cheer, clashing their swords on their shields, an ear shattering crash of metal on metal, as if in answer to Troy's drums of war.

Soon we were indeed on the march, sallying out of the camp gates. I was mounted now and leading my corps of men from Pylos I set my sights on the Sigeum Ridge, a high outcropping covered with gnarled ancient trees, from the top of which we can, if the king's plan is right, sweep down on the Trojan forces in the shallow valley below.

I urged my horse to a gallop. The king, Menelaus, my father, Odysseus, all the commanders, are already waiting on the hill. Opposite us across the plain, broken by scrub pine and thorn brakes, are the Trojans. Their commanders have taken a position a top Thorn Hill, while their captains ride back and forth along the lines, like us shouting and cursing while trying to create a formation out of the mass of men and horses and chariots that mill about in the clouds of dust.

Their troops pour out of the city and cascade down the wide causeway in seemingly endless numbers, some drawing up on the far side of the river, others crossing at the ford to the near side—*our* side—of the Scamander. I can now see the Trojans clearly, recognize tribes by their banners, even make out some faces, for after all this time we know our enemy, often by name. There are men from Zeleia, near Ida led by Pandarus. They are all, like Pandarus himself, famed as bowmen. They carried their huge bows made from ibex horn, and quivers full of long feathered arrows with points of iron. Adresteian men march side by side with those from Pityeia, led by Adrestus and Amphius, sons of Merope the Seer. Several cohorts of grim-faced men from Percote and Practicos march out; they chant while they quick march, a low, rhythmic, guttural and sinister song, like the beating of a heart. I see the fabled

Prince Asius, lordly and very grand, the head of a huge posse of glossy horses ridden by tall and handsome men from Arisbe, Sestus, and Abydos, three of the cities Asius rules. Coming in from the left flank and joining the veritable river of men moving toward the rendezvous appears a seeming forest of long spears, moving toward the staging site. Who could not know them, these men from Larissa, whose rage at our butchery was clear in the grim set of their faces as they passed. They could be counted on to fight to the death, for they had little else to lose. Thracians and Paphlagonians tramped next to rough Carians, whose lands extended over a vast terrain, as a rough as they, and marching next to them elegant Phrygians playing the shrill flutes they used to accompany their marching, all wearing their distinctive caps. A cheer rises from the marching infantry as a splendidly mounted troop of Trojan horsemen clatter by, spears tipped with the banner of the king, the horses as heavily armored as their riders. And there are the Dardanians, Aeneas' tribe, in battle formation, their chariots drawn up harnessed and ready, with warriors mounted in them, armor aglitter, shields embossed with images of Dardanus and Tros, who founded the city and the land that they march to defend.

Like a vast corps of dancers performing a huge martial choral dance at a festival honoring the god of War, the forces—Achaean and Trojan--jockey into position, until finally the lines are drawn up on either side, line captains standing in front of each of their cohorts, chariot horses pawing the ground in anticipation of an exciting run. On the heights the senior commanders wait—they on Thorn Hill—I see Hector, Aeneas, Anchises' son, who might have been king had fate been more kind, and Paris, Sarpedon and Glaukos. On our vantage, on the highest rise of the Sigeum Ridge, amidst fluttering banners is Agamemnon and Odysseus, Nestor and Menelaus, on account of whose wounded honor some of us here today might win—or lose all.

At last the forces are in place. As if the anxious and hurried gathering of the forces has exhausted us all--Trojan and Achaean—by mutual consent a strange long silence has fallen upon the field of battle. As they look toward our side the Trojans can see our line stretch long and unbroken, various with the multi-colored flags of the allies. Our shields catch the sun and reflect it back into their eyes so that we must seem to glitter like a golden wall. I look along our line and realize that what the Trojans see are legends. Line upon line of armored men from lands that few of them have ever seen, standing silent and grim, the plumes of their helmets floating in the breeze like defiant flags, their shields, some as tall as a man, locked together in one long defensive wall.

Amidst it all flows the silver Scamander, the sacred river, glinting like a silver necklace in the sun. Across it for eons Trojan shepherds have taken their sheep; across it their horses have wandered free looking for pasturage. Across it since time out of mind Kings of Troy have passed to and fro from one corner of their realm to the other. Now it is guarded by us—by fierce Achaeans— who the Trojans call invaders, despoilers of their homeland, desecrators of their sacred soil, just as we call them our enemy, a malevolent power bent upon destroying the peace of the world, a hideous threat to our families, our temples, our homeland.

The air is silent; no wind stirs; the sun stands now at mid-day. Just a short distance away from the front of the Trojan line I can see a rabbit, unconcerned with the wars of men, foraging amidst the low grass. Then, a sudden flash of red, a muffled shriek. A fox appears from nowhere and falls on the hapless hare, gripping it in his jaws. Blood spurts and the fox disappears. In the battle about to come I wonder who is fox and who is hare.

Chapter 24

The Trojans are advancing toward us. They move raggedly—they have much ground to protect--and they are spread thin—too thin I hope. Their line moves unevenly forward, in the midst of a constant din—some units chant a rough marching cadence, others beat on drums or clash spears on shields, others, perhaps to keep their sprits up, sing bawdy songs, or shout taunts at us as we advance toward them.

We march in steady, almost mechanical unison, without a sound, the heavy tramp of feet punctuated only by the shouted orders of the officers. The entire front of our line has locked their shields and lowered their long spears so that they present a bristling row of long and deadly spikes, a moving defensive machine.

Then with a clash of shields and armor the bronze clad troops collide, a great cacophony of sound rises up; men shout with triumph as they thrust their swords into the stomach of an onrushing foe; others scream in agony as a spear cleaves them between the eyes and their blood flows where they fall. The huge mass of men is a disciplined army no longer; the ordered ranks dissolve into a boiling melee of swords rising and falling, spears thrusting into flesh, the screams of the dying mix with the taunts of their killers. The ground becomes slippery with blood as bodies fall and are trampled underfoot.

Our solid line begins to waver, as soldier meets soldier in close quarter combat. I see this and signal my cavalry to charge. I ride headlong down the Sigeum slope, shouting a war paean, and rush into the battle. I see the Trojan Sarpedon coming in from the left leading the chariots. And there is Hector, Priam's son riding into the center of the fray, his sword whirling like a great scythe as he comes—toward me. I swerve away to avoid him and ride towards a small group of Trojans fighting a handful of our men, both sides on foot. I shout at the top of my lungs as I headed right at them so as to run the Trojans down. They scramble to get out of the way and that

174

gives me the surprise. I jump from my horse, my shield up, spear ready to thrust. I spit one of them; our men rally behind me. I see another; I try for a hit between the eyes. Breastplates are hard to pierce, but between the eyes and out the back of the skull always drops them where they stand.

We had engaged them just after sunrise. We didn't catch them as much by surprise as we hoped. They were ready and when we came at them they came at us. Now its full tilt: two huge swarms of ants battling over a piece of rotten food. Some men all alone race toward the enemy, hoping for glory and a quick kill. Some only get a quick death. Swords rise, fall and slash. Cut, parry, thrust. Again. And again. Someone screams. Someone falls. Blood spurts. There's a man staggering; his arm has been lopped off. There's another. He's on his knees over a body, trying to cut the straps on the fallen warrior's helmet so he can claim it for himself. Then he has a spear in his back, and now someone tries to take his armor.

Chariots. There are Trojan chariots coming in from the left flank. We're falling back. The king makes a sign. A soldier standing on a high outcrop a few yards away waves a huge signal flag. Someone sees it. Our chariots advance. Their cavalry rides in to a melee of our infantry. Men fall. Horses scream. From here it looks as if the gods are moving pieces on game board, and like so much of what they do, there seems to be no reason in it, just killing and carnage.

Back and forth the battle goes, first one side then the other taking the advantage. Mid-morning, mid-day, afternoon, the fighting continues without a halt. Fresh forces are sent in from both sides, the dead are pulled away; chariots race here and there. No clear advantage can be seen. It's a stalemate. There are dead men everywhere. Trojans and Achaeans lying stretched side by side, face downwards upon the earth. The sun is setting. We can fight no more today. The Trojans are of like mind. I hear their trumpet sound retreat to quarters; then I hear ours as well.

I got back into camp as the dusk fell. No army fights after sunset, for aside from the tactical difficulty of doing so, and the need for rest and food, it was said that the spirits of those who had met their death during the daytime carnage walked the battlefield at night. No man dared to confront them. Somehow I managed to escape harm, though death came close many times. I was covered with blood and the mud of the field and tired to the bone. My father rushed immediately to my tent. Concern was written upon his face that became delight when, as Mecisteus helped me out of my armor and washed the blood and gore away, he saw that I was unharmed. He wanted me to tell him every detail of the battle. I told him what I could, but one horror blended into another. When the rage of battle comes upon you there are no details, no fine discernment, just the carnage, screaming men, blood, and death. And tomorrow would be the same. I slept as if I were dead that night.

Chapter 25

Mecisteus lies next to me, I feel him stir and rise. He must have shared my bed, but I did not know it. I pull myself up, sitting stiff and exhausted on the edge of the bed. Mecisteus comes and sits next to me and massages my shoulders. His hands are strong and warm. I want him never to stop.

I feel myself becoming aroused. I half turn to him; he pulls me to him and we kiss, his strength flowing into me. I want to touch him everywhere, to take him, have him in turn devour me.

We fall back on the bed together, bodies close, desire at its height. It has been so long; so long that he has waited for me, so long that I resisted what I have always known I wanted. Nothing stops us now, and we wrestle together in the passionate battle of love, lips touching, tongues exploring, hands and bodies engaged, the smooth curve of his stomach, my hands on his strong broad back, his breath on my neck, the thrust of his loins, the taste of his skin, his tongue caressing me into pleasure.

I am flying; we two fly together; together we rise up above the world and together unite and like a thousand suns we burst into glorious light. There is music: brilliant, insistent, a triumphant fanfare as we descend and fall and fall and fall into each other's arms.

I lie back, all the pain washed away and hold him close to me and only realize after the dual beating of our hearts begins to quiet that music I heard is the trumpet calling Greece to arms.

Mecisteus jumps up. The moment is gone. With a sheepish look at me and yet with satisfied half-smile he brings me a basin of water. I forage for some food, find some ground millet with a bit of honey, some goat cheese and bread. Somehow he gets me into my armor and I we rush out to the command tent. Agamemnon is laying out the strategy for the day as I enter.

"Its simple, men. We have to keep them fighting till they can fight no longer. We have to tire them out, so killing is the key to it.

But they don't have our discipline, so we need to demoralize them. Letting blood does that. The objective is to breach their line so we can make a charge at their walls. I'm sending Diomedes today. I held him back yesterday. But he's ready. Ready to kill and you know he can. I will ride too, and so will the Lord Menelaus. My Lord Nestor, you remain behind in command." I could see my father was not happy with that. But he is too old to fight. And we need that wise head on his shoulders.

A guard from the north watchtower—the one that looked toward Troy--comes racing to where we stand around the king.

"The Trojans Lord, they're advancing on all fronts." At the same moment we hear the shrill and distant call of their trumpets sounding the advance, answered by ours calling our troops into battle. Another day begins.

I ride just behind Diomedes. He is a giant of a man, standing several hands taller than I and as strong as they say Heracles must have been. I've seen him lift the prow of a ship and push it into the waves. He is not handsome the way Achilles is. But it is hard not to look at him. His craggy face and deep set black eyes are framed by a mane of shaggy black hair that flows out from beneath his helmet almost to his shoulders, shoulders that seem broader than those of two men. He doesn't speak much and never talks about himself. When men sit around the fire and boast about their courage in battle, Diomedes never joins in, never shares his exploits. He doesn't have to. He's a legend. Everyone knows he was one of the seven who captured Thebes. He courted Helen and the gods know it might have been better for all of us had she chosen him. Men always argue whether he or Achilles is our best warrior. Who can know? Diomedes is as brave as Achilles and even stronger, and like Achilles, in battle he is a ruthless killer, pure and simple. But oddly, when you sit with him and talk by the fire passing a wine cup, just two soldiers together, he is soft-spoken, thoughtful and very kind. I get the feeling too that he is wise. Hubris has no place in that great heart. If anyone escapes alive from this long war, it will be he. He is the youngest of the great lords who came here, and save for Agamemnon, he brought the most ships and men from far away Argos, where he is king. Without Achilles, he is our best hope.

As we spur our horses to a canter and then a gallop, I see a cloud of dust rolling down from the Trojan walls. It is a line of Trojan chariots in the lead of the infantry. Our front lines are on a course to collide with the chariots. The two sides come close, closer, then with shouts and the crash of armors and weapons they meet. In front of me, Diomedes gallops ahead; I follow. The sun breaks through the early morning clouds and glances off his shield and helmet, reflecting like a beacon that envelopes him in a fiery aureole as he speeds into the thrashing heart of the fight. He suddenly reins in and leaping from his horse, gives it sharp slap upon the flank. The animal rears up and speeds away. Diomedes fights, spear plunging and rising, thrusting and withdrawing, with horrific rapidity. All around him men fall, blood spurting, crimson fountains falling to earth.

From Diomedes' right a chariot speeds out from the main body of the Trojan chariot line and bears down on him. In it are two young Trojan warriors. I think, its not an even contest, he's on foot and they are fighting from their chariot. I pull my horse around and try to fight my way to Diomedes, but the press of men is heavy and I have all I can do not to be pulled from my horse. I cut and slash, and began to get closer to where he fights, but I can't reach him, though I can see him clearly now. I shout to him because one of the Trojans has taken aim. He hears me and the Trojan spear flies over his left shoulder without hitting him. Without an instant's hesitation Diomedes whirls and throws his spear. It hits the young Trojan on the breast and he falls from his chariot. The other springs from the chariot, but instead of defending the body he takes flight. There are more like Paris I think. Diomedes rushes to the chariot and its two fine horses, seizes the reins and throws them to an Achaean soldier—one of his own men--who has rushed in to back Diomedes up. "Take them to the ships," Diomedes shouts.

When the Trojans fighting in the immediate area see that one of the chariot-warriors is dead and the other has fled, and that it is Diomedes on the field, they begin to waver, and then to panic. I see some of them look back toward their own lines for an avenue of retreat. Seeing this, Diomedes rallies his men and with horrific war cries run at the Trojan infantry and begins to drive them back, even as several of our own chariots, led by Agamemnon and followed by Idomeneus, thunder in the pursuit of the Trojan chariot detachment that had been hovering on the edge of the battle to back up the their infantry. Seeing that the odds are rapidly deteriorating, both Trojan infantry and chariots wheel, draw back and flee, with ours in pursuit. I race beside the king's chariot as he gains on what is clearly the Trojan captain. Agamemnon's spear catches him between the shoulders and slices through his chest. His armor rings and rattles around him as he falls heavily to the ground just as Agamemnon's chariot wheels pass over him. He does not stop, for he is in pursuit of the next chariot. As if in a race, another chariot pulls parallel with the king. It is Idomeneus, king of Athens. His squire whips his horses; his chariot passes Agamemnon. The two kings shout encouragement to one another as they pass. As they race by I think I can see the bloodlust in their eyes. No doubt it gleams in mine too. Before us the Trojans are in retreat and we are moving toward the walls of Troy, bathed blood red by the slowly setting sun.

Chapter 26

No matter what the poets say when they write about the titanic battles of superhuman heroes who never seem to rest, real armies can't fight on and on without ever stopping. Horses need food and water. Chariots need to be repaired, swords re-sharpened, spears points re-honed. Men have to eat and rest and most of all the wounded must be tended. When a battle is done, it is everyone's task to clean up after it all is over— to clean and dress the bodies of the dead so they can be burned on funeral pyres and sent to the fields of heaven where heroes eternally roam.

Yesterday, after yet another indecisive battle, the day's carnage ended at sundown, for no one fights at night, and as is always the case, the Truce of the Dead is called between Greek and Trojan. The dead lie strewn across the landscape, their blood making every patch of soil sacred ground. They must be found. This is a job for both slaves and soldiers and an honor for men of any rank. And so I, a prince, go from body to body, looking for fallen Greeks, and for dead Trojans too, tending to my enemy.

To the victor belong the spoils, they say. When defeated blood spills out upon the ground and the eyes can no longer see, no warrior who has lived to see his enemy die--whether he is Trojan or Achaean—will leave that treasure, armor made of bronze, swords chased with gold and set with precious gems from distant lands, upon the ground to rust and molder and decay. And so the dead lie stripped of their armor, naked on the ground where they fell. I go from body to body. If a man is wounded, we do what we can to ease the pain until soldiers come to carry him back to the camp. We close the eyes of the dead; if they still have eyes to close, and with the water we carry wash their battered faces so as to tell if we can whether they are Greek or Trojan. If Greek, our soldiers carry them toward our camp where the funeral pyres await. Sometimes we have to hail a Trojan soldier to come to take one of their own. On the field of death, an odd comradeship exists as Greeks and Trojans, who that morning fought against one another work together to find and honor the dead, some of them may have helped to kill. Greek and Trojan soldiers and their slaves move across the field, collecting their dead, digging trenches into which the bodies of horses are dumped, lifting dead men into carts, and trundling them to lie on the huge pyres upon which the bodies will eventually burn.

Before night the priests, and detachment of soldiers, both Greek and Trojan, under the flag of truce will burn the dead. This is a sacred protocol of war, mutually agreed upon, and the only decency that all observe. Finally at day's end, the remains will be gathered and buried in a common grave. And so along with the smoke from cook-fires and sacrifices, smoke rises from the pyres on which dead men lie, broken bodies, men disfigured and unrecognizable, common soldiers and commanders, for death levels all on the battlefield.

Even as I care for the dead, soldiers go about the business of their day. I hear them shouting; hear the horses whinnying, hear men cursing or laughing, even hear the clank of cook-pots and utensils as they make their meal. Once in while a Trojan soldier on death detail looks up and waves with a jaunty arrogance as if to say, "Look your fill, you will not live to see another day." If the Trojans breach the walls of the Greek camp I suppose they may kill me too, but I will die with my sword in hand. When we are done with the dead we return to the tents of the living, safe, for now, behind our walls.

Chapter 27

We camped last night in front of the city so as to keep the advantage we had gained when the Trojans were driven back to their walls. In the morning we took a cold morning meal hastily. There was no time to light cook fires. Before us stretched the field upon which this day's battle will be fought. Before their city the Trojan army also camps, readying itself as we were doing. Behind us toward the sea stretches the huge expanse of the Trojan plain, over which we had fought yesterday, sloping toward the river, open and unprotected. Because of our success in that bloody battle we now consider it to be ours.

As the sun moves higher both armies begin to form lines, commanders shouting orders, chariots wheeling into place, horsemen mounting. Priests of both sides stand before their ranks praying and searching the sky for omens. But the sky is clear, no bird can be seen, no clouds scud across the silvery blue. It seems as if the entire earth waits for the battle to begin. In the front of our line the commanders wait in their chariots, Agamemnon at the center, Diomedes and Idomeneus on his left, Odysseus and Menelaus on his right. Rank upon rank of foot soldiers is ranged behind each commander. I am at the center with my men. Mecisteus rides by my side. As I have done so often I look where Achilles and his Myrmidons might have stood if things had been different. How we could use them now.

Everyone waits, tensely. After yesterday, the men can smell victory. Perhaps to bolster their sagging hopes some men in the Trojan lines shout taunts at us, hooting and catcalling, making obscene gestures, hoping to move us to anger. But we do not respond to them. In fact we are ordered not to do so. Instead we face them with deliberate grim silence, a tactic we have found especially effective against less disciplined troops. For an army that fled from us in panic on the day before, they seem remarkably arrogant and confident today. I remember what my father always says about an over-confident army. Rising above the Trojan din, I hear another sound. What is it? Women's voices. They are singing. From the highest point of the citadel where the great temple stands, rises the smoke of sacrifice and the women's voices, hundreds of them raised in a hymn of supplication. The Trojan women have gone to pray for the safety of their men. Will the gods hear them?

Then the moment comes. There is never any sign to herald it. There is no parley between opposing commanders. No signal from the heavens is discerned by any priest. But somehow, both sides know when the time is ripe to begin the attack. One commander or the other raises his hand. Trumpets sound. The whole vast assemblage on either side begins slowly to advance, picks up speed, and soon the two forces are racing toward one another, battle cries sounding, chariot wheels raising dust, horses' hooves drumming a thunderous tattoo that you can feel beating in unison with the rapid beating of your heart as you ride or drive or run toward the advancing foe to a meeting with some man whose face may be the last you will ever see.

I ride pell-mell, heedless, the drumming hoofs beating in my brain, my heart racing, looking for a man to kill. Shield clashes with shield, and spear with spear. The noise is unbearable. No one who has not fought knows what it is like to be in the midst of such terrible clamor as men press hard against one another, the death-cries of the dying and the shouts of triumph of their killers mingling in a horrible chorus as the earth runs with blood.

All morning we pressed the attack, all morning they fought us off, weapons clashing against weapons. All around me men are falling. It is hard to see who fights with whom. I have lost sight of Mecisteus I am on foot now. My horse has been struck by an arrow. He fell, the arrow protruding from his chest, blood spurting like a pulsing fountain, legs kicking in the air. With a kick and final agonized scream he dies. I send up a prayer to the God of Horses for him. I want to find the bowman who did this. I see him, just a short way away. He has his back to me. He is fitting another arrow to his bow. I cannot see his target but I can see him. I throw my spear and it strikes him full in the back. With a guttural cough, spitting blood, he falls face down. I do not care whether he is noble or common, what matters is that he is dead.

I think I see Agamemnon raise his sword against Sarpedon, but then Sarpedon wheels and drives off toward the right flank at the northern end of the lines with Agamemnon in pursuit. Menelaus rides against Antenor. But a cohort of Trojan foot interposes and Antenor escapes into their midst. The Trojan Prince Deiphobus rushes toward Diomedes. Diomedes moves to attack but his way is blocked by the swift incursions of Paris, resplendent of course, who rides towards him, but at the last moment wheels and gallops away to the right as well, calling taunts to Diomedes, daring him to follow. Which he does. Everywhere it seems that whenever an advantage is about to be secured by an Achaean it is snatched away by Trojan. Agamemnon, Diomedes, Menelaus are all fighting on the right flank now where the Trojans seem to have concentrated their strongest forces, and I suddenly realize that our center is weak and that is why the Trojans are so ferociously confident, as eager for blood and battle as yesterday they were to flee from it.

It is as if Zeus himself has intervened and raised the scales in which he weighs the fate of men. Holding them high above the men at war below, in one side he has placed us, the Achaeans. In the other the Trojans. All morning the scales have been tilting one way, then this, and then back. But now as if he has added a golden weight to one side, the balance has tipped and it is not in our favor.

Whether gods or men make our fate, no man knows though many pretend to.

With horror and with a sinking heart I see that the gates of Troy have been flung wide open. From them issues at breakneck speed a line of huge war chariots at full gallop. I am close enough to the front to see who rides in the first chariot. It is Hector, leading the charge. And behind him in the next—Aeneas. I need to save myself for the onrushing juggernauts are headed toward the center where I stand and where our line is weakest. Their speed is incredible. The horses that draw them are Troy's best and most powerful. Huge chests heaving as they rush forward, mouths flecked with foam and teeth bared, nostrils flaring and black eyes staring and wide, these fearsome creatures gallop toward us. They ride so fast they will overshoot our position.

Then I realize, that is their intent. They intend to ride us down, catapult over us and through us, breaking our line. Behind them is the next surprise, a racing phalanx of Trojan infantry; they are the Royal Guard, bred as killers, who will fight to the death if need be. They will fight us while the chariots ride on. Ride where?

Then I see it. They are riding toward our camp.

We have only two choices, neither good. We must keep fighting where we stand or we must retreat back to our camp to save our ships, which in our over-confidence we have left only lightly guarded. I make my choice. A Trojan horseman is riding toward me. I throw up my arms and plant my spear in the ground as if I will surrender. He canters to a halt and as he comes abreast of me I use my spear as a pole to vault upon the horses back behind the rider. In a breath I draw my dagger and with a swift clean cut slash his throat, push him to the ground and gallop toward the camp. The same choice has been made by the other commanders. Trumpet calls sound the retreat to quarters. Men on horse, on foot, in chariots, turn and join the retreat. I ride like fury toward the camp. In my ears I hear the victorious shouts of the pursuing Trojans, mixed with jeers.

A day has passed. The Trojans have contained us inside our own walls. They now control the entire plain in front of their city and with impunity race their chariots within hailing distance of our camp. What is worse they occupy the area in front of our ships. From any vantage point—looking north, looking south, looking east--we can see their army. How has this happened? Over-confidence for one thing. Agamemnon's over-eagerness to attack collided with the Hector's superior strategy. And now they are at our ships. How easy it would be for them to mount a full-scale onslaught and burn them. I wonder why they haven't. Then where would we be? Lambs ready for slaughter. While the Trojans keep watch, we huddle inside our camp walls and shudder in the grip of panic. I lie that night in Mecisteus' arms. Thanks the gods he is safe. His arms are strong and he comforts me. But we both know we cannot win this. Not without Achilles.

Book Nine
Achilles' Fatal Pride

And Achilles said: The son of Atreus treated me like a slave. I will not think of arming for war again.
    —Iliad 9. 791-95.

From: Dionysos of Tenedos, A History of the War at Troy

The Greeks followed Agamemnon because he is High King, though he was too quick to anger, too rash, and too arrogant by half. What he knew was this: he wanted Troy, he wanted the gold that went with it, he wanted to destroy once and for all that great city. He also knew that he hated Achilles and had hated him from the start.

And Achilles? He was just as proud as Agamemnon. And he was a better soldier and a better man. Indeed as all the world knows he was the greatest warrior of them all. His mutiny, for such it surely was, was beyond a disaster. It was tragedy.

With Achilles gone Agamemnon believed that he was, as it were, at last master in his own realm, a mastery that always seemed in doubt when Achilles was there to outshine him in battle and in all other things outdo him at every turn. But at the heart of it all lay a contradiction. A contradiction that is, if you believe in priests who claim to know the will of the gods—as Agamemnon did!

It was just after Paris had stolen Helen and Agamemnon was sending heralds all over Hellas recruiting for the war, that a message came to Agamemnon from the priest, Calchas, saying that he had foretold Agamemnon's victory. If Agamemnon really wanted to know more, it would help it along if Agamemnon would take him into his service.

"How can you know that I will prevail," it is said that Agamemnon not unreasonably asked?

"Because I have seen the future in the entrails of birds and the god speaks to me, coming to me in the night in dreams and in the smoke of the sacrifice." Calchas replied.

And he told Agamemnon that he had prophesied that if Achilles took up arms against Troy that it would surely fall.

But now Achilles was not in arms.

Chapter 28

At last! Odysseus has forced the king to call a council of the high command. For days we've been cooling our heels, but by necessity for the Trojans surround our camp. But there is no fighting. By unspoken consent both armies have paused; we all need rest. Agamemnon keeps to his tent, drinking and whoring I imagine. That's his answer when things go wrong. Pretend the problem isn't there. Well this just won't do this time. Our backs are, literally, against the wall. We're in a pretty pickle and everyone knows it. And everyone knows that Achilles is the only answer. For the Trojans will soon attack again.

"Achilles is the only answer. We've got to go to him again, beg him—again--if we have to, to help us. If we don't, it's all lost."

Idomeneus relinquished the speaker's staff and returned to his seat. He was only one of many voices that have been saying the same thing.

"What good will Achilles and his Myrmidons do us now?" the king said, his voice was tired, his eyes dark. Defeat seemed to weigh him down and he slumped in his chair, barely looking up as he spoke.

"We have only one choice, take to our ships and sail away from this accursed land. I see the hand of heaven in this impasse. Calchas has taken omens: Zeus has snatched that victory from me. Why? If the gods are against me, what is left for me? Nothing but to go ingloriously back to Argos, even though I leave so many dead behind. It's the will of Zeus, and who am I to battle him? I say we must sail back to our own country, for we will not take Troy."

189

Everyone broke into talk at once; some loudly agreed, others as vehemently objected. Among the latter Diomedes leapt up and in a fury grasped the speaker's staff.

"Agamemnon, it's my right as a king to answer you. This is folly." He paused, and then: "And worse, it's cowardice." A stifled gasp went up; the room was as tense as it was silent. We were but a step from rebellion.

Amazingly the king did nothing. He did not leap up, sword in hand to challenge Diomedes. He simply sat staring into the distance as if he had not heard.

"Listen to me," Diomedes shouted at the king, "if we do what you say, then all of us, all the Achaeans, will be branded by all the world as cowards! If you want to abandon us now, do it. Go"—and he pointed to the entrance to the tent—"the way is open to you; your ships are on the seashore. But for myself I say this. I will stay here till we have sacked Troy."

The room broke into cheers but the king remained silent, seemingly unaffected. Then my father rose to speak.

"Diomedes, in war your prowess is beyond question and no one among all the Achaeans can argue with what you say. But there is more to this. Forgive me—and all of you, my lords—if I speak plainly, but I am older than any man here and have been a king the longest and fought upon more fields of conquest than most."

Then to Diomedes he said, "you know as well as I that you are still young--you might be the youngest of my own children. You have spoken wisely and what you say to the king I would say myself."

I saw that this hit home; the king looked at my father as if struck.

"But though you have said it—and though many a man here may think it," here my father spread out his arms as if to embrace the entire room--"yet I will tell you this, and let no man, not even King Agamemnon, disregard me: he that foments discord among this alliance does no service to our cause. It would be better for such a man to be sent into the night alone, an outcast from his kin and nation."

I could see that he had had captured the room. Diomedes looked crestfallen and stared at his feet, sheepishly. I could see agreement written upon the face of some men, uncertainty upon others. The king's face now showed the beginning of a triumphant smile as he began to think that old Nestor had come to his defense.

Then my father threw the last dice and they were loaded. He addressed the king.

"Agamemnon, you are king over all the world. Zeus has given you the scepter as a token that you are to uphold the law, rule fairly, and do the best for your people. And so it's your duty to listen to those who counsel you. And now I shall say what must be said. I tell you this: from the hour when you angered Achilles our enterprise has been doomed. In your pride you dishonored a hero who heaven itself has honored. You were wrong then, and you will be wrong now if you do not appease him and apologize for your error."

The color drained from the king's face. He stared at my father, and then around the room, as if trying to divine in the faces of the assembled men what his answer should be. I could see his pride struggle with the dawning realization that he had no position upon which to fall back. My father was right, and the king knew it. He beckoned to Calchas and Odysseus. The three of them huddled together, speaking in low tones. Would he turn back to us from this conference white with rage, call us traitors, or dismiss us with cold hauteur as he has done in the past when what he has been told is not what he wants to hear? He returned to his chair, Calchas and Odysseus ranged on either side of him.

It was a standoff. The king seated, his face a mask, his eyes dark. Standing facing him Diomedes, my father, me and the other officers.

Silence.

My father approached the king. He did not kneel before him. Instead, he reached out his hand and held it out to the king, looking intently at the seated man. As if impelled to do so by the steadiness of my father's gaze, the king slowly rose and took the proffered hand.

191

Then like a father to an errant and sulking son, my father, almost gently said: "We have no choice. We must beg Achilles to return to battle."

The king stiffened and then, like a puppet whose strings have been cut, he fell, not sat, back in his chair.

"Do it," he said.

Chapter 29

The next day, slipping out of camp in the still morning darkness before the dawn, Ajax, Odysseus and myself—for we had been chosen to be the last ambassadors, indeed the Achaean's last hope-- arrived at Achilles' camp. His tent was pitched on a low rise of ground a few dozen paces from his ship. Around it were the smaller tents of his company of troops, the Myrmidons. A few pack mules grazed on the sparse beach grass, and Achilles' war chariot stood nearby. Achilles himself sat in front of his tent, polishing his sword. His long spear lay on the ground by his side next to where he sat; his shield was propped against a small table by his side. Both, one could see, were in very easy reach. It was not an encouraging sign.

Patroclus appeared from inside the tent and caught sight of us and made a gesture to Achilles who turned to look where Patroclus pointed. We expected black looks and rejection. Instead his face lit up when he saw us and he bounded down the slope like a young antelope.

"You must come upon some important matter, my friends." He said with a quick flash of his handsome smile and embraced the three older men. Then he came to me and took me in a bear hug of an embrace.

"Ah, Antilochus," he breathed into my ear. "Come to my tent. I will give you wine and food."

"Patroclus, bring a larger wine bowl, and don't stint on the wine when you mix it for my friends. They are very dear to me, so bring enough food as well."

Patroclus reappeared and set a chopping-block in front of the fire, laid the loin of a sheep on it and held the meat while Achilles chopped, sliced, and salted it and put the pieces on spits over the fire. Patroclus mixed the wine—strongly as Achilles said--and passed cups of it to each of us. Before drinking we all poured a bit in the ground as a libation to the gods. I am sure Odysseus prayed that

193

our embassy would be a success; I fear that I—Mecisteus gone out of my head—prayed to have Achilles in my bed again.

As if to demonstrate that my prayer was in vain, Patroclus took the now sizzling meat off the fire, set it on platters, and handed bread around, while Achilles dealt out portions. I watched this all too domestic scene with envy in my heart. Just like an old married couple, I thought. I wanted that.

"Eat up, men," Achilles said.

"A toast first," Odysseus said.

He opened his knapsack and took from it a golden cup, wonderfully worked and chased with figures of gods and men and scenes of battle. He filled it from the wine bowl and raising it, toasted Achilles. We all raised our cups to pledge him good health and fortune, and as is the custom Odysseus passed the cup to Achilles, who we had honored, indicating that it was a gift. Achilles raised the cup in return.

"A generous gift, my friend," he said. "But now you must tell me why you have come with such a gift. Is it to bring me news of war?"

"We have no good news to bring, I fear, my lord. To put it plainly we face a great disaster. The Trojans have pushed us back to our camp just when we thought that we had pushed *them* back to their walls. Their army is spread out across the plain in front of Troy, and they have even bivouacked detachments near the ship station. They have lit watch fires all around and sentinels are posted day and night. They wait for the opportune moment to attack and when they do I fear that there is nothing that can prevent them from taking our ships and even burning them. We have lost many men in battle, food is in short supply and we are penned up in our camp. Only the shoreline remains ours. Daily the Trojans taunt us: come out and fight, they shout. But what is there that we can do? Mount a full-out assault to drive them back to the walls of their city? We do not have the strength; what is worse, we do not have the will. The king wavers, the men know it and they are losing confidence in him. There are many who would take ship and run. Here's the long and short of it, without your help we don't know if we can save our fleet or lose it, or even save ourselves. We need you. You must come and fight beside us again."

"And if I do?" Achilles said.

"Then the king will reward you beyond your dreams," Odysseus said, "for that cup is only a fraction of the treasure the king will give." Odysseus listed the vast reward—or was it bribe— that the king offered.

Achilles turned the cup over and over in his hands, held it up so that it caught the sunlight. The battling warriors on it seemed to move as the light glanced off them, their raised swords thrust; their spears seemed about to fly from their hands.

Then he handed the cup to Patroclus and said: "Let us eat and drink. Tomorrow there is time enough to talk about this."

We could not argue, though we knew there was no time. We ate and drank until the moon rose and then we were shown tents that had been made ready for us. But I could not sleep.

I got up and went out into the moonlight that silvered the beach, the sea, even the mountains beyond. I walked among the small tents and came to the tent of Achilles and Patroclus. I walked quietly thinking them asleep. But I saw the dim light of a lamp and saw their shadows cast large by it and etched on the canvas tent wall. They were shouting at one another. Never has this happened. Patroclus and Achilles have never raised their voices in anger to one another.

"I will not fight; let the king ruin it all." I heard Achilles say. "There are some things a man won't do and I won't bow down to that drunken sot."

"But our men, our brothers, our friends, they are dying, and we sit here. We might as well be killing them ourselves." This was Patroclus and his voice trembled with anger and frustration.

Achilles did not answer.

I stood outside the tent. I knew I shouldn't, but I was transfixed. For I realized that if Patroclus could convince Achilles to fight then the war might yet be won.

"Every day they move closer to the camp and to the ships," I heard Patroclus say. "What then? Will they burn the ships and leave the army stranded to be picked off like rabbits? I won't allow it."

195

"We have our ships here, on our shore. They will not burn those." Achilles said coolly.

"I see," Patroclus said, and the anger in his tone was even more intense. "So will you cast off and leave Troy, leave your friends behind, dead? Is that what you call honor?"

"Don't preach to me about honor," Achilles answered. "I have no stain on me nor will I ever. If I have to I will storm the walls of Troy myself, at the head of my brave men, but I will not do it as a vassal of Agamemnon until he abases himself in the dust before me to pay for the insult he has given me."

"And meanwhile our men die and without you they cannot win."

"That is my choice, "Achilles said coldly.

"Then let me make mine," Patroclus said.

Then in desperation Patroclus played his final card.

I could not believe what I was hearing.

The next morning as we prepared to leave, breaking bread by the embers of last night's dying fire Achilles was ready to talk He reached for Odysseus' hand.

"Odysseus, noble son of Laertes, and my good friend, I know the plight of our army, for rumors fly like the wind even here far away from the battlefield. But no matter how you try to convince me, each of you, one after the other, you cannot. The king has sent me treasure before. I refused it then, I refuse it now. I reject his gifts. They are a shameful bribe to assuage his guilty conscience. He can promise me gifts as numerous as the sands of the shore, but he will not move me. Nothing that Agamemnon offers will appease me

"If the king wants to save his ships and his army and even his crown, then tell him to come here and look me in the eye and beg *my* forgiveness, not me his. Then he must ask for me to fight again by his side. But he will not dare do that, because he knows already he is wrong. And you my friends, take my advice. Go home, for you will not take Troy. Zeus holds his hand over that city and protects it. Tell the princes of the Achaeans what I have said."

We were struck speechless by the vehemence of his rejection. Achilles and Patroclus sat on one side of the fire that was by now beginning to smoke as the flames died out. I sensed the tension between them. A dying fire. A suitable omen, I thought, for our failed mission. We sat on the other side; I could not look at Achilles.

Then Ajax, rose, threw up his hands in a gesture of frustration.

"There is no further point to this. Let us go and take this bad news back to the king."

Then turning to Achilles.

"It is bad enough that you refuse to come to the aid of your comrades, who love and admire you. Some god has hardened your heart and filled you with an unforgiving spirit. I am sorry to see it, for of all the Achaeans, we here today want to remain your closest friends."

"Ajax," replied Achilles, "perhaps you are right. Perhaps my heart is hard beyond reason. But no matter what I will always be your comrade. But this I will say. When I fought among the Achaeans, Hector did not dare to leave the shelter of his city walls because I was there. Now Hector sits before your camp.

"Know this: If Hector comes to *my* tents and to *my* ships in his murderous course, and destroys *anything* that is *mine,* then will I fight. Do not doubt that. Then I will kill Hector where he stands."

We saluted him with sorrow in our hearts. The others turned and headed back toward the shore. I hesitated for a moment, wanting to say something, or just reach out and take his hand. But he and Patroclus made no move, and stood together, their faces grim, on the other side of the dying fire. I hated what Achilles had done, but I knew that despite that the fire that I had kindled for him so long ago would never really die. I raised my hand to him. He nodded and his face seemed lined with a sadness as deep as mine.

Book Ten
The Prophecy Fulfilled

Antilochus, son of great-hearted Nestor, send him out to run with a message to wise Achilles, how one who was far the dearest to him has fallen.
-Iliad 17. 655-56

From: Dionysos of Tenedos, A History of the War at Troy

The Greeks were forced to prosecute the war without the one man who could win it, for not all the riches in the world could convince Achilles to swallow his pride, for Patroclus was at his side and he wanted nothing else. But the gods care little for the will of men and they, as the legends say, had other plans.

Let it not be said that the Greeks fought half-heartedly or admitted defeat. They went into battle and killed and killed and killed. Antilochus was among those seized by the rage for battle. But Achilles refused to fight.

Chapter 30

It is hopeless. But I will fight on. Even before the sun rose, so as to take the advantage, our forces streamed out of the central gate and into the massed army of Troy. Our plan was simple as it was daring. We would fling open our gates and attack them head on, in one glorious all-or-nothing charge. We came out like a pack of wolves and our desperation gave us strength. All morning we fought, and then with a cry that rang through all the ranks, Agamemnon swept into the lead in his great war chariot. It was as if he had shed the burden that his treatment of Achilles had imposed upon him and now was free to take out all of his accumulated rage against Achilles upon the Trojans who stood in his way. His charge brought him on a collision course with an oncoming chariot, a commander's I think judging by its size and the battalion banner fluttering from it. In it, two men, one the charioteer the other the spearman, and sworn lovers it appeared since each wore the other's favor on his helmet, came careening recklessly at the king who cast his spear and hit the driver. His comrade sprang from the driverless chariot and came full towards him; but Agamemnon struck him on the forehead with his sword and pierced both bronze of the helmet and the bone so that his brains were battered in and he was killed in full fight. With that kill we broke through the battalion of the enemy that fronted our gates. Agamemnon was like a lion that leaps from his hiding place and attacks the fleeing deer, crushing it in his jaws, robbing it of their life. The Trojans were the deer and flew in panic before the king who killed and killed and killed.

As if he were a man possessed by a war demon come out of Hell—and perhaps he was, so furious was he at Achilles' rejection—the king sped onwards, calling out to the Achaeans to advance on the city. He flew by the tomb of Ilus, son of Dardanus, making for Troy. I raced behind him, Mecisteus riding close beside me. The Trojans he was pursuing flew over the middle of the plain like rabbits maddened with fright when a wolf attacks them in the dead of night. The king slaughtered them as they fled pell-mell before him, and as he pressed forward in his eagerness to be ahead of all the others., shouting at his charioteer to lash the horses in to even greater effort.

And this was his mistake. We were still behind him; he was ahead of us all, his chariot now a lone glittering target. Not running like the others but waiting in his chariot as the king pushed recklessly on, a huge Trojan warrior was obviously bidding his time until he could get a good shot at the king. When the king came close he threw his spear and hit the king, wounding him in the side, the point of the spear going right through his armor. I threw and hit his attacker who stumbled and then fell back from his chariot, but was tangled in its reins, and was dragged away by the panicked horses.

The king's charioteer had halted the chariot when he saw the king fall. I rushed up, leapt from my horse and into the chariot. I could see that the king was convulsed with pain and blood was welling from his wound. the driver was trying to comfort him. "My lord," I shouted, "you must retreat." I pushed him down to the platform of the chariot and shouted to the driver, "Get him back to camp." The chariot wheeled and I frantically signed to the horse-guard detachment that had been running with us to give the king cover back to the camp. The charioteer turned his horses towards the ships, and they flew forward, their chests white with foam and their bellies with dust, as they carried the wounded king out of the battle.

I turned back to the killing fields, but when those in the immediate area where the king fell saw his chariot fleeing toward our camp with Agamemnon in it, they faltered and began to pull back. How news travels so quickly in the midst of the chaos and horror of the battlefield I do not know. Perhaps some malicious goddess descended to trumpet the king's fall and fill our hearts with fear. However it happened, it was soon known and men fell back, the retreat became a rout, and then a panic. My horse gone, I was afoot. I fought my way back toward our camp and vowed as I cut and thrust, ran, turned, cut and thrust again, ran more, that if my time was upon me, that I would die a hero's death before the gates.

The Trojans are determined to break through. Again and again they attack the gates, the breastworks, any place where they think they can get a foothold. They shoot fire arrows into our battlements. But we do not give ground. From above our archers rain arrows down upon them. Blood flows everywhere. I am directly in front of the camp gates. My arm rises and falls rises and falls. I know I have sustained some wounds, but none mortal, though all around men I know are dying. We are trying too stall for time, to keep them from taking the main gate and rushing the ships. If they take the ships we will be lost indeed and be driven into the sea.

Someone shouts: "Hector is coming" and a huge war chariot thunders toward the us, its charioteer lashing the horses, in it a giant of a man in golden armor raises his sword in a sweeping gesture as he passes us within a hair's breadth and the wind rushes in my ears as the sword descends. Lycophron, the lover of Aias, who is standing next to me, is killed by Hector's sword. His blood spurts out of the neck wound and some of it stings me in the eye. The poets like to claim that Hector was wrapped in the mantle of Zeus.

I was in that battle; I saw no god, only that huge terrifying man. I stand my ground with the men, but the odds are too great. We retreat back, closer to the gates. The soldiers inside open a postern and we rush in, safe as it turns out, only for a moment. I race to the ladders and mount the wall. Right behind me is our bowman Teucer who springs to the wall and careless of whether he will be hit or not, draws his bow for one last clear shot at Hector who is riding right at the gates. It is said that his bow is one that Phoibos Apollo himself had given him. I see him draw that sacred bow. The bowstring breaks as if snapped by the hand of the god.

Hector springs towards the wall shouting as he did so, "Trojans, charge the gates, break through and fire the ships." As if suddenly given double strength, in one body the Trojans rush our position, heading straight for the gates. Hector leaps from his chariot and seeing a huge boulder, so big that it should have taken two men to raise it, lifts it and with it held high above his head runs toward the gates and with his whole weight behind it he uses the stone as a battering ram. There is splintering; the hinges break; the great bars no longer hold; the gates fly open and Hector leaps inside with a face as dark as night and his eyes glare like fire.

We are in full retreat toward the beach, a last ditch attempt to protect the ships. The Trojans are scaling the walls and pouring through the gates. We fall back towards our ships, and all is uproar and confusion. The Trojans advance in a dense body, with Hector at their head, careering through our tents trying to reach the sea in his murderous course. Our battalion hastily reforms, but Hector and his soldiers are coming at us. Then horror of horrors. The Trojans are shooting fire arrows toward the ships. Some are hit; some ships begin to burn. The battle rages as the fires rage.

We have our backs to the sea and the distant ships. A couple of them are burning now, the smoke rises like a beacon of doom against the sky. Then I hear a sound.

At first I thought the sound was the wind rising. Then it was shouting, cheering, the voices of a thousand desperate men suddenly seeing hope. I heard his name being hoarsely shouted, then chanted, then raised to heaven like the Paean. "Achilles! Achilles! Achilles! Achilles is coming." And come he did, cleaving into the mass of swirling men like a shaft of the silver dawn, cutting a path before him, the chariot wheels and horses hooves sounding like thunder from the throne of Zeus. Achilles stood in his chariot, his armor a flashing beacon of victory, his sword making great deadly silvered arcs while with the other hand he thrust with his lance drawing black blood. Achilles had come, slayer of men; there was no hope for the Trojans now.

Achilles' chariot swept in our direction, scattering in its wake the dead, the dying, the rumble of its passing overwhelmed by the cacophonous shrieks of hideous death. His Myrmidon's raced after and beside him. The Trojan lines wavered, broke, panicked. A terrible sigh went up from the Trojan ranks, became a shriek of fear, rose to heaven as a wail of defeat.

Our men took heart; we charged. I shouted a paean of victory and thrust my spear direct into the skull of a beautiful young man coning at me with blood in his eyes. I later learned it was Atymnios, Amisodaros' son. The battle had turned. Achilles' chariot swept in our direction, scattering in its wake the dead, the dying, the rumble of its passing overwhelmed by the cacophonous shrieks of hideous death. The slaughter was terrible.

But in the midst of it I drew up short in amazement. As Achilles' chariot bore down on us I could see clearly its two occupants, Achilles and the charioteer, descending like avenging chimera. As they drew near, passing within feet of where I stood deep in blood and mangled bodies I saw that the charioteer was Automedon! Automedon was not Achilles' driver. Automedon always held the reins for Patroclus. They were *never* separated.

With all the strength I could command I ran after the chariot, pacing it for just long enough to see that though the armor indeed was his, it was not Achilles in that armor. But the armored man was one I had also served, and washed and dressed. It was Patroclus who wore that armor; Patroclus who rode there; Patroclus who had come out to make the enemy believe that Achilles had sallied forth to kill.

I was overwhelmed with a torrent of mixed emotion. How could he? How could Achilles send anyone in his place, especially his lover? How cowardly! And how brave of Patroclus to go. How terribly, stupidly wrong it was for Achilles, when his comrades were dying, not to give up his stubborn pride, not to forget his vain quarrel in order to save his men. And how unworthy of a hero to engage in such duplicity, even though as was evident, the ruse was working. This was worse than hubris. He would be punished by the Gods. That terrible certainty struck me like that javelin must have struck young Atymnios, a brutal thrust to the brain.

But there was another emotion, a dreadful one that overtook me too. I am ashamed to say it. It was this: Patroclus was brave, but he was not Achilles. Soon the deceit might be discovered. Hector would attack him directly. No one could stand against Hector, save Achilles. Patroclus would surely be killed.

Did I lament? Did I rush to his side? Did I shout for him to turn back?

No, I did not. Deep within me a terrible voice whispered, the soft whisperer drowning out the din of war: "Patroclus will die. Achilles will be yours." For that thought surely I will be punished and deserve whatever death the gods have in store for me.

And I knew in my heart the most terrible truth of all: Patroclus dying meant Achilles dead.

And as it was decided long before the foundations of Troy were laid, so it came to pass, and I——I numbly fought on the Dardanian plain, fought against shadow warriors, heard no sound, felt no emotion, my arm rising and falling, mutely dispensing death, thrusting, parrying, killing, in dumb, dreadful, sorrowing silence, hating myself, knowing what was to come, unable to help. Unwilling to help.

It happened.

Patroclus had indeed, it seemed, carried the day. As the sun move toward setting he seemed to gain new power. Three charges he made, each time dealing death, slaying it was later said nearly thirty men himself. The sun hovered in the sky near the horizon, as if breathlessly waiting to see the outcome of the battle. The field was bathed in red: blood and dying sunlight. The hordes of men still surged back and forth. Across the field, Hector was, I could see, fighting his way towards where Patroclus stood, his back to the chariot. Achilles' chariot, Achilles' armor, Achilles' lover, the symbols were there, the man was not.

Hector literally cut his way across the field. It seemed to me in the hazy glow of the fading sun that beside Hector was a comrade fighting with him, a golden young man, seemingly luminous, fighting with a grim and cold determination, unwearied, bearing Hector before him, as it were, by some invisible force. My heart went cold. If there are gods, surely this was Apollo himself come to take vengeance on the pride of Achilles and the presumption of Patroclus.

As if sensing the terrible event about to happen the fighting men cleared a broad path, almost a processional way. At either end stood the real Hector and the false Achilles. They paused, sighting one another, then with dreadful battle cries rushed, spears leveled. It seemed then that the terrible god at Hector's side, if god he was, dissolved into a mist and enveloped the two. Patroclus stumbled as if struck from behind.

Hector stopped, startled, unsure of what had happened. He had not delivered a blow. Then Patroclus was struck again, this time by no supernatural weapon. A Dardanian spear struck him between the shoulder blades, thrown from behind. Patroclus staggered, turned, blindly moved toward his own lines when Hector with a triumphant cry lunged forward and ran his spear into Patroclus' belly. Without a sound he fell.

Hector stood over him. He lifted the bloody head and stripped off the helmet. When he saw that it was not Achilles, his face contorted into a cold and triumphant smile, knowing that he had destroyed his foe in a way more terrible than death. A ghastly silence took possession of us all. The fighting simply ceased. The sun, Apollo Himself surely, painted all the players in the bloodiest red. Hector stood over Patroclus, saying something to the fallen but still living warrior. I caught only a few words: some terrible boast, some vaunting cry of victory.

"Patroclus is it? You thought you could sack our city. Your Achilles was of no help to you now. Did he send you here to strip the armor from my back?"

Even though he was dying I could hear Patroclus' words: "Boast if you will, Hector, for you do not have long to live. Death and fate stand beside you. Achilles will avenge me. He will lay you in the dust."

Then he was cut off, his voice suddenly stopped. He fell back. And I swear, though I do not think I believe in such things, that I saw his spirit rise, hover, and descend into the earth on its way to Hades, as the sun darkened around us.

There was absolute silence now. Hector turned, shrugged as though the prophecy were nothing, and brutally ripped the spear from Patroclus' body. Men watched in horror, and then insanity swept us and the killing began again.

What followed is almost too terrible to relate. I was swept away from the place where Patroclus fell by the fury of the renewed fighting, but not before I saw that there would be a battle for the body, and especially for the armor, the armor of Achilles. The last thing I saw before I had to defend my own life against an advancing Trojan pikeman, was Menelaus bestriding the body of Patroclus, spear leveled, shield before him, ready to kill anyone who should attack. I saw too that Euphorbos, whose spear had struck Patroclus, was closing in. Then the pikeman was upon me, and I sent my own spear home, crunching into his chest, releasing a crimson spout of Trojan blood.

The press of men carried me away, but later I heard that there was indeed a battle over the body. Menelaus killed Euphorbos, but soon Hector furiously returned with a large company and Menelaus was forced to retreat, leaving body and armor to the grimly victorious Hector. He stripped the body of the armor and began to drag it away when Menelaus returned with reinforcements, determined to save the body. Hector out of policy retreated, leaving the mangled corpse on the field, but in cruel mockery, retired behind his lines, put on the armor, and wearing it, charged out again with the intention of capturing the body and defiling it. The battle over the poor corpse was furious, bloody and hideously insane: men literally pulled the body one way, then another; it became no longer human, but instead a horribly mangled thing, broken and torn. Menelaus, who had been fighting near me, came quickly to my side and pulling me into the shelter of an overturned chariot commanded me to go to Achilles. I could not speak. With eyes filled with tears. I nodded dumbly. I felt the chill hand of fate touch my brow and I knew that Achilles must be told and that I was the man who must tell him, I who in my selfish and obsessed love had reason to rejoice at the news I must carry. How I despised myself, and how I wept: for Patroclus, for Achilles, for us all.

I threw my weapons to Mecisteus and ran as I had never run before, out through the crowds of still dumbstruck soldiers, Greeks, Trojans, friend or enemy I did not care. The faces of the soldiers blurring as I passed, the bloody ground seeming to be no longer under my feet, my heart hammering against my breastplate.

I ran through the lines, out of the crowds of killers and the killed, along the smooth crescent of the shore towards the tent where Achilles lay knowing nothing of the blow that was about to fall upon him, unknowing that a world was about to die and a legend to begin.

I ran, the messenger of the grimmest tidings, hoping that like all such messengers, I would be allowed to die, for shortly I must throw myself at the feet of the man I loved more than all others, to tell him that the man he loved beyond all others and now beyond hope, the man who had from the beginnings of time been the half that made them whole, was dead, a victim of Achilles' fatal pride. Would my name echo down the sad and hollow years, I wildly wondered, as the man who told Achilles that Patroclus was dead?

Chapter 31

There are now differing stories explaining why Patroclus came to that field. Some say that it was Odysseus who went to him and put the idea into his head that led to his death. Others that it was Patroclus alone who made the choice, so horrified was he by the slaughter of his comrades that he dared to brave the wrath of Achilles the man he loved, and went to him to suggest the fatal plan. Alas, I know the truth, for I was there and its consequence was tragedy.

Patroclus went to Achilles and begged him to go into battle. The Trojans were at the ships; close perhaps to capturing them. But Achilles moodily refused. Patroclus argued, saying that without Achilles defeat was sure. Still Achilles refused. In desperation Patroclus turned to his last resort and asked Achilles to lend him his armor so that, charging into the fray, Patroclus would dupe the Trojans into believing that Achilles had come to war. For then they would surely scatter and retreat.

Achilles, strangely, agreed. How he could do this? Who can know? What evil possessed him? What blindness overcame his reason?

But, and this is important: Achilles *commanded* Patroclus—*commanded* him! —"make no forays, no charges, slay no men."

"Even" he said, "even if the gods offer you the chance of winning glory for yourself, *you must not* seize it. You *must not* fight. Turn back when you have saved the situation at the ships. And leave the rest to do the fighting on the plain."

But Patroclus did not. Was he headstrong, suicidal, helpless in the grip of fate? I do not know what *daimon* filled him. But he charged direct to his fatal rendezvous with Hector and the gods.

How could Achilles not have known that Patroclus would do just that? How could he not have known that Patroclus would see this as a chance at last to equal or even surpass his lover in bravery, and that he would do that, for him, for them, for their legend? And most terrible of all, how could Achilles not know that it was his pride that had sent his lover to death?

And the horror. Patroclus died alone, without his friend at his side, the friend who if he had been there might have saved him, or died gloriously with him. But at least Patroclus died with glory. It was for Achilles to live, knowing that all the blame was his.

As I ran all of these things, some certainties, others perhaps a foreknowledge momentarily granted me, whirled in my head. And so when I saw the tent of Achilles in the distance my own petty emotions seemed to be washed away. I no longer cared that he did not love me. I no longer cared that I did love him. I felt then only terrible, terrifying pity for that soon-to-be wretched man, and I was filled with fear at the spectacle of grief that I knew I must surely witness. I was desperately glad that I was not in his place and this tangled mixture of emotion filled me at once with anguish and a profound sense of release.

As my feet flew over the blood-sodden ground my soul flew up and I no longer hated Patroclus. I no longer felt the sickness of my selfish and murderous love. I was saddened, but I was free as well. I would be to Achilles whatever the fates decreed I must be, not what my vain lusts demanded. I would fight destiny no longer; I would welcome it, whatever it might be.

But it was as I feared. I came panting into camp, my sides wrenched with the agony of my exertions, barely able to speak. I instantly saw him, standing by the tent door, a look of dark concern on his face as if he half-suspected. I fell at his feet and had no more strength left save to inartfully, brutally, gasp out what I had to say:

"My Lord, it is Patroclus—he is dead, his armor taken. They fight for his body even now. Hector is to blame."

He stared at me, through me, toward the distant battle, and I am convinced, into time, the future, and eternity. A moment of chilling silence, a sudden intake of breath, and then a cry, low, rising, increasing, then torn out of him, torn out of the depths of Hades, a cry like a damned spirit wailing in desolate agony, rising up, up to heaven, forming a word, nearly indistinguishable as it echoed across the Dardanian plain, reverberated off the Trojan walls, filled the world and sky around us and resounded against the foot of the Olympian throne, the word was one word only. For Achilles, the *only* word: "Patroclus."

He threw himself on the ground, writhing as if in a seizure, throwing the dust over his head, sobbing, moaning like a wounded dog, howling like an animal that has lost his master. I did what seamed to me the only thing to do. I pulled him to me, taking his hands in mine, comforting him as best I could, holding him while he sobbed, trying to enfold his trembling body with my own exhausted arms. He wildly looked around. He reached for his sword. I feared that he was indeed about to slay the offending messenger, but instantly I also knew that instead he was about to take his own life. I threw him down on the ground, threw myself on top of him and pinioned him there.

I wrestled him into stillness; bringing what strength I had left to silence him. Then our battle ceased and my mastery turned to solace and I held him, cradled him, loved him. We lay there; he in my arms, and the only sound was the rolling sea.

Then it seemed that from the very depths of that sea I heard a cry of sorrow, and I remembered who his mother was. Men have said that Achilles sprang from immortal loins, that Thetis, sea-goddess, bore him, but this had seemed to me only the fond praise that people like to heap upon the exceptional among men. But at that sound, coming it seemed from the deep sea itself, at that moment I was suddenly not so sure. Perhaps I held divinity in my arms. I let him cry.

Then slowly he sat up. I let him rise. He left my arms. I rose, following him closely for fear that he would again attempt violence to himself. But instead he looked out toward the rolling ocean. I followed his gaze. At sea there seemed to be nothing there but a rising mist shimmering above the waters.

But for him there was more.

"Mother, Mother, Oh help me," he cried.

And then we were enveloped in that mist. I could no longer see him, but I could hear his voice, fragmented, the words disconnected and around us there reverberated a low musical hum, deep and melodic, and an aroma of richest potency, like ambergris from the sea.

"Mother, he is dead, who I cared for more than my own life. I will die too. I will never go home. What is left for me now? Though I know I will shortly die, yet I will kill Hector. But die I must, my friend was killed and I was not there. He died far from home and I was not there to aid or protect him."

The mist began to swirl more swiftly around us, its music growing louder, the throbbing chord penetrated to my heart. Surely I now knew what it was to hear the Goddess speak.

Then, silence. The mist cleared, Achilles still stared out to sea. I went up to him and gently put my arm around his shoulder and we stood thus for a time until the mist finally vanished.

Then, as if awakening, he turned to me and gripped my hand. "I will make peace with Agamemnon," he said, and strode off.

"My Lord, " I called, " where are you going?"

"To battle," he said without breaking stride.

"But you have no armor" I said almost desperately. I feared that he had become unhinged.

"That will come," he said, "Follow me."

He leapt into his chariot that stood, ready, horses harnessed and waved toward one of the warhorses tethered nearby, indicating that I should mount and ride.

I, exhausted, followed him.

What came after has already been taken up by the bards and turned into legend. Achilles rode like fury toward the plain where the battle now raged again; I following at a gallop. As he drove an incredible thing seemed to happen, or so it seemed to my exhausted eyes, for I was dizzy with fatigue and from the terrible intensity of what had happened.

I rode behind him, and then, giving my horse his head came up next to Achilles. It seemed to me that as he careened toward what was surely a rendezvous with fate that he actually began to grow in stature and the air around him became luminous, began to glow with a white-hot incandescence. He raced across the plain, wrapped in light toward the spot where his Patroclus lay dead, warriors—Greek and Trojan—all around him, killing to claim his battered body.

His chariot, with me following, bore down on the melee and as he rode into the fight this is what all that fought there saw: fate and vengeance rushing towards them like the Furies in the person of Achilles, separated from the world by the fire of divinity, not man now, but a god. As if this figure cast a tremendous ray of light across the battling men and transfixed them in its blinding glare, one by one, group by group, company by company they turned to stare. The astonishment and the spreading fear were palpable. It was an incredible spectacle. A thousand men who moments before had been engaged in the hysteria of slaughter turned and stared, Trojan and Achaean, at the blinding pillar of flame that enwrapped Achilles, slayer of men.

And then he raised his voice. It was a trumpet call. It was a summons to death and vengeance. It was a clarion sounding the crack of doom. There were no clear words, though I was sure that it was the name of his beloved that he called, but the power of his voice and the sheer terrifying presence of this fiery apparition, enfolded, the priests later said, by the aegis of Pallas Athene Herself, so terrified the Trojans that they fled pell-mell, in panic and terror, leaving the body of Patroclus, pitiful and alone, lying on the field of war.The Achaeans, seeing they had somehow achieved a miraculous victory simply stopped where they stood. All motion stopped. It seemed as if even the earth stopped turning and the sea itself was silent. The army stood silent, creating a circle around the body. Patroclus, alone, lay dead on the ground. Around him the greatest army of the world stared in shock and horror.

Achilles brought the chariot to a stop, leapt out and ran to where the crumpled body of Patroclus lay. I dismounted and rushed to his side. He knelt in the dust and looked for one long agonizing moment at the bloodied corpse. Praise the gods, the beautiful face, at least, was unscarred. Then Achilles bent, put his arms around and under Patroclus, raised him up, lifted him, and stood with the body in his arms. His face was a mask of anguish; his eyes promised a terrible vengeance.

Then without a word he carried the body of Patroclus through a wide lane of his comrades, carried the poor, mutilated, bloody thing to his chariot, motioned me to come with him and drive. Holding Patroclus' body as if it were a holy image, he stood as we drove, followed by a procession of the living and bloodied, across the plain to our camp.

There the terrible news had preceded us. Reverently, carefully I helped him carry the body to a makeshift bier quickly raised beside the sea. Achilles laid Patroclus on it and stood silent, immobile, before it. The flaming aura that had enveloped him before faded, flickered, and was gone. He was a vengeful giant no longer, now a man again, weak with loss, weak with grief.

He approached the bier, knelt before it and reached out and brushed the cold hand with his own. In all the repertoire of their passion, that gesture was the most achingly, intimately tender.

Then the hot tears came. The evening deepened into dusk and then into purple shadows as if it was in mourning too. Achilles lay prostrate before the body of his friend. The sun, as exhausted as I, paused for a moment on the distant rim of the darkening sea, and then slipped behind the horizon.

For Achilles too, the light had gone out and the world was dark.

Chapter 32

All know the events of the next dreadful days. The bards are no doubt already trying their skill at this story, singing their various versions around the camp fires, finding which gains most approval, which lines most essentially capture a scene, a battle, a tear. They will tell how Achilles mourned Patroclus, how he made his terrible vow that would send the souls of many heroes down to Hades, while their bodies lay as meat for the dogs and carrion birds. They will sing how, for Patroclus, he vowed to slay Hector, bring his armor and his head as blood-price to the bier and shed the blood of twelve noble Trojan youths as recompense for those dear wounds.

He said: "I will cut their throats and their blood will pay for his."

And in the days following the stories of wonders began to be circulated in the camp, as Patroclus' body was washed and perfumed and laid out in fine linen upon a bier of fragrant wood. Some said there were miracles: that the body was saved from decay by Thetis, that an amazing suit of armor made by the gods for Achilles suddenly appeared. Some described the tense scene between Achilles and Agamemnon and their reconciliation. When the poets write about this war, indeed they will tell in terrible detail the hideous truth, the tale of Achilles' mighty slaughter, the men he killed as a vast and bloody sacrifice in Patroclus' name. All their songs will be about the horrible consequence of the wrath of Achilles, who killed for love.

In the dreadful battle that followed the return of Patroclus' body, Achilles, garbed in the shining, and by now in everyone's mind, divinely made armor, sallied thunderously forth to kill. Men claimed—and the bards eagerly seized upon these claims and the priests later wisely said they foresaw it and validated the tales—men claimed that they saw the gods themselves in full array, battling on

215

the field in aid of their favorites, carrying out the inexorable law of fate.

Perhaps this is so. I saw nothing like that. I only saw men die. And I saw Achilles grimly calm, but to my eyes clearly insane, slaughtering the flower of men: Demoleon, Polydorus, Priam's youngest son, Lycoan, another son of Priam, Dryops, Mulios, Deucalion, Dardanos, Echelos, Khigmos, all, all dead. He drove a group of men into the river, leaping into the water after them, turning the water to life's-blood. A dozen of them he pulled out like weeds, bound them, and sent them back alive, with the grim assurance that they would die before the sun set, throats cut for Patroclus. Only Aeneas he did not slay.

But it was only for Hector that he sought.

And of course there are a dozen versions of Hector's death as well. But there is truly only one, and it is grim and it is shameful. It is best told quickly, without the embroideries the poet's use. They met; they fought. The battle was cruel. Gods may have aided them, but it was Achilles' strength and his anger that gave him victory. One can go to any bard to hear the details, to hear the description of thrust and parry, of hacking blades and plunging spears. It is enough to say that carried before the inexorable power of wrath, Troy's great hero fell to Achilles' raging sword and spear.

Achilles bent over his fallen enemy, bent close as if to hear his final words. Then standing erect he dealt the deathblow. With that, in grim imitation of the past, he stripped the body. Then his men came and shameful to tell, each of them thrust their sword into the lifeless corpse.

But most shameful of all, and an offense to every decency, Achilles pierced the sinews of Hector's ankles and tied the body behind his chariot. Then, whipping his horses to their greatest speed, he dragged the thing around the walls of Troy, his dreadful shouts of victory playing indecent counterpoint to the wailing lamentations that rose from the many towers of Ilium as the Trojans now foresaw their fate and the inevitable end. High on that tower reserved for kings I could just barely see ancient Priam, a King of Kings, now a shrunken old man. Next to him a feeble woman. No one needed to tell me that this was Hecabe, mother of princes, now bereft of her favorite son.

Patroclus has been dead for several days. Hector was killed yesterday. Both armies observe the sacred truce of the dead. Last night I lay in Achilles' tent on a rug at the foot of his bed. I gave him honeyed wine with a drug in it to make him sleep. He needs me now. He has no one. People avoid him. His grief has been beyond comprehension; his treatment of the body of Hector beyond forgiveness. Men fear that the gods will exact some terrible punishment for these excesses, and I am sure they are right. We all know what the prophecies tell us, and so we wait, we wait. Everyone has some theory, pretends to know some secret or special fact.

Only I know that he says he has had a vision of Patroclus. That is why I drug his wine for fear that he will be awakened again by such things, though the funeral will be soon and the uneasy ghost will at last be laid to rest. Did he in fact see Patroclus? I do not know. I was in his tent that night, resting near him. I saw nothing, but I know that he started suddenly from his sleep, eyes wide and filled with tears. He spoke, but I could not understand his words. He reached out, tried to grasp something in the air, nearly enclosed it, then fell sobbing to the floor. I rushed to his side, thinking he was having a seizure. "Tomorrow," he said. "It will be tomorrow." Then he fell into a sleep as if dead.

Indeed, the funeral did happen the next day. Achilles rose in the early hours and roused me, insisting that it must happen that day.

"But my Lord," I ventured.

"No, I promised him, don't you see? It must be done. See that it is done."

Somehow I caused it to be done. It was of great magnificence. No bard has yet done it justice. The sands were drenched with the tears of lamentation, with the wine of libation, and the blood of sacrifice. Patroclus' dogs, his horses, all were slain. Bulls, sheep, and boars were sacrificed around the bier, and as he had grimly promised, Achilles himself slew the twelve beautiful youths he had taken from the Trojans, scarcely looking at them as one after the other, with terrible efficiency, he cut their throats.

217

What stunned everyone was the gesture made before the pyre was kindled. Achilles cut off the long golden curl that had been reserved since his youth as a sacrifice to the Gods. But he did not offer it to them; he cut it off for Patroclus, and laid it in his dead hands. No one need be told the terrible meaning of that gesture. Everyone knew that it had long ago been vowed that if Achilles returned safe home he would sacrifice that lock of hair as thanks to the Gods, a gift of the symbol of his youth, a testimony to his achieved manhood.

He knew, we knew now, he would not go home. Patroclus would hold that token for him now, forever.

Finally the pyre was lighted. It took time. Prayers were made for the fire to burn. It did not. There was muttering. It was an omen. The gods were refusing the offering. But Achilles' mother, so the bards will no doubt say, caused the winds to kick up, and soon the pyre was a mass of flame, licking high up to heaven, the hot blood sputtering, the meat of sacrifice, animal and human, turning to an acrid billow of smoke that marked the final voyage of Patroclus, a pillar in the sky to show how heroes died.

All day and all night that pyre burned, and all day and all night Achilles stood alone in front of it, pouring beaker after beaker of wine upon the ground, calling aloud to Patroclus, if anything more frenzied than he had yet been. Finally, there could be no more, and he fell to the scorched earth, heedless of the heat, sobbing, groaning, dying a little

It was over. The flesh was consumed. Only the bones remained. They were reverently gathered up and placed in an urn, a golden urn, the finest of all Achilles' treasures. As these rites were being consummated, I stood next to him. He leaned on me; I gripped his arm.

"I will lie with him there one day," he said, not to me, but to history.

The funeral games are to begin soon. My horses, sensing the contest, are pawing the ground. I can hear Achilles from here, his voice hoarse from shouting, hoarser from weeping, exhorting the crowd to do honor to Patroclus. I will enter the chariot races and the footrace. If I win one, or both, he will see that I am worthy to stand beside him, to comfort him now that he is alone. Will he see? Will he care?

But I must go. I hear Achilles calling me for the chariot race. "Antilochus, Antilochus," I hear him cry out in that trumpet voice that so terrified the Trojans before their walls, that voice that lifted a nearly insane lament to heaven and threw reproach at the foot of the throne of Zeus.

"Come now, Antilochus," he calls, and it is the same voice that defied Agamemnon the Great King, and when softer, gentler, it is the same voice that one night I heard say to Patroclus the only words that any man ever wants to hear as they lay together in the Trojan darkness a thousand miles from home, while I stood desolate but shamelessly listening outside their tent. There I had come hoping to catch a glimpse of the legend to whom I had given my heart and for whom I had left my native land, for whom I had come unbidden and against my father's will over the wine dark sea, not for politics, not for war, not for glory, but for love.

Yes, for that is why I came to this windy Trojan plain and camped beneath the beetling walls of Ilium, and why I am here now: not because I cared a fig about Agamemnon's war, not because I am a Prince of Pylos and hungry for glory, but because I knew of Achilles, the greatest hero. I had seen him once, and I loved him. I always knew that his destiny and mine must cross, and so I came to Troy to find him.

At the funeral games I lost in the chariot race, and came in second in the footrace. I am the fastest runner in Pylos; surely I was being punished for my pride as well. But I didn't care, for as he gave out the prizes for the footrace, and I standing next to him handing him the treasures he had chosen as rewards, I said that no one could have won the race against Odysseus, the victor, save Achilles who fortunately had chosen not to run. I don't know what crossed his mind then, but he looked at me intently, almost as if he had never seen me before, and took a golden ingot from the pile of prizes and said: "Thanks for your words Antilochus. They have not been in vain."

The scene must have seemed foolish to onlookers, he holding one end of the ingot, I the other, neither relinquishing his hold, I clearly dumbfounded, staring deeply, no doubt longingly into his eyes. I know that all he saw was Patroclus, but in those steady eyes I saw my own reflection already becoming part of him, sinking into his soul. As he let go of the ingot, his eyes cleared, and he said again: "No, not in vain, Antilochus, not in vain."

There remained one thing more for him to do. Penance. To kill Hector anyone could understand. It was the blood price. It was fair. To defile the body as he did, dragging it around the funeral pyre, throwing it in the dirt at the foot of his dead lover's bier, that was an insult to the dead; it was hubris; it challenged the laws of every god. Of course he was unhinged, possessed by a demon of grief. Everyone saw that.

But there are many more who feel that after the rites were over, when old Priam came to beg for the body of his boy, of his Hector, of his now dead hope, many people feel that all of Achilles' desecrations were erased by what can only be called his magnanimity.

I was there, for I was always by his side now, and when the ancient Majesty of Troy, kneeling before Achilles, lifted his hands in the gesture of the suppliant to the man who slew his son, no strong man could forebear weeping.

Gently Achilles took the old man's hands in his own, as he had taken Patroclus' hands in his own, and he wept while Priam crouched before him, weeping too. Surely Achilles wept then not only for Patroclus but for all the dead. Surely then he knew that fate had woven this web for both of them, for Priam and himself, and that there could be no more rancor.

That scene, an ancient King humbled at the feet of the greatest hero of our age will forever remain graven on my memory, like an image hammered and embossed on a golden shield. Graven there too is the noble gesture of Achilles as he raised the king to his feet, holding Priam's trembling hands in his, and by that gesture, so filled with ancient meaning, took his broken enemy under his protection.

And then, astoundingly, enriching the almost unbearably poignant scene, Achilles made his low obeisance, not to Priam, but to the dead Prince lying at his side, and then lifted him, gently, like a lover might, and bore him to the cart that Priam had brought for his son's last journey. In all the ranks of men there drawn up to do honor to a King there was no eye that remained clear of tears. Surely the gods wept too, and in their eyes this last act of manly and decent mercy must expiate and wipe away the shame.

I am under no illusion that I can replace Patroclus. But perhaps for a little while I can share what time remains to Achilles. Of course, he will die soon; we all know that. He knows that. It has been foretold and destined before time began. It is only a matter now of watching it unfold, of participating in destiny.

The great ones have always been playthings of fate. It is the price of greatness. Achilles, Hector, Agamemnon, Priam, Patroclus, their lives have never been their own. They play the roles assigned. Some do not know their Fate. Others do. Achilles did. I wonder how he must have felt knowing that his men sat around the campfires telling the old stories of what was to come, rehearsing his future and their own. We would never speak so in his hearing of course. Then, if at all, we would laugh at such things, calling them old wives tales, the fables of priestlings. We would never even think such things if he and Patroclus were together, leaning negligently against one another, passing a cup with an affectionate glance, or letting hands linger against tanned flesh as they reached across the table to share their meat and barley. No, at those times we talked of war and heroic deeds, of captured gold, and home. In the face of their love we had no heart for prophecy.

Those of us who do not have immortal parents, like Achilles, or whose lives, like Patroclus, were not interwoven on the loom of time with the fatal threads of another's destiny, have to advance bravely toward our own fate with no knowledge of it.

But as for Achilles, he knows. Oh yes, the prophecy gives him illusion of choice. He can choose which road to take. He can choose to fight before the walls of this accursed city and inevitably die and thus assure that his name would forever be on the lips of men. Or he can go home to long life—and obscurity.

He had been given the choice before the foundations of the earth were laid. But he was Achilles, and he was in love, and so there was no choice. And finally, it was Patroclus who answered the question for him. It was Patroclus, headstrong, suicidal or just helpless in the grip of fate, who rode wildly to the city walls and his encounter with the gods.

All of us who knew him knew how he would choose. He is so alive, the animal power coursing visibly through him, that such strength must not, could not last long or be spent slowly wasting over a long and pointless life. But there is this too: always, as if it were a faint aureole around him, the ashen sheen of death faintly glows.

My question, my only question, is if I will follow him or precede him to Hades. I will surely die here. We all think that we will die here. I do not know my fate, but I can guess it. I will surely die in battle in some horrible manner: a knife in the vitals, a spear through the brain. Men go out into battle, great men, heroes. They do not return. Both sides lose huge numbers. We hear constantly from the Trojan walls the wailing of the women, and no day goes by without the smoke of one, two, or a dozen funeral pyres blackening the sky.

If I die before Achilles I can precede him and walk the Asphodel fields with Patroclus, making ready for the man we both loved. Of course if I outlive Achilles and follow him after a day, after a lifetime, to that haven of heroes, I will find them together in death as in life.

I will be then what I once was: tolerated with affection, allowed to share the moments which are not too intimate, used by one for quick play when the other was gone, but finally, in the face of their overwhelming love I will be as I was: unnecessary.

I simply wait now, for the inevitable to occur. I am constantly with Achilles. I sleep in his tent, though we do not make love. Yet in a strange way we are lovers. Patroclus' ghost is quiet, though late at night I sometimes feel him hovering near when Achilles and I share wine before we retire to our separate beds for uneasy sleep.

Often he cries out in the night. I arise and go to him, waken him, comfort him. He always looks up and smiles and says "Thanks, Antilochus." But sometimes his sleep is too deep and then I do not waken him, for I know full well that the name on his lips will not be mine.

Oh, I should say that Nestor, my father, has had an oracle that I must be protected from a black god--an Ethiopian. But we are all Achaeans here. There are no Ethiops. Mecisteus says that no Trojan would fight next to an Ethiop.

Chapter 33

It begins again. With Mecisteus helping, I arm as the early morning sky goes from darkness, to gray, to pink. As he helps me into the armor, he averts his eyes. He does it, I know, to hide the tears, to hide the pain of knowledge of what life could have been for the two of us had not Achilles intervened. Not Achilles the man, but Achilles the myth, the ideal, the very image of unattainable love. I pull Mecisteus to me, hold him tight and kiss him, wiping the tears away. He too will go into battle today. Who knows if I will see him, living, again.

Everyone thinks this will be a decisive battle, maybe *the* decisive battle. But no one really knows. Both sides are evenly matched. Calchas makes encouraging prophecies—or at least the king says they are encouraging, though no one ever quite knows what they actually mean. It is rumored around the campfires that Odysseus has come up with some brilliant plan to take the city of the Horse Lords, as Trojans are also called because of their vast herds of them. Disguised as horses, someone joked. We all laughed.

Now that Hector is dead, Achilles is arming to return to fight. I will go with him and fight by his side—by his side at last. He is convinced we can take the city.

We will march within the hour. Our scouts say that the Trojans were not entirely taken up by grief during the twelve days of Hectors' funeral, for two days ago several huge ships docked at a northern town the Trojans still hold, and a large company of men marched to the city.

They are led by Memnon, the Ethiopian King. He is reputed to be a giant and beautiful, and as black as ebony.

Chapter 34

The rage of battle is upon me. I raise my sword and bring it down on flesh; I thrust and parry, just like Achilles taught me. A few feet away Achilles fights too. I throw him a look. In his eyes is the same exaltation that must be in mine. I feel possessed, as if through my veins flows the fiery golden nectar of the gods. I feel as if I am surrounded by a halo of light, just as is Achilles too. Who fights nearby. He hovers in cloud of glory, Achilles slayer of men, a god on earth.

Oddly, it is all silent. The usual sounds of war have gone. I raise my sword, I bring it down; it hacks through flesh; I see the man fall, see his distorted face, his mouth agape in pain, but do not hear his scream. The hordes of men around me are like shades, ghosts dimly perceived as they weave and move and rise and fall in a silent dance of death. We dance too, Achilles and I, as we deal out death on the blood-soaked plain of Troy, fighting side by side at last, he and I alone, against the world. I have never been happier.

And then, the horror.

In the melee of battle I had been separated from Achilles for a brief time, and after making a kill turn to see him fighting alone against two others. I race to help, and with a blow decapitate one of his attackers, even as Achilles spits the other through the throat. Over his shoulder I see another Trojan soldier coming up behind him. I shout and Achilles whirls in time to thrust his sword into the man's stomach; he falls dead on the spot. I throw Achilles a grin, and he says, "Thanks, Antilochus," and seems about to speak again when a sudden hiss and whirring cuts him short.

He looks down. I follow his gaze. An arrow protrudes from his heel. He bends down to pull it out with a look of annoyance and then his face goes white. He staggers and falls to the ground. Black blood gushes from the wound. I leap to him, kneel by him. He looks up me, astonishment on his face; he tries to speak, to rise, raises his

225

hand to me for help. I grasp it; he slips back and I cradle him in my arms. Then the grey eyes cloud. Then the light goes out.

Some of our men nearby see what has happened, even as did the Trojans. With shouts of triumph, the Trojans rush toward us, intending to strip his body of its armor and defile it as he had defiled Hector. Whether his divine mother Thetis protects his fallen body or our men are brave enough without the help of gods to rescue his poor battered corpse, some poet will someday no doubt tell. I, like a madman, slaughter those who would despoil him.

And so into our camp his body came, borne upon the shoulders of his men, weeping Myrmidons, and with them were Ajax and Odysseus, and me, his friend.

How could I not have foreseen it? I knew the prophecy. I knew it had to come. I knew of his fatal vulnerability, the heel left untouched by the water of the Styx when his mother, Thetis, dipped him in that sacred river and made him, save for that one small part, immortal.

But in my delirium, my ecstasy, in my happiness at my final possession of Achilles the man I loved, I ignored what the gods had decreed. I did not believe, would not believe that it could happen even though all things are destined and foreordained.

Our failures, our triumphs, even the common round of our daily lives, were long ago decided by the Fates who weave all the strands of destiny upon their loom. And thus that tiny spot upon the heel of a newborn babe, left untouched by the water of the Styx, became the target on the body of the man. Death found him and delivered its final fatal sting.

In the raging heart of the battle, just as our army fought its way to the gates of Troy and would have taken it, Achilles met his doom. Did Apollo, who hated Achilles for what he had done to Hector, guide the hand that shot Achilles? Or was Paris unaided when he fired that swift deadly arrow? No matter how death came to Achilles, it came. His life is ended. Mine is meaningless. In the distance as we fought, just before Achilles received that fatal arrow, through the dust of battle I thought I saw Memnon, the black Ethiopian king.

As he lies there, bloody, cold, dead, I will kiss my Lord and love one last time. Then I will return to the battlefield again. Two men wait for me: Memnon on the Trojan plain; Achilles in eternity.

Epilogue: Funeral Games

"Achilles, you died on the fields of Troy, a world away from home, and the best of the Trojans and Achaeans died around you."
–Odyssey 24.38-40.

From: Dionysos of Tenedos, A History of the War at Troy

Indeed on that day, the same on which Achilles fell, Antilochus, Nestor's son, as fate intended, also died on the battlefield, and as prophecy foretold at the hands of the Ethiopian king. When his bloodied body was finally recovered it was carried into the Greek camp and laid next to Achilles. Achilles' men, knowing what had passed between them, lay them side-by-side, cold hands touching. Mecisteus washed the body of the man he could never have and grieved, silent and desolate And there also stood Nestor, face drawn, eyes blank, staring at the body of his son, Antilochus.

The funeral was magnificent. The flames licked at the base of the pyre, then like red and gold serpents slithering up its sides, began to catch and then devour the logs—cedar, oak, and ash-- soaked with oil and perfumed with all the unguents and scents that remained in the camp. Erected in the center of the parade ground with the sea at its back, the pyre stood as high as ten men.

Achilles' body, wrapped in a linen shroud, rested on the top on bed of pine branches and aromatic herbs and seemed to float there as the smoke began to rise and wreath around it. Agamemnon, Menelaus, Odysseus, and Ajax stood at the base of the pyre, which Odysseus had lighted with a flaming brand. At attention and forming a hollow square with the pyre at its center, the army of the Achaeans stood, and first among them, closest to the fire that consumed their lord and commander, were his Myrmidons, spears grounded point downward in the earth, heads bowed, standing motionless like grieving rows of statues. On a lower tier, his armor heaped around him, another body lay. Antilochus, beautiful and swift of foot.

Soon the entire pyre was engulfed, the heat was unbearable. The smoke blackened the sky and mixing with the aroma of the funeral perfumes, it masked the odor of burning flesh. The sounds— the explosion of the wood, the crack of the flames---joined now with the sullen and angry crash of the sea. The melancholy calls of swarms of birds that circled overhead blended with the laments of the soldiers, for no man could now hold back his tears as Achilles' body turned to ashes and his spirit mingled with the smoke rising to

229

heaven. Mixed with the terrible music of the roaring flames, it is said another dirge was heard by some, a divine mother wailing for her son.

In the days thereafter the funeral games were celebrated and for many days the Greeks mourned him—and for days a truce prevailed, honored by the Trojans just as the Greeks had done for them when Hector died. Sacrifice after sacrifice was made, and as is our custom men competed in the games, running, wrestling, in all manner of sports, to honor the dead by the exploits of the living.

Finally on the last day, at dawn, the whitened ash and bone was gathered. The remains of each hero were steeped in oil and unmixed wine. On an altar three urns stood. In one the ashes of Antilochus were laid with tenderness and reverence, and ancient Nestor, his grieving father, through blinding tears set the golden cover on it and sealed it with wax and pitch.

In the second and largest of the three, a great two-handled urn made of the purest gold and chased with silver, Achilles' ashes were placed by Calchas, who chanted ancient prayers for the departed spirits as he reverently did his office.

Then Calchas took the remaining urn and broke its seal. Holding up it up before the assembled army he said: "See Achaeans, here is the urn and in it the ashes of Patroclus, who loved our Lord Achilles better than any man. He died in Achilles' armor to save us all. Reverence him"

Then taking Patroclus' urn he slowly poured the ashes from it into that of Achilles, mingling the ashes of the heroes, and sealed it.

He lifted the urn in which Patroclus and Achilles now lay together in death as they had in life and displayed it to the mourners. "Reverence them," he said.

An anguished, desolate, and barely stifled sob rose from every corner of the field. Soldiers turned helplessly to one another and strong men who had never wept, sobbed upon the shoulders of their comrades.

Agamemnon himself ordered the salute. With a crash of arms the men came to attention and saluted Achilles, Patroclus, and Antilochus for one last time. Calchas began the dirge, a sweet chant

230

like the song of spirits flying to their rest, and it was said that with it men heard the lament of the Holy Muses, the Nine who had never sung for men, till now.

As perhaps his own act of expiation, Agamemnon set a huge detachment of men to build a tomb for Achilles, a giant mound of earth faced with stone, rising on the headland that thrusts into the Hellespont. There Achilles lies with Patroclus and Antilochus, who loved him.

Afterword: The Reality of Troy

For Homer, Troy was no myth and the war that destroyed it was real, an event that resonated down the ages from the time that Troy's walls were razed by Agamemnon to Homer's own, some four hundred years after the time that most in the ancient world believed that Troy fell. Nor did other ancient authors doubt the historicity of Troy and the war that destroyed it. The Greek historian Herodotus assigned the date of Troy's fall to about 1250 BCE. Eratosthenes of Alexandria believed it to be about 1185, and a marble tablet called the Parian Marble, discovered on the Greek island of Paros, dated the fall of the city precisely to June 5, 1209 BCE. From Thucidydes, writing in the fifth century BCE to Josephus writing in the First century AD, Homer's story was accepted as an accurate depiction of a real place and of real events. Indeed age after age has believed the story of Troy, and so over two millennia, in art, in music, and in literature, and lately in film and in shreds of popular culture, Troy and the terrible war that engulfed it and the names that made it an all-too human tale, has remained a story that is central to our understanding of those times and through them of ours.

Homer probably wrote the *Iliad* about 850BCE. In it he—or they, for some still claim that "Homer" is a collective name for several poets—tells the story of the last days of the ten year war that ended with the fall of Troy to a coalition of nations led by Agamemon, King of Mycenae, the most powerful of all the kings of the ancient Greek world. Coming from dozens of tribes, nations, petty fiefdoms and kingdoms all around the Aegean Sea--on mainland Greece, on the shores of Asia Minor to the east, north to Thrace and Macedonia and south to Crete and variously called Acheaens, Argives and Danaans by Homer--for the words "Greek" and "Greece" were not used by him--this huge coalition sailed, Homer claims, in more than a thousand ships to the shores of the Troad and the sacred city of Troy. Their mission was to bring back Helen, wife of his brother Menelaus of Sparta, who had been abducted by Paris, Prince of Troy, son of Priam, Troy's king.

Homer's story begins only a few weeks before the end of the war. In twenty-four books he describes the plague that nearly decimates the Achaean army, brought down upon them by the arrogance of Agamemnon, and he details the wrath of Achilles that arises from a dispute between him and Agamemon which in turn led to a crippling stalemate in the war. But once the deadlock is broken, there follows--told in excruciatingly gory detail—descriptions of bloody battles during which Patroclus, Achilles' special friend—and as ancient authors believed, his lover and companion--is killed by Hector, heir to the throne of Troy, who then is slain by Achilles. There follows the agonizing funeral of Patroclus during which Achilles vents his grief. Finally, Hector's body is returned to Priam by Achilles. For the end of the story—the death of Achilles, the wooden horse, the fall of the city, the death of Priam, the abduction of Hecabe, Andromache, and Kassandra, and the aftermath of the war including, primarily, Odysseus' twenty years of wandering, one must turn to Homer's *Odyssey.*

The *Iliad* and the *Odyssey* are among the oldest texts of ancient literature to survive intact into modern times. They were for the Greeks--the descendants of Homer's Achaeans—virtually sacred books. The Greeks believed them to tell the real history of their race. They read them to learn about war and its conduct, and found in Homer's epic codes of conduct for the ideal hero and cautionary tales about greed, impiety, cowardice, and deceit. They learned there too about the power and unpredictability of their gods, and the death, whether terrible or glorious, that must eventually come to all men. And the two books enshrine the tales of the war against the greatest city of the world and bring to life the heroes who fought, lived, and died there.

For the ancients, Troy was a sacred city. Its light and sanctity shone across the ancient world, and its reputation for unrivalled riches, military power, and as huge and impregnable, was a staple of ancient descriptions of it. Homer describes it as "holy" and a "well-walled" city with four "lofty gates" and "wide streets," and "fine towers," one of which was the "great tower of Ilios." He describes its huge royal palace with fifty chambers for the king's fifty sons.

Modern research has confirmed that Troy stood in Asia Minor in modern-day Anatolia near the seacoast of northwest Turkey and southwest of the Dardenelles, and thus at a crossroads of major

233

trading routes upon which it could send a large variety of goods and receive riches from the entire Agean and beyond. Thus, whether or not Helen's abduction was a fact and sufficient cause for an invasion, Troy's power, size and wealth was enough to tempt the Achaean forces to invade and destroy it so as to seize its riches and remove it forever as both a military and commercial threat.

So powerful and real was Troy's legend to the ancient world that the city became a revered site for visitation. According to Herodotus, Xerxes, the Persian king, visited there in 480 BCE when crossing the Hellespont, and sacrificed to Athena. Alexander, who carried with him everywhere a copy of the *Iliad,* and who admired Achilles as a paragon of heroism, visited the city in 330 BCE and dedicated his armor to Athena and laid a wreath at Achilles' tomb, famously declaiming "Oh fortunate youth, to have found Homer as the herald of your glory."

But three hundred years later, when Julius Caesar visited the city, there was little left to see. The small city that stood there, he must have thought, could not have been the glorious city of Homer's tale and the city from which Aeneas set sail to found Rome. Caesar toyed with the idea of rebuilding it and the Emperor Constantine imagined his new capital as rising on the site of old Troy. The Emperor Julian, who so detested the Christianity that Constantine brought to the Roman Empire that he was called the Apostate because of his rejection of the faith and his attempt to revive the worship of the old gods, was pleased to discover upon his visit to the remains of Troy in AD 355 that the shrine of Hector and the Tomb of Achilles were intact and that before their altars fires of sacrifice still burned to show that the memory of Troy had survived even after a thousand years.

That memory has indeed survived intact and untarnished down the ages. From the fall of Rome to the Italian renaissance, into the sixteenth century and until the nineteenth, the "matter of Troy" as medieval writers called it, provided the subject for a huge body of literature and images in the visual arts. From Virgil's Latin *Aeneid* to Saxon writers of the middle ages and to romances of the twelfth century like the *Roman de Troie,* to Chaucer's *Troylus and Criseyde*, through Chapman's translation of the *Iliad* in 1598 to

Shakespeare's *Troilus and Cressida,* and to Alexander Pope's great verse translation in the 18th century, the story lived on. Like the ancient Greeks, British Victorian students found in the *Iliad* inspiration that helped them found an empire, and even now, American movie stars don armor to become Achilles.

Even as the myth survived, the remains of the city disappeared beneath the shifting soil of two millennia. Some came to think that Troy was only a myth and that the city and the war were a figment of the imagination of a poet whose identity was itself in doubt. The story of how that perception has changed over the last century parallels the rise of archeology as a branch of exact and rigorous science. The names and work of a dozen explorers—some dreamers, some careful scientists, some part charlatans, figure in the resurrection of Troy. So exhaustive has been the research to unearth this ancient city that it has now been proven that Homer's account is a remarkably accurate portrayal of the physical location of the city and there is now little doubt that Troy was real, a great city that war destroyed. Indeed the story of Troy tells of a violent clash of cultures that has come down to us as a dreadful exemplar of the horrors of war and the folly of those who engage in it. But as the ancients all knew, Homer's story of Troy was also a tale of love between men—of the devotion of Achilles for Patroclus and of Achilles' nearly insane grief at Patroclus'death.

From both the *Iliad* and the *Odyssey,* as well as from the legends of Greece that tell about the events that led up to the war, I have taken the events that I recount and the people to whom I give a voice in this book. I narrate the tale in the first person voice of Antilochus, son of the wise King Nestor. Antilochus appears only briefly in the *Iliad* and the *Odyssey,* but in both epics Homer hints, tantalizingly, at intimacy between Antilochus and the great hero Achilles.

In the *Iliad* Antilochus is described as brave and fleet of foot. And it is he who has the terrible task of telling Achilles about the death of Patroclus. After the death of Patroclus it was Antilochus, as Homer says in the *Odyssey,* who was the closest to Achilles once Patroclus was gone. Indeed, the companionship became more intimate in death, for Homer says that Antilochus' ashes were interred in Achilles' great tomb on the Trojan shore along with those of Achilles and Patroclus. Thereafter, as Homer tells in the *Odyssey,* the three friends are re-united in the underworld and walk together in the eternal fields. Thus my title: *Achilles: A Love Story.* From these few lines of Homer I have written a tale told, so far as I know, by no other writer.

The voice of the Fifth century BCE Dionysos of Tenedos is also my invention, as is his text, *The History of the War at Troy,* "excerpts" of which preface each of the books of this work. But had he existed as the historian I imagine him to be, the story of the war at Troy would have been for him the most gripping tale he had to tell.

Byrne Fone
La Millasserie
France

Byrne Fone is the author of the three novels in the *Trojan Trilogy* (*Achilles: A Love Story, Trojan Women,* and *War Stories*). His other works include *American Revolution,* a look into the future about a gay American Presidential candidate, a historical study: *Historic Hudson: An Architectural Portrait,* and several books in Gay Studies including *A Road to Stonewall; Homophobia: A History;* and *Masculine Landscapes: Walt Whitman and the Homoerotic Text.* He is the editor of *The Columbia Anthology of Gay Literature.* He is Professor Emeritus of English at the City University of New York. He lives in France.

Manufactured by Amazon.ca
Bolton, ON